NORTHWEST CORNER

**Center Point
Large Print**

Also by John Burnham Schwartz
and available from Center Point Large Print:

The Commoner

**This Large Print Book carries the
Seal of Approval of N.A.V.H.**

NORTHWEST CORNER

John Burnham Schwartz

CENTER POINT PUBLISHING
THORNDIKE, MAINE

This Center Point Large Print edition is published in the year 2011 by arrangement with Random House, an imprint of The Random House Publishing Group, a division of Random House, Inc.

This is a work of fiction. Names, characters, places, and incidents are the products of the author's imagination or are used fictitiously. Any resemblance to actual events, locales, or persons, living or dead, is entirely coincidental.

The text of this Large Print edition is unabridged. In other aspects, this book may vary from the original edition. Printed in the United States of America on permanent paper. Set in 16-point Times New Roman type.

ISBN: 978-1-61173-175-0

Library of Congress Cataloging-in-Publication Data

Schwartz, John Burnham.
Northwest corner / John Burnham Schwartz.
p. cm.
ISBN 978-1-61173-175-0 (library binding : alk. paper)
1. Large type books. I. Title.
PS3569.C5658N67 2011b
813'.54—dc22

2011019271

For Aleksandra & Garrick

There are heroes, and there are the rest of us.
RESERVATION ROAD

NORTHWEST CORNER

PART ONE

SAM

"ARNO—BUS."

Coach dips out of the locker room. Sam listens to the footsteps echoing down the long corridor and only now, knowing he's the last, removes the towel draped over his head. He picks up the thirty-one-ounce aluminum bat lying by his feet, jams it into the UConn duffel with the rest of his gear, and zips the bag closed.

The bus is already running when he climbs on. The row in front belongs to him now. The doors fold in with a sigh, and Old Hank shifts into gear for the three-hour trip back to Storrs.

Evening is falling. Sam slides his headphones on and tries to become just another shadow.

Into the athletic-center parking lot the bus doors open: high fluorescent lights, pools of blue night. A gangplank waiting, all lit up. He's sitting right behind Hank and should go first, but it feels less bad to stay where he is, headphones on, eyes nowhere, deep in the stump of his own mortification. Teammates start to shuffle by, smells of glove leather and greased eyeblack, hail-like rapping of spikes.

A hand on his arm. It's Jake, his roommate. Sam lifts one side of the headphones an inch.

"Heading back to the room?"

Jake's voice is almost insultingly tender. The comfort you receive when, bases loaded and two out in the tenth inning of the college playoffs, you strike out without taking a swing, ending your team's season.

"Shower up, at least. You look like shit."

Sam shakes his head gratefully. The bat never even left his shoulder.

"Okay . . . see you later."

"See you."

Then the bus is empty, except for himself and Hank.

"This ain't your goddamn limo, y'know." Hank's voice a gravel bed, snowy buzz cut and jowly neck turned round on him from the driver's perch. The dash clock reads 10:20. Out of respect, Sam pulls off the phones. A sigh from Hank as he levers the doors closed. "So, fuck it. Where to, DiMaggio?"

Where to is O'Doul's, off-campus, third-choice watering hole in town, nobody's date-night destination. The school bus pulls up outside. Neon fizzing through the windows, fun-housing the gloom.

He tells Hank to hold on, takes off his game jersey, and buries it in the duffel. He wishes the bag didn't say UConn in big white letters—it's not that kind of bar—but there's nothing to be done about it now. He's already down to the two-tone undershirt with the sleeves hacked off below the elbow and the dirt-stained away-game pants worn low, no stirrups, and the spikes that make each step sound like he's chucking bags of marbles.

"You're a million bucks," Hank growls. "Go get 'em, tiger."

"Thanks for the ride, Hank."

"We all got bad days, Sammy."

"Yeah." Suddenly, he's blinking back tears.

"Stay out of trouble, now."

The bus doors start to close before his foot touches the curb. By the time he passes through the entrance to the bar, Hank and his caravan are gone.

O'Doul's is hot and crowded, the walls painted dark. A long time, Sam stands drinking by himself. When a stool at the bar finally opens, he slides onto it, the UConn duffel shoved down into the sawdust-and-gum shadows at his feet. A Bacardi mirror with fogged glass hangs above the backbar next to a St. Pauli Girl clock, the clock's hands frozen at twelve minutes to six, permanent happy hour.

" 'Nother?"

The bartender, wiping under his empty bottle.

"With a shot of J.D. this time."

"Right up."

He keeps forgetting. Trying to get back to just

before—on-deck circle, pure ritual, mechanical drop of vinyl-covered doughnut over aluminum barrel, stretching the bat down his back and around, beginning to swing nice and loose. Watching the pitcher and timing the swing. Watching and timing till it's *second nature.*

No such thing, he needs to tell Coach. Just the nature you're born with, handed down through the generations.

He was thinking too much, even in the on-deck circle, before the first pitch was thrown. He can see it now that it's too late. Not empty as he should've been, cleared out; too much junk in his attic. Thinking about what he'd do if the big chance came, what a game-winning hit would feel like. At the plate Stemkowski's just taken ball three and Coach is in the dugout barking, "Good eye, Stem. Good eye, buddy!" The crowd (attendance announced at 683), roaring their heads off, as Stem watches ball four ride in tight under his neck and starts jogging up the first-base line, loading the bases. And Sam stakes the bat handle into the packed dirt, dislodging the doughnut, the weight slips off and the bat becomes a *killing staff.* And for about half a minute a raw brute strength he's never personally experienced before comes surging through his shoulders down to his hands, and he strides into the batter's box believing for once that it's going to happen. The strength fills him, blotting out the past; till it takes him too far, tips the meter into the red; and because it's raw and threatening and not really there, this illusion of power, already leaving, leads him to his father. It makes him think of his father. At which moment, the first pitch on its way, he knows in his sinking heart how it's all going to play out.

DWIGHT

AT 11:47 A.M., a man in a patterned vacation shirt not unlike mine steps out of his Lexus SUV, followed by his young son. I watch them through the front window from aisle seven (baseball, softball, more baseball) in a moment of commercial respite and quicksand reminiscence, a Rawlings infielder's glove cupped over my nose, its hefty price tag flapping, inhaling the bicameral whiff of factory-fresh leather. Trying, as ever, to situate myself in actual time and space. Call it a voluntary hijacking: I'm no longer in SoCal Sports in Arenas, California, in the year 2006, but in Pat's Team Outfitters in North Haven, Connecticut, circa 1966. Not fifty years old but ten. Staring up into my old man's wide creased face. Absorbing that shark-skinned voice as he tells me he'll buy me the glove I want, so long as I swear on my life to treat it right. But if he ever finds it food-stained or left out overnight on the lawn, abused in any way, he'll thrash me

17

with it, that's a solid promise, and my playing days will be done. Do I understand? Already this dark shadow he's casting over me and the thing I've always wanted. Which dooms me somehow, the little poisoned apple he's offering. And still I crave the glove so much I'm going to give him the price he demands.

And then, before my first season of Little League is halfway over, early one morning he finds the Rawlings, that holy object of calfskin perfection, on our shitty, dew-soaked lawn. Just as he foresaw. I'm still in bed asleep, fielding grounders in my dreams, when he bursts into my room and beats me with it good.

Listen to me. These are the sorts of thoughts that too often come back while you're spending thirty months in the hole. And after, too. There's violence in the air, even when nothing is happening. The idea of personal control is just a noble pipe dream. What comes at you feels bitterly, in the end, like some echo of what's inside you. Like any vessel only more so, a place gets defined by what's in it. A hive hums and buzzes. A fist is nothing without rage.

The glass doors open: in come the man and his boy. I pull the glove from my face and replace it on the shelf. Dust myself off, as it were. The boy trailing off his dad's hip at four o'clock, but looking up into that trusted face and smiling. The guy turning back over his shoulder—a joke just passing between them, or a story, say, about soggy doughnuts, wafting in from the parking lot like a cool breeze in summer. Their outward physical details less interesting to me by comparison, though still notable: the dad's big expensive watch, like a hunk of gold bullion clamped to his wrist, the boy's pro-model Dodgers cap and special-edition Tony Hawk slide-ons. Upper-middle-class family, I'd say. He a rising associate in one of the investment boutiques in the recently developed Arenas business park or a tax lawyer taking a much-deserved post–April 15th day off; his boy, at ten or eleven a promising private-school student with an easy, winning personality, though perhaps too enamored of skate culture and the slackers down by the piers and so already being prophylactically primed by his parents for a future boarding spot at the exclusive Thacher School. Lacrosse, I decide, this kid's going to learn lacrosse, as the father checks their progress at the front of the store, the better to assess the aisles of merchandise and the somewhat dubious prospects for service. He spots Derek stacking boxed volleyballs in aisle three. But a first lacrosse stick is serious business, and possibly Derek, who takes night classes in diagnostic massage at UCSB and is today wearing a purple sun visor backward, doesn't look quite up to the task. So the man's gaze turns ninety degrees—passing over Sandra, my boss's fetching twenty-year-old niece, at the register—to land on me in aisle seven. I suppose that, ignorant of my résumé, he mistakenly considers me the safe bet for attentive shopping assistance in the store. And who can blame him? I am fifty years old, relatively fit yet comfortably substantial. My red plastic SoCal Sports tag says DWIGHT ARNO, MANAGER in clear white letters. Under expected circumstances I would be a figure of rectitude and probity.

To which I can only add that I still want to be. I still remember what it feels like to be that man, and not a morning goes by that I don't see his striving, confident image in the mirror of my thoughts. Which maybe is why, watching this father and son approach, caught in the glow of their radiant connection and prosperity, I can only stand in aisle seven, my mouth slack and my heart in lockdown. Still unable after all these years to relinquish my phantom grip on what I had and lost—a wife and son, whose health and happiness were my charge. I wore a suit to work and brought home year-end bonuses that make my current salary look like chump change. My young son and I used to walk into stores like this one and elicit from glove-sniffing, minor-league salesmen like me silent cries of want and memory. Because, for fuck's sake, the goal of life must not be to lose it all, to cause other people grievous harm and suffering, to wholly give up one's pride and respectability. To drop so low in the order of things that years later in an outpost far from home, clocking in for work and stepping forward to help a customer and his boy, you find yourself besieged by ghosts and mauled by a crippling need for atonement. When, let's face it, all the good folks really want is a lacrosse stick.

SAM

A GIRL SQUEEZES IN next to him at the bar, orders two drinks. Afterward he won't be able to say what the drinks were or anything about her except that her hair was brown and medium-long and he never asked her to be there.

Leaning into him, her right side against his left, she hooks a heel over the rung on his barstool.

"You guys win?"

He shakes his head.

"So, next year?"

A month from graduation, there's no next year for him. "Yeah, I guess."

"You know my boyfriend?"

She gives a name, kind of foreign, that he won't remember till later. He just shakes his head again, not looking at her, but she presses closer anyway, her right breast indenting against his biceps.

"He got cut from the team freshman year. Don't tell him I told you, okay? He's watching us."

She's drunk—he sees it now. Her face so close

her lips are misting his left ear. Faintly repulsed, but not meaning harm, just needing space, he gives her a tiny nudge with his shoulder—to shake her off.

Too hard: his soft touch unbalances her. As if the wasted strength that earlier coursed through his body has cruelly lingered, turning back to waste. Her heel catches the rung of his stool and with a low cry and a surprising heaviness she tumbles sideways into the black woman on her left.

He's in the process of standing, about to apologize, when a hand grabs his shirt from behind and jerks him violently backward: for a moment, eyes rolling wildly over the browned ceiling, he is airborne.

His spine slams the floor, the back of his skull thuds into ungiving wood.

Dazed, internal flares dilating his pupils, he comes to on his knees in the rank-smelling sawdust: his brain fogged like that mirror, past the bartender's betrayed glare, which continues to serve down his own stunned reflection.

To his wonderment, a small clearing has formed around him. People staring from a safe distance, as if he still has teeth left to bite.

Stupidly he kneels there, pawing at the back of his head for blood.

The lugged sole of a boot splits his shoulder blades, catapulting him over the fallen stool into the bottom of the bar.

He lands on the UConn duffel, the aluminum bat crowbarring his chest—a blow so ferocious it's like smelling salts, waking some older, vestigial pain. Rage rises in him like animal blood. And suddenly everything but what burns inside him is underwater-quiet. He doesn't think; at last he just becomes. In one swift move he unzips the duffel, pulls out the bat, and, levitating to his feet, turns on his assailant—just another young buck like himself, and so beneath his pity—and drives the bat two-handed, with all the strength he's ever wished for, into the guy's stomach.

RUTH

PERCHED ON THE EDGE of the bed in her underpants, ivory-colored bra dangling like a shot pheasant over the back of a chair, she slowly massages the ruinously expensive homeopathic cream into the notched side of her left breast.

The surgical wound has healed well enough, leaving the excised spoonful of private flesh invisible to the uninformed eye in sixty-three percent of all lighting situations (her estimate). In any case, at this point it's the Hippocratic approach, not the awkward visuals, that she believes matters most. Her healer in New Milford—as opposed to her oncologist in New Haven, whose relationship with the nonscientific branches of medicine is at best dismissive and at worst insulting—explained that the most important benefits of the cream, which contains some rare Peruvian or Senegalese bark and is of unknown medical efficacy but certainly can't hurt, might well come from its application, the simple yet mysterious possibilities of human tactility performed in a manner harmonious with the ancient Eastern wisdoms. An elderly Romanian with dark haunted eyes, the healer went on to suggest that perhaps this laying on of hands was something her husband could perform, would perhaps even relish doing on a nightly basis. (He claimed to have received anecdotal evidence to this effect from other patients.) And, sitting in his tranquil, pleasantly scented office with the fourteen potted plants, Ruth couldn't muster the courage or spunk to disabuse him of this idea, to tell him that, despite or because of the havoc wreaked by her rebellious cells last winter, she had sent poor Norris packing without informing him of her condition, and so would henceforth be establishing an unlicensed massage parlor of one.

Coming to the notch of missing flesh now, her fingers instinctively jump away, still refusing to acknowledge. She forces them back to the task at hand, to which they go reluctantly—showing, she guesses, that her mind is still strong enough to enforce its confused will. Nonetheless, the moment is disheartening. In the parlance of healing this is called spiritual, this not knowing whether something is going to kill you dead, this wool-over-the-eyes perplexity. And maybe it's that. But, more than that, it's simply a disgrace. At forty-seven, she has long accepted gravity's attack on her better parts—she had great tits once, and the ass to go with them—but this cutting out of herself with a blade, this cold-blooded removal, however precise and necessary, is more than she can take. It makes her feel, unbearably and every day now, how little of her there was from the start.

The TV is on across the room, tuned to *Good Morning America*: a commercial for frozen pizza; another for hemorrhoid ointment. She is waiting with a certain embarrassing passivity for the preposterously jovial weatherman to come on and tell her where today in our great and hopeful nation there will be rain, and where there will be sun.

Where, indeed.

The cream is gone, traceless. She takes her fingers away. And the breast remains, inert yet screaming. She'll try not to count all the things it's saying to her—the stage whispers and threats, the self-pitying beseechments and raging monologues—because they are hers. Somehow, without ever intending to, she's become the mad ventriloquist of her own body.

She thinks about Sam. Who is hers, too. Who will bring her back to wholeness, if anyone can. So many times during their years together (which seem to her now the only years she can remember with any color), no matter what was happening to her personally, this small victory or that massive mistake, just the thought of him, mother to son, was enough to situate her in his life rather than in her own, to grab her by the hair if necessary and yank her out of the self-regarding muck of her own existence and into the fertile, ever-changing garden of his.

In order to see him she's had to imagine him. To imagine him she's had to truly love him. To truly love him she's had, by some alchemical extension, to love herself, the mother she can be.

SAM

THE SCREAM BELONGS TO THE GIRLFRIEND.

The barroom hums with shock.

On the sawdusted floor of O'Doul's, a young man is slumped.

Sam feels the air around him contract. Whirling blindly, bat still in hand: people large and small scatter to safety.

A muffled groan draws him back to the room's sickening center, where the body writhes on the floor.

"Nic," the girlfriend begs, "stay down. Stay *down*."

Sam opens his hand. The metal bat strikes the floor with a cracked bell's dead echo. A second later, he feels his arm roughly grabbed, as behind him the bartender grunts, "And don't you fucking move."

Silently, with everything he has, Sam wills the hurt guy to get up.

"I called the cops," someone shouts from the back.

With sudden urgency, groaning and huffing, the hurt guy forces himself to one knee. "No cops . . ."

"Nic, stay *down*."

"No cops."

"You crazy fucks." The bartender again, in Sam's ear. "You crazy, stupid fucks."

With brutal effort, like a man trying to scale a shifting heap of garbage, the hurt guy claws himself almost upright. So threatening a few minutes ago, crouched and panting now, he will look no one in the face; his eyes are wounded pits of shame. A Chaplinesque wobble, three stumbling steps—then, clutching his stomach and gasping curses, he abruptly folds at the waist.

"Wait for the goddamn ambulance," implores his girlfriend.

"Shut the fuck up."

A wild arm flopped across her shoulders; the deadweight almost drags her down. Somehow, the entire room staring on mutely, they shuffle out of the bar like a single wounded animal and disappear into the night.

In O'Doul's, awkwardness and confusion follow. With no body to point to, it is not entirely clear what has just happened.

From the floor nearby, the UConn duffel gapes at Sam like a judging eye, its letters glowing white.

There is still a narrow pathway, carved by violence, to the door. Another moment or two, he thinks, and it will close.

EMMA

WHEN SHE THINKS BACK to the beginning, she can't remember meeting him. He is simply there, part of the general fabric, her brother's schoolmate at the Sherman R. Lewis Public School in Wyndham Falls, two years older than her, kind of small for his age, with hair the color of sun streaming on a yellow-sand beach and white teeth that rarely see daylight. He plays the trumpet but not very well, despite the fact that his mother is the school's music teacher. His talent on the trumpet never comes close to equaling Josh's on the violin. Not that it has to, but later on, no fault of his own, there will be no getting away from the comparison. Sometimes she sees him waiting for the bus after school, always off by himself a little, carrying the instrument in its black padded case like some weary vacuum salesman. The difference being that he's still just a little kid, not at the end of his life but at the beginning.

Then, in '94, after a thirty-eight-year-old lawyer from Box Corner named Dwight Arno finally turns himself in to the police for the hit-and-run killing of her brother, the killer's son—that boy in Josh's school, Sam Arno, the loner, small of stature and shy to smile, the boy she's never paid special attention to and can't remember meeting—becomes, locally, a negative celebrity.

Think of the backside of a billboard along I-95, with its ugly scaffolding and hidden graffiti: if you happen to get a good look at it, you are by definition heading the wrong way into hostile, oncoming traffic.

And she knows she is no different, not really.

They are like two satellites: hurled into space to orbit the same barren moon, once in a while catching curious glimpses of each other through the ash-colored murk, but never stopping to question their weirdly shared circumstances or motives.

Which maybe is understandable: by then his father is in prison; and, deep in the thrall of their emotional devastation, so are her parents.

SAM

IT IS CLOSE TO FIVE IN THE MORNING when he returns to the dorm. The leftovers of his uniform stink of old beer and frightened sweat. His body hurts in many unseen places. Since fleeing the bar, for the past couple of hours, on familiar streets and unknown fields, he has run, walked, run, and sat for long periods of stillness that are like falling, not knowing what to do or where to go.

Now, in the common room, a single lamp is on. His roommate, Jake, slouches unsmiling on the broken-down vinyl couch.

"It's my fault. I should've stayed with you."

"I really need to crash," Sam mumbles, but his legs won't move.

"I was at a party at McMahon. An hour ago, guy showed up saying his buddy'd just gone for emergency surgery. Bar fight in O'Doul's. Internal hemorrhage or something. Very fucking serious." Jake leans forward, his gaze nailing Sam into frame. "Somebody gut-whacked him with a baseball bat. The rumor already going around is maybe it was you."

The duffel in Sam's hand has begun to feel like fifty pounds. He sets it down.

"And don't fucking try to tell me how he hit you first. I don't give a shit. I told that asshole at the party, I swore to him on my mom's goddamn wedding ring that there was no way—no fucking way, Sam—that my roommate would ever be stupid or crazy or just plain wrong enough to do a fucking thing like that."

There is more, but the words turn fluid. Part of Sam absorbs their acidic implications; part repels them like accidental rain.

Until, at some point, Jake stands and says he needs to take a shower; it will help him think. After that, they will head to breakfast. Over breakfast, they will come up with a game plan.

A game plan, yes. Sam nods at his friend, or believes he does. He takes the UConn duffel into his bedroom. He closes the door.

Alone with himself, he stands looking at the brightening stain of sunrise that spreads from the window to his feet.

Something inside him has ruptured; something hideous has come out of hiding. He is leaking enough poison to kill another man, or himself. What toxin he can't identify, but he'd swear that he now understands, at the level of blood, the meaning of the word *ruin*. A sudden conviction, like a dog's yelp, impales him: to keep running and never look back. To find someone as far away as possible who might take him in and hide him from the clean world.

For the second time in twelve hours, he thinks of his father.

Unzipping the duffel, he dumps the contents on the floor. Amid the day's profane waste are the clothes he was wearing before the game.

Quickly now, he begins to pack.

DWIGHT

TWELVE-THIRTY ON THE NOSE, I look out the store's front window and see Tony Lopez's cream-colored Mercedes coupe pulling into the lot.

Tony gets his car washed every other morning on the way to work. I watch him now, stopping to inspect a recent smudge or scratch, invisible to me from this distance. A quick buff with his shirt hem and he's on the move again, eyes critically scanning the store sign; the front window displaying the impressive collection of trophies that he and his brother Jorge amassed on the baseball diamond and football field of Arenas High School; the security gate I left not quite rolled up. He frowns to himself and corrects my error, then enters the store and, shooting a look at Sandra behind the registers, orders her to get some clothes on, pronto.

"What?" she complains, hands on her hips.

He's got a point, I can't help noticing: her halter top a Day-Glo display case for her own particular trophies; her name tag an extreme-sports enthusiast about to tumble to a happy death off the face of Mount Shasta.

Sandra shouts to Derek to cover for her, before strutting down aisle nine and through the security door into the stockroom.

"That girl," Tony grumbles, shaking his head. "She thinks she can just show it like a free movie and everybody's happy."

"Some people probably *are* happy," I venture.

"She's my niece," Tony says, ending the subject.

Once every couple of weeks, Tony and I have lunch together at a nearby Mexican cantina that's another small piece in the modest business empire he's gradually building. The lunches began not long after his hiring me as a sales assistant six years ago—no doubt as a way for the boss to keep tabs on a rookie employee with a certain kind of track record. But, to Tony's credit, the meals don't make me feel as if Big Brother's watching. A few years younger than me and exponentially more set on his feet, he seems to have no interest in overtly contrasting our situations, save for the obvious reality that I now work for him. He respects the fact that, prior to my troubles back East, I went to law school and for a while was a practicing attorney. (And possibly, out of a desire not to cut off this unexpected avenue of goodwill, I've been guilty of not giving him a fuller picture of my former professional vicissitudes.) He also takes a sincere interest in my estranged relationship with my son.

For beyond the snappy shirts and expensive summer-weight slacks and the gold-rimmed designer shades perpetually perched on his bronzed, balding head, Tony is a genuine family man. His pretty blond wife, Jodi, and their twin seven-year-old daughters, Ruby and Jade (Tony and Jodi are fans of a certain Home Shopping Network strain in the naming of American children that would now seem to be the norm), are his delight, and he's given to handing out wallet-size photos of them to near-strangers. He often mentions his beloved mother (Papi cut out when Tony and Jorge were still in Pampers) and the Los Angeles barrio he grew up in, and to me, anyway, it never feels like just a line. As Tony and I have become friends over time—he's near the top of my very short list of guys to watch football with—I've occasionally gone to his and Jodi's home at the foot of the Santa Ynez Mountains for big, festive family dinners that, after a couple of tequilas, always make me feel as if there are balloons and piñatas tied up everywhere, even when there aren't.

At lunch today, I order the large chicken taco salad (it comes in a kind of crispy sombrero that you're free to wear out of the restaurant if you're in the mood) and silently vow to ignore the chips. Since moving out to California, Diet Dr Pepper has become my daytime beverage of choice and, on the whole, I try to eat like a native. I exercise most days and am not averse to fresh fruit.

One of the ironies of enforced institutional life is that the hours of nothing time that threaten to drown you can also lead you to get yourself in pretty good fighting shape. It's possible in certain locales to see a murderer's handprints—or, for that matter, a tax evader's, and wouldn't you know it, they look much the same—faintly worn into the grimed cement floor. He's been doing his push-ups and crunches for months now, years, day after day, preparing himself for some test with no name or prize money attached to it. There our man sits, lats and delts and traps getting bigger, finding abs he hasn't seen since he was a high-school virgin, but the truth is he ends up scaring no one but himself. Because for all the work on his body, the rock-hard carapace he daily attempts to fashion, the absolute mystery of the overall scheme—the tragedy by which he got here in the first place—grows no plainer to him, and never will.

Then one stupendous day, according to the calendar that never lies, he gets spit out by the state. And if our man is unusually lucky and tenacious he'll eventually find his way to some situation that looks a lot like human society. A diorama, but with real sunshine. And there he'll continue his daily exercise routine—we won't call it a "regimen," which might suggest good health and a required monthly membership—that he learned inside. A certain number of reps, a certain series of poses. Disciplined man that he is, he'll order the salad and stay off the chips. And the irony of it all won't escape him: how he's keeping himself strong in order to endure, or fight back, the very thing he can't understand. Which, like the fine California weather, keeps coming at him, relentless. At this rate, he could live for a very long time.

"Hey," Tony says mildly, snapping his fingers. "I'm talking business here."

"Right."

"Want to be more involved, you gotta be on the ball."

"I'm on the ball, Tony."

"Yeah?" He eyes me skeptically, in no rush whatever. A hint of ownership in his gaze, as if I'm a second car and he's checking me for dings. And it occurs to me, and not for the first time, that he's the only person in the state who knows my official record. Information that from the start he's promised to keep confidential, so long as I live up to the responsibility given to me. As it's turned out, I've earned his trust and we've become friends. Not partners but teammates of a kind—the way I guess the lug man in the pit crew is a member of the team, due his share on payday, even if not cut out for the bright lights of the winner's circle.

I take a swallow of diet soda and prepare for Tony's verdict. In my position I seem to spend a lot of time simply waiting, stuck on like a limpet, for other people to give me the news.

Finally, he flashes his *telenovela* smile. "Just keeping you on your toes, hombre."

I smile back.

"That bakery out near the 217 overpass? Feeling they getting ready to sell. Low foot traffic and rising value of the underlying asset. I could do better with that site. Maybe time to take a look."

"You thinking sporting goods?"

"Maybe a gym. Athletic center. Start a chain."

"That would be a new direction," I reply carefully.

"New and not new." Tony finishes his mineral water and cocks a frowning glance into the kitchen, where a disorganized clatter can be heard. "Matter of branding."

I nod, because it seems the right thing to do at the moment, and because I have nothing worthwhile to add to the conversation. He isn't asking for my opinion, anyway. There was a time—as a young lawyer in Hartford (my first stint in that beleaguered northeastern city), billing hundreds every hour—when I had something to say, for a price, about almost anything you could imagine.

According to the law, as I still recall it, words

are our fate, perhaps our character, too: they will make us or break us. But the gloomier truth is that the breakage usually happens in an instant, life changing in a single wordless act. The words are the last thing you hear before you slip into the darkness of afterward, mere nails in the coffin.

RUTH

BY HER STANDARDS, she believes, the message she leaves this evening on Sam's cellphone—the only phone he has, its monthly contract paid through his summer-job savings—is unimpeachable in its lack of emotional Velcro: he can bounce right off it if he likes, and never think of getting stuck.

She does not say: *I am looking increasingly like a woman I would give a dollar to on the street.*

Nor: *The real reason I play the piano so often and with such desperate zeal at home is not because of my lifelong passion for music but, rather, to rule out the possibility—more and more likely—of conversing aloud with myself, which, as we both know, would be embarrassing.*

Nor: *I was thinking of you yesterday morning, and then couldn't stop. All day long, you understand? Though I have gone about what I've needed to do like a normal person—don't worry, I'm not broken. I just wanted, now, to hear your voice.*

Here is the message she actually leaves, in its entirety:

"Sam, hi, it's Mom . . . Just, you know, checking in . . . Nothing urgent . . . Wondering how you are—Oh, stupid of me: How'd the big game go? I'm sorry I couldn't be there. Let me know everything when you have a moment . . . Okay, well . . . Sending love . . . Bye . . ."

There are speeches that have started wars and led to suicides. This would not be one of them. It is a penny dropped down a very deep well. Ruth has loads of pennies stored up; she is that kind of woman.

You let it go and then wait for the splash and echo; you hold your breath or pray. The rest is in how you choose to think about it.

She sits down at the piano in her living room to wait.

SAM

THE GREYHOUND TERMINAL IN VEGAS.

No one in the world knows where he is. This could be freedom, except it pretty clearly isn't.

From a waiting-room bench, three days of stubble on his jaw, he watches half his fellow losers grab their rucksacks and worn suitcases and slink off into the deathless light of the Nevada morning.

Vegas, baby.

No one around to greet them. When they're gone, he misses them, broods over them henlike, though during their cross-country ride together he stubbornly avoided all contact. These poor unwashed bus creatures have reached their destination, apparently.

The glimpse of his own nature that abruptly comes at him then is a mental sucker punch. He almost goes down, but doesn't.

DWIGHT

BY FIVE O'CLOCK, with an hour till closing, I'm loitering behind the store next to the hulking dumpster, at my feet a tidy pile of half-smoked butts. One a day my prescribed limit—perfectly reasonable, I'd argue, given that I'm probably the last nicotine junkie in the state and bear responsibility for single-handedly keeping the industry alive. Leaving the pile visible is my way of showing whoever might be interested that I'm not only keeping with my program but can restrain myself from smoking the death stick all the way to the filter. I personally sweep up the mess every Saturday afternoon, thus to start fresh again on Monday. Creature of habit that I am. Dog urinating on a bush.

Officially at present, however, I'm overseeing the unloading of a Nike truck backed up to the store's open rear port: large industrial-strength boxes of Nike golf clubs and Nike soccer balls and footballs and Nike track shoes and field cleats and high-tops and all manner of Nike equipment and apparel, Lycra and cotton, tight and baggy. Call it legal pornography—a man allowed (no, paid, though not richly) to ogle in broad daylight the unveiling of humble but sacred objects (balls and sticks and nets) that, in the right hands, on emerald fields of dreams, might one day become the heroic stories of his unlived life, memories better than his own.

The sound of basketball dribbling then, childhood's echo: it's Evander, Tony's nephew by marriage, twenty-six going on thirteen, who works the stockroom and does odd jobs for us when he isn't chasing skirts and getting high down at the piers. Tony, being a family man, makes room for all sorts so long as they're blood, or nearly, casts a wide financial umbrella and is generous with his shade. Evander, wearing lime-green Nadal clamdiggers and a violet striped Pacific Sunwear tank, does a through-the-legs crossover with head fake, goes round the back, and pulls up for an imaginary jumper.

"Ooosh. Gi-down." He mimes the ball going through the invisible net, and one of the Nike truck guys—heavyweight division, with a shaved noggin—turns to get an eyeful of this Majorcan-dressed man-child. The ball in Evander's hands a Nike, of course, fresh off the truck. The

cardboard frame it came in lies in torn pieces on the ground—just one more thing in his life the kid has no intention of ever paying for or picking up.

"Evander?"

He shoots me a grin, right wrist still down-flapped as if he's just sunk the winning trifecta at the Staples Center.

"Is there something more constructive you could be doing right now besides playing air hoops?"

"What, like *smoking?*" The grin turning stiletto—as if to say, in his fake homeboyese: *Yo, hoss, I'ze family and you ain't.* "Getting, like, cancer?"

"It so happens I'm working."

"Yeah? So *happens* I'm Kobe."

"I hate to break it to you, dude, but you're white and short."

"*Dude?* Man, how old're you, anyway?"

Dribbling leisurely, the kid sways and jukes his way into the building.

"I'm half a fucking century, you prick," I say to no one in particular.

The huge truck guy cocks his cue-ball head at me. I shrug and ground out my cigarette, tossing the butt onto the pile by the dumpster.

Reentering the premises, I can feel the air-conditioning on too high. This is a sore spot with Tony, who has to pay the bills. I walk through the stockroom into the mechanicals room and adjust the thermostat three degrees warmer. I'm functioning, doing things, but in my head I've moved on to thinking about Penny Jacobs, the pretty and refreshingly forthright UCSB English professor who'll be coming over to my house for dinner the next evening—and, if the stars are aligned and the gods mildly tanked, maybe some romance as well.

I met Penny right here in the store, in aisle six (aqua sports, camping), the week before Christmas. She stopped in to look for snorkel equipment for her daughter, who, she mentioned with a faint note of feminine irritation, was going to Florida "to see her father." A phrase and tone that caught my attention, as did her short brown hair, pert nose, and tennis player's slim but muscular legs. As did the big fat book she was lugging around (only customer to do so) in her ringless left hand. Upon inquiry, the book turned out to be the collected letters of Elizabeth Bishop, a poet I'd never heard of but who, I was assured, was one of the greats. By which time I was listening hard while saying things like "And your daughter's shoe size is?" and staring into this woman's hazel eyes as she told me about this literary genius who'd lived in Brazil and been a lesbian while also probably being in love with (though apparently never screwing) another great, pretty much insane poet named Robert Lowell, and who—this was Bishop she was talking about, not Lowell—sometimes spent up to fifteen years working on a single poem, drafts of which she kept stuck to her refrigerator door. And I responded, pulling a pair out of a box, with something like "These are the best fins in the game," or some such inanity, because that's my job. She gave me a little smile then, though not at all condescending—something to the tune of "It must be sort of a kick to say things like 'These are the best fins in the game,' which really, when you get down to it, in its fine American banality, is just another kind of poetry." All of which seemed pretty unusual and appealing to me under the circumstances—namely, our being in a sporting-goods store—and struck me meaningfully, and not just because I'd been a near-monk for so long that I'd begun to feel like Thomas Merton (the only monk whose name I could reliably recall).

And so, before I knew it, I'd rashly offered Penny Jacobs twenty-five percent off the merchandise (top of the line and rated a Best Buy by *Consumer Reports*) in exchange for her phone number.

A deal she took, though only after due consideration.

"Boss?"

Lost in my reverie, I've wandered out to the sales floor and am now being greeted by Chang Sook Oh, former manager of the UCSB varsity tennis team and by far our most conscientious employee, emerging from the stockroom with two boxes of hockey skates for a waiting customer.

"What's up, Chang?"

"We're out all Merrells between eights and eleven and a halfs. And Salomons are low. Should I place an order?"

"Check with Derek first to see what's low his side. And when you talk to Mike at distribution tell him we need that bulk discount. They scrimped us last time."

"Got it, Boss."

Chang wears his clothes and hair neat, goes to church every Sunday, and is the only person in America who calls me Boss.

"How's your mother, Chang?"

"Doing better today, thanks, Boss."

I watch him walk away, duck-toed and light on his feet. His mother has kidney problems that will probably do her in soon, but the kid never complains about it and never misses a day's work. A good son. I can picture him washing her swollen feet in water scented with some Korean herb; making a Tupperware lunch for her before heading off in the morning; checking the connections on the dialysis machine to make sure that, within the sad, sinking chaos of her last years, this one necessary thing will function according to the warranty.

45

Of course, such ruminations by a man in middle life about a young man his son's age are prone to a high degree of subjectivity. Like most guys of my ilk (whatever that means), I'm in all likelihood just another salmon narcissist, ever returning to the corpse-strewn spawning ground of me, where one day, unless something even worse happens, I too will quietly expire.

What I can say for certain is that watching Chang Sook Oh approach his seated customer at the end of aisle nine (skis, snowboards, winter-sports apparel, ice skates, hockey equipment), squat down, and enthusiastically present the merchandise as though on a silver platter, a suckling pig at a feast, hearing his low, genuinely congratulatory murmur of "These Bauers are top of the line," I can feel myself already eddying off into a backwater of personal regret that, in truth, has nothing to do with this upstanding young man or his dying mother and everything to do with my own internal weather.

At the register, Sandra's just finishing ringing somebody up: "Thanks and, you know, have a good one."

Exit customer, bearing two cans of Penn tennis balls, rolls of Tourna Grip, a pack of string grommets, and a Wilson sun visor.

"What*ever*," Sandra mutters to herself.

"Tony come in?" I ask.

"Had to take his dog to the vet. Some sort of diarrhea thing? Poop all over the house."

"Sounds ugly."

"Like, what kind of name is Dudley for a dog?" Sandra grabs a SoCal sales catalog and begins fanning herself. "It's so motherfuckin' hot in here. Can't you turn up the conditioning or something?"

"Just turned it down. Ever pay your own utility bills?"

"Tony can be so cheap sometimes."

"I'm going to get some air for a minute."

"You already got some."

I look at her.

She puts her hands on her hips—her lippy pose. "What, like you think you're invisible on the security camera back there? You got a nicotine problem, Dwight. That's *bad.*"

I grin. "I know."

I head out the front doors. Weekdays can't touch weekends in the sporting-goods trade, and the parking lot is only a quarter full.

For Chang's ice-skate customer, I pick the Mercedes SUV, and a Subaru Outback wagon for the schoolteacher type I saw poking around the Patagonia fleece vests in aisle three. Just a little game of mine to pass the time. A palm tree is growing out of a clump of green between the lot and the four-lane Calle Real, and high up its leaves are shimmying in a breeze that, down

47

where I'm standing, I can't even feel. A hallucinatory taste of the evening's first cold beer starts climbing the back of my throat, and this is not an unhappy thing.

Then a yawn convulses me, and the moment it's over I feel doomed by fatigue.

SAM

HE COLLECTS HIS DUFFEL from the luggage well. The driver points him in the direction of the municipal bus stop half a mile away, and he starts to walk. Late afternoon, a fog of exhaustion in his head. Moving, after three days of sitting, still bruised from the fight, like an old man with rickets.

He observes that Santa Barbara is a clean and prosperous town, not entirely real. Half the street names are in Spanish. The few people he sees are sun-browned and mostly blond, dressed in shorts, T-shirts, slip-on sneakers, or flip-flops. They appear to regard him, if they regard him at all, with curious suspicion, as a ragged and somewhat embarrassing spectacle from the Far North. An assessment with which he cannot disagree. He thinks how the nights back East will still be cold. The fog in his head slowly beginning to lift, he remembers Emma holding him that night two years ago, her hand burning down the front of his jeans as she presses him against the rusted feed trough of the abandoned farm in Falls Village. The feeling of being, just this once, a single body, two broken pieces forged together in the secret, dew-ridden dark.

His arm has begun to ache, and he stops to switch the duffel to his other hand. A light breeze blowing in from the west. In it the fermented whiff of his own body and what he hopes might be the briny breath of the Pacific. Though right now he can't see his way to the ocean; just the sourceless egg-blue light everywhere and the vertiginous, faintly swaying palms along the broad sunbaked streets whose brightness has begun to infect him like the onset of motion sickness.

He remembers sitting on a sofa next to his dad and watching a ballgame, the smells of furniture leather and cooked popcorn, his dad's heavy arm resting on his shoulders, pulling him in; but which year and which game he doesn't know and will never trust.

And so it goes: the duffel switching hand to hand, the mind clear but seeing backward, the angled sun anointing him like a troubled pilgrim who's journeyed to the far edge of the continent in search of a blessing that he doesn't believe in but can't stop looking for.

PENNY

THURSDAY OFFICE HOURS RUN FORTY MINUTES late because her toughest, most confident student (the brassy, probably gay, raven-haired junior who starts at point guard for the women's varsity basketball team and who for some reason seemed to believe, until today, that a poem, no matter how well made, is just a simple equation with a plug-in answer), Angela, while reading aloud some Louise Glück lines on the death of the poet's father, bursts into tears, right in her office. Not so discrete or containable after all, this big, intelligent, well-defended girl, whose own father turns out to be on his deathbed. There she sits, gasping with sobs, stripped right down to the interior—the soft tissue, where the pain resides and the words, if they're true, take root. Nothing for Penny to do but comfort her and pass the Kleenex and say, *I know, I know.* Because, dammit, she does know. If not these specific lines—*My father has forgotten me / in the excitement of dying* (no, Penny's dad, tough nut that he is, is still out there making a nuisance of himself)—then the more communal experience of being knocked flat, your liver ripped out, by a handful of lines on a page.

On her way home she stops at Vons to buy fresh herbs and arugula, a baguette, for dinner. She'll make an omelet and a salad, fruit for dessert, and then while Ali works on her report on the Biafran War (bit of a stretch for a twelve-year-old, it seems to Penny), she'll go into her little study off the kitchen, sit on her Eames lounge chair and ottoman (the set, which she loves with an embarrassing ardor, a fifth-anniversary present from her ex, Darryl, one of the only unselfish acts she's inclined to credit him with in retrospect), take her original copy of Glück's *The Triumph of Achilles* off the shelf and, poem by poem, immerse herself in the pure early work as in a pool of deep, clear water whose underground tributaries, bearing news from distant mountains, she can feel but never accurately source.

Parking the car, she enters the house through the back door, straight into the kitchen.

"You're late." Ali's greeting the hooded gaze that appeared on the girl's face about six months ago and never left. She's sitting—brown-haired and, in Penny's opinion, way too put-together for someone still under five feet tall—at the kitchen table with a bottle of Vitaminwater, a bag of Gummi Bears, a metallic pink laptop, and a heavy tome on the Biafran conflict.

Setting the groceries on the counter, Penny goes to the refrigerator for the eggs. "Sorry, student meltdown."

"Over poetry?" The sarcasm implicit, impressive, without a single note of strain.

"As a matter of fact, yes." Cracking eggs into a bowl and beginning to chop the herbs.

Ali sniffs, pops a Gummi Bear into her mouth.

"You'll ruin your appetite," Penny hears herself say automatically, remembering, even as she speaks, a line from another Glück poem: *Once we were happy, we had no memories.*

"The Biafrans had to eat their dogs when there weren't any more goats," Ali declares. "They ate their parrots."

"Please move your things and set the table."

"Whole families were brutally murdered with machetes. Some were burned. It was, like, one of the most savage wars in history."

And another Glück: *I had come to a strange city, without belongings: / in the dream, it was your city, I was looking for you.*

"Would you like your baguette heated?"

Was it seeing Angela, the tough jock, break down in her office that makes her feel so vulnerable now to these internal waves of words about being freed from the past? Penny thinks about Dwight, how the thing about him, right from that first day, meeting him in the sporting-goods store, getting picked up by him really, is his categorical difference from the rest of the cast of her life. He's not some hotshot linguistics professor like Darryl, not a blazing preteen sharpshooter like Ali. He couldn't care less about stupid academic politics or, for that matter, what's cool or uncool in junior high, wouldn't know a good poem from a bad one if it hit him on the head. What he is, she senses intuitively (and still can't say why), is solid, tangible; a man, lived-in, sure of himself, respectful, decent. She doesn't have to go looking for him with blind hands in the dark to know what she has or whom she can trust. Doesn't, as in the old days, have to spend precious emotional capital that she isn't sure she has in trying to one-up him, or outmaneuver him, or, worst of all, lie to him.

Scraping the eggs onto two plates, adding a piece of baguette for each of them, she splashes olive oil and lemon juice over the arugula.

"Sit," she says to Ali, who sighs and rolls her eyes but in the end, being twelve and having no other option, joins her for dinner.

SAM

AT LAST HE TURNS, the arm carrying the duffel by now numb and roughly five feet long, onto a short street called Hacienda. His GPS a torn-off remnant of a much creased and fingerprinted envelope marked by return address in his father's chunky scrawl: the original having contained a Hallmark Christmas card of a hockey-playing snowman with the same seven words as every year added at the bottom—*Think of you often.*

Love, your dad—along with a check for a hundred dollars.

The card he threw out like the ones before it. The check, like the other checks, he cashed at the deli on his way to practice. The gift money he squandered on a denim shirt with fake mother-of-pearl buttons.

Not part of his traveling kit now, the shirt. Left behind with so much else. Just the envelope with this street name: *Hacienda.* Single-story stucco boxes in various shades of pale, no garages, patios probably in the back. Out front tidy, bright-eyed flowers, clean little middle-class Southern California street.

Not the dad he remembers from twelve years ago, not possible: these cupcake houses that have never known the cold, dull weight of snow or remorse.

The house is beige, same color as the one across from it. He stands between them, middle of the quiet street, looking from one to the other. A less-than-new Chrysler Sebring convertible parked in front of No. 28.

He passes through the low gate, onto a cement-block path. In the center of the door floats a knocker in the shape of an amputated hand holding a smaller-than-regulation baseball. Funny, almost. Sam recognizes the grip on the pitch as a two-seam fastball. He puts his hand over it for confirmation, a private reenactment. Can't help himself. The white-painted metal still warm from the afternoon sun.

The last pitch he'll probably ever see was a two-seamer.

Now, on the far side of the country, it comes for him again, living thing, rising and tailing away the closer it gets to home.

The bat still on his shoulder.

The bat sinking into another man's flesh.

He takes his hand off the knocker without making a sound. There's a doorbell, too, but he doesn't try it. He stands frozen. It's dawning on him in painful stages how his running all the way here is a pathetic tracing of his father's running from his crime twelve years ago. There is no such place in this world as "away." Nothing for him to do now that he's here but stand outside his father's gingerbread house like some paratrooper mistakenly dropped from the sky. What he needs is X-ray vision. To glean through this firewall door some early warning of the radioactive force within, the human trouble waiting there.

Exhaustion is suddenly upon him like a caul: so many hard, pointless miles traveled, and Hacienda Street just a snow-globe desert like any other.

He should've made some kind of plan. This is not a plan.

He puts his hand on the door, turns the knob and, to his surprise, feels the latch give; and, before he can regret himself a moment longer, he's through, into his father's house.

EMMA

FOUR YEARS AGO: her father, Ethan Learner, once admired literature professor and critic, stands in front of the sagging bookshelves in his study, an open poetry book in his hands. Emma is sixteen; her dad forty-six, plenty of salt in his dark hair, a ragged beard, too, grown by neglect, and, above the round bookish glasses, black Russian eyebrows in need of a trim.

She has stopped in the doorway of that room whose quality of doomed penance makes even seasoned visitors, even family, pause and reconsider.

A long silence: digesting a poem, he raises a finger in her direction, but not his head.

"Dad, I'm spending the night at Paula's. I'll see you in the morning, okay?"

He doesn't seem to hear. Then, slowly, the head comes up, blinking her in; it is always a long way back for him. In the past eight years, his son's killer has gone to prison, been released, and disappeared somewhere, maybe to his own little hell. But here at home none of it has made any difference that Emma can see, except for the beard.

"Let me read you something," her father says, with more intensity than the occasion requires.

In the window behind him, past the huge dusk-shadowed limbs of the old oak that has stood in the yard since God knows when, Emma observes the glowing brake lights of her best friend's car.

"Dad—"

"Just the first couple of lines. Her name was Katherine Philips."

"Dad, I'm going, okay? I'll see you tomorrow."

Imperceptibly his head falls back, as if by interrupting his train of morbid thought and robbing him of his feeling (though she wants to point out that the feeling isn't really his but rather belongs to just another dead writer) she has cruelly cut him off from his one source of comfort. Stung, his liquid dark eyes quickly drop back to his book, and a guilty heat begins to creep up her face. He's Sisyphus, for Christ's sake, can't she see? And once again, selfish girl, she's chosen not to help him climb his mountain.

She leaves him there and goes outside.

This time of year, late fall, the dusk is as dark as night. From Paula's car, she glances back and sees her mother watching from the open front door. Just watching. Backlit, wearing a stylish cardigan, her blond hair expensively cut: outwardly, at forty-three, the talented and

57

successful garden designer that some of the people of Wyndham Falls still remember from the days before the tragedy.

And yet, upon closer inspection, there's something a bit off about her. She isn't waving and calling out "Have a good time, girls!" like the other mothers. Instead she murmurs, so softly it's like a wounded bird spiraling toward you in the dusk, "Be careful!" Followed by the totally unnecessary "Drive safely!" Which makes her daughter want to hug her, and also to throttle her. Because it's been like this for so long—half Emma's entire life—that the memory of that earlier, supposedly happy time is like an old sheet that's been washed too many times: thin, stained, torn, in places translucent—you can see right through it.

And that's what life is now.

Her mother, Grace Learner, turns, closes the door. Shut up again, the house is briefly no more than it would seem to be—a "dignified" old Colonial, according to the Realtor, who in a few years will unsuccessfully put it on the market.

Smell of exhaust: Paula waiting. But Emma can't bring herself to leave anymore. Continues to stand hypnotized by the scene, a frozen lake studded with frozen lives, her gaze pulled back through the black limbs to the glaring window, where her father still stands by the bookshelf reading poems that exist only thanks to the deaths of children.

And in a few moments, as she already knows will happen, her mother appears in the doorway of her father's room and stands there waiting, as earlier her last living child waited, for the man of the house to look up from his tears and recognize her.

DWIGHT

AFTER WORK, I go home and take a long shower. I hold myself as still as possible and let the hard, calcified water come down. Then I put on a terry-cloth robe and head for the kitchen to get myself the evening's first beer.

The house is empty when I enter the bathroom, but it isn't empty when I come out. The sense I have of another man in my house is kinetic and alarming: I feel him before I see him. My muscles tighten, and I take small, charged steps to the edge of the living room.

But, to my confusion, instead of a stranger wielding a kitchen knife or carrying off my TV, what I find is a handsome, leanly muscular, not very clean young man sitting on my sofa, his long legs splayed before him.

I stand in shock. With his mop of greasy sand-colored hair, prominent cheekbones, and wide-apart eyes, the young man looks like his mother, except for the dimple in his chin that's mine.

"You left the door unlocked."

We haven't seen or spoken to each other in twelve years. His voice now not high and sweet as when he was a boy but a sandpaper dirge, deep and a little flat. (Missed that, I think with a sodden feeling in my chest—and his first shave, his high-school graduation, and every other thing he's gone and lived through without me.) His tone, for starters, as if I've just accused him of something, though I haven't.

I take a few moments to compose myself as best I can.

"How are you, Sam?"

The question may be too existential for his taste: he sits looking at his hands.

"You thirsty?" I hear myself persisting. "Want something to drink?"

He is ten years old again, lying in bed in our house in Box Corner. Outside it's snowing and the sun is just coming up, but you can't feel any warmth behind the snow. I help him under the covers, his smell so innocent I can't believe I ever had a hand in the making of him. I tell him to go back to sleep. Everything will be fine, I say, though it isn't and hasn't been for a long time and, indeed, never will be again. And Sam believes me. He asks if I'll take him sledding later, and I promise I will. And then he closes his eyes and I kiss him goodbye and step out into the hallway, where the face of what I've done and whom I've hurt is waiting for me.

And that is the end, and the beginning.

"D'you have any beer?" he asks now.

In the kitchen, out of his sight, I lean against the wall.

The refrigerator with its undrunk bottles and cool bright-lit air: sometimes this is all you find yourself trying to get to.

I get there, and bring back two bottles of beer.

He's pulled in his legs, is sitting up now like a guest. Staring at his hands, which are as dirty as a boy's. Nothing looking right to him in my rented California house, but then why should it?

I hand him a beer and sit across from him, not too close to scare anybody. An anxious penny taste on my tongue. My hands aching with the need to touch him.

"So. How's school?" A stab at general conversation, to give myself a fighting chance. A safe enough place to start, it would seem.

"I left." He says this to his hands, quietly.

I sit looking at him, dumb as a stick.

"There was a fight."

He takes a deep, needy swallow of beer. Angrily he wipes the sweating bottle on his T-shirt, leaving a wet spot.

"In a bar."

He swallows more beer and stares at his hands again.

"This guy hit me from behind, and I . . ." He shakes his head. "I just kind of lost it."

"Lost it how?"

Now, solemnly, he nods—a gesture so out of sync with himself and the story he's telling that my heartbeat lurches with a panicked clamor into my head.

"I hit him with a baseball bat," he says.

"What?"

"He came at me first."

"A *bat?* Jesus, Sam, are you out of your mind? How bad was he hurt? Was he conscious? Bleeding?"

"He got up and walked out on his own." His voice has turned suddenly stiff, and he's blushing—from shame, I imagine, at having to admit to me, of all people, how badly he lost control of himself.

I breathe out, feeling my pulse slow a notch. "Did anybody press charges?"

"No."

"Thank God. Christ, you're lucky."

His eyes snap up and fix on me, bright and hard with disgust.

The room is silent. I watch my neighbor, Ramón Hernandez, drive past my window and park in front of his house.

Sam gets up. I almost say something to stop him, but then I see that he's not actually going anywhere: his shoulders are hunched in defeat, and he's left his duffel behind. Halfway to the front door he stops and turns, aimless—not old or brave or mean enough, I'd swear, to have attacked another man with a baseball bat in a bar.

"I wanted to hurt him."

His voice is so quiet I can't be certain I've heard him correctly.

"What?"

He looks away and doesn't repeat the remark.

"Does your mother know?"

"She's got enough on her plate."

"Meaning?"

"Nothing. I just want to take a shower, okay? I've been on a bus for three days, and I just want to take a shower, if that's okay with you."

Like a sinking, poisonous balloon it lands: the answer to the question I've been too scared to ask. Why, after all the years of locking me out, he's finally come to my doorstep.

This feeling of dirt. Unable to wash it off because now it's inside him and untouchable.

In the bathroom, behind the closed door, the shower begins to run.

I can hear the moment he steps under the stream, my ears still attuned that way. Imagining my son's long, carelessly muscled torso and the water beating down on him. The outside dirt running off, different from my dirt and particular to himself.

At the same time, listening to him try to scrape himself clean, thinking about his being here at all, I find that I'm having trouble shrugging off the nagging fear that it's some dark, sticky notion of me and my life that led him to run away from what he's done, as I ran years ago.

But what can you do with a thought like that, except turn away from it as fast as you can? I go to my room, drop the terry robe (suddenly preposterous under the circumstances), and pull on whatever clothes are at hand. I sit on the bed and hold myself still while I count off thirty seconds.

Old trick from the downtime.

Two years since I've used it, but Sam's mother's number comes back now without fail. (It was my house, too, once.) First digit, then the fingers walking the rest. Which only proves, maybe, that there's no such thing as an ex-wife. The long, slow ringing is almost soothing till it stops.

"Ruth, it's Dwight."

Her silence is so long I lose track of it. I begin to think I hear a TV somewhere, and some slithery movement followed by a papery flutter— probably her closing a magazine she's been reading in bed.

"Ruth?"

"I'm here."

"Sam's in my house."

"What?"

Before she can say any more, I jump in and tell her the gist of it, along with what scattershot details I know of the matter.

Her shock, understandably, is many-sided. She bombards me with questions that I can't answer. Still, I do my best.

When I'm finished, Ruth observes—not meaning it as praise—"You sound like a lawyer."

I'm about to halfheartedly defend myself when I look up and see Sam standing in the hallway, a towel knotted at his waist and his torso glistening with water. A bruise like a beanpole eggplant across his muscled chest. His beauty, even so, simple and astonishing to me, a shock to the paternal system: as if the boy he used to be, beautiful, too, but miles different, fits inside this bruised man without meaning or wanting to; as if this creature is both man and boy.

"Where is he? I need to talk to him. Please, Dwight, for God's sake, put him on."

I reach out the phone. "It's your mother."

Sam shakes his head.

"Talk to her."

The shake of his head grows fierce, almost violent. He turns—I catch a glimpse of a second nasty bruise on his upper back, this one fist-size—and disappears into the guest room, shutting the door.

"He doesn't seem to be up for talking just yet, Ruth."

"I still don't understand what he's doing there. He should be *here,* dammit." A castered, fumbling noise on her end, and I picture her hunting for something—Ambien or chewing gum—in the drawer of her bedside table. "I always knew something like this would happen."

"Ruth, listen. I don't understand the situation any more than you. Just give me a little time with him and let me see if I can't sort him out, come up with some sort of plan."

Her laugh is so grimly sardonic it causes the skin on my back to prickle.

"Who's going to sort *you* out, Dwight? That's the question."

And then, before I can attempt an answer, she hangs up.

RUTH

FROM THE BED, still holding the phone, she makes her way quickly to the bathroom, unsure whether to pee or throw up. In the end doing neither, choosing by default, because she's already there, simply to stand at the sink looking at the haggard scarecrow the mirror gives back to her. A purple cardigan over her checked flannel nightgown, little patches of scalp gaping whitely through the sparse new growth of hair on her head. Were she to witness such a picture of another woman in a bathroom at night, she feels certain—the cardigan and nightgown, the henpecked coiffure, the tag-sale regalia—she'd have to draw a host of ungenerous conclusions about her and her life situation, starting with her ability to be a good and responsible mother. For if you can't take better care of yourself than this—if, certainly no longer young, you let yourself go to the extent of wearing pilled sweaters to bed and having hair that resembles a mostly empty bowl of popcorn; if, peering into the bathroom mirror at an hour when most women should be snuggling up with their husbands in front of *An Affair to Remember* instead of *The Daily Show* alone, what you see staring back at you from the looking glass is, in effect, not yourself as you once recalled her but an answer to one of the more absurd questions in the Sunday *New York Times* crossword—well, you do the math. And she has; she's done the math. Which is why, probably, standing now in the bathroom, she finds herself suddenly chilled despite the cardigan and the thick rag-wool socks, feeling the April cold in her poisoned bones to a degree that goes way beyond the seasonal meteorological average (not for nothing is Bow Mills called "the icebox of Connecticut") or the fact that, responsibly for a woman who some months ago decided that she would rather live alone and sick than with a silly man who too often made her want to laugh at rather than with him, she's turned the thermostat down to sixty-two degrees for the night.

The hand still holding the phone is trembling—again, nothing to do with the cold. She sets the black plastic instrument on the sloping clamshell rim of the sink and lets go, only to watch it slide down into the bowl and come to rest on top of the dulled chrome drain. She stands looking at this, the earpiece out of which her ex-husband's voice with his terrible unhappy news has sprung at her, her urge to turn on the tap and electrocute the thing ferociously strong.

DWIGHT

WHEN SAM'S DOOR REMAINS CLOSED, I take a second beer out to the patio and, zoo-like, pace back and forth. Some ominous little weeds have sprouted around the cement, I see, and I make a mental note to spray the hell out of them with Roundup over the weekend. Meanwhile, someone's grilling chicken in his backyard a couple of houses over, the marinated smoke rising up plump and fragrant; and a neighbor's dog begins to bark hungrily, then another. Then both animals' voices abruptly fall dead, and the evening is still again.

Minutes pass like this, the dusk settling in—the lazy, arrogant, slow-moving dusk of Southern California, where the world is your oyster and there's time enough for any dream. And I remember that my son, who until an hour ago I stubbornly continued, against various odds of my own making, to think of as a sensitive boy forever young, is now twenty-two years old, a grown man who has violently struck another man with a baseball bat. A physical expression of some roiling darkness in him that I surely recognize, because it is mine.

And, at some point, one has to ask: What are a kid's odds going to be growing up, when his father does time for killing a boy, accident or not? What are his odds going to be, anyway? Not even my old man did that to his family.

My bottle is empty. I sit down heavily on the one chair in my backyard.

Tomorrow I'll buy another chair, I finally almost decide; and more plates, and maybe a bigger freezer, too. I'll think about what's happened here today and make lists toward change and attend to those lists with a hopeful urgency that I cannot in fact recall in myself.

I get up and go inside.

The house is quiet. I walk down the short hallway and stand with an ear against the closed door to the guest bedroom, hearing nothing from inside. After a few moments, I knock lightly and open the door.

My son is lying on his back on the bed, mouth agape, still in the towel he was wearing, his right arm dangling off the edge. There is no movement in him at all, and for a terrible moment I believe he is dead. I think he has killed himself somehow, that he crossed the country to do that in my house.

I'm halfway to the bed, stepping panicked over my set of dumbbells strewn across the rubber-matted floor, when I see his chest rise.

I stop to watch him breathing in and out, until I'm sure. And then, slow and careful as a heart-attack patient, I back out of the room and leave him to sleep a while in peace.

EMMA

LOOKING BACK ON IT, theirs is not a house of dramatic battles; it is a house of forced retreats across mountains and down through bitterly cold rivers. Ever retreating, ever glancing over your shoulder for the invisible enemy, who is a ghost. The war long ended; there is no front to fight on. The cause of the unholy conflict—the death of a child, a son, a brother—is unmentionable history.

Ah, but: a living child remains. Not the chosen one, however. No, that was her brother.

Unlike some other kids she knows, Emma never wanted to be an only child, with the only child's lonely, obsessive burdens, the need to stand for everything and everyone. But that's what, for its own reasons, life has turned her into.

Her parents were close and loving once, she is almost certain. There are photos that stand as, if not proof, then emotional attestations to familial and marital happiness, what human lives produce instead of proof. Two parents, two children, a dog, a fine old house. Her mother a creator of exquisite gardens for other people. Her father a teacher of impressionable minds and the author of brilliant elucidations of important works of literature. Her mother beautiful and still young. Her handsome father . . .

She is seventeen and applying to college when he packs three suitcases and departs for Chicago—a "practical relocation," her parents call it, as if she's a head case and can't tell the difference: separation, divorce, the long, cold withdrawal into an ever smaller and more isolated chamber of the heart. What else can you say about a man who's given up teaching the novels of Henry James and the poems of Wallace Stevens to write a book on twelve—no, sorry, eleven—sentences of the Talmud?

It is early morning. There is mist; this is not an illusion. A taxi pulls up outside and beeps its horn. She carries one of the suitcases. Her mother has not come out, and cannot be seen at any of the windows. A coldness has seeped in everywhere. The house's eyes are closed; the front lawn overgrown with weeds.

Her father kisses her, not tenderly on her cheek as he once did but on her forehead, penitentially. Some sort of Old Testament thing, she guesses.

She tries hard not to cry, and is successful.

The taxi gone, she returns to the house. Her mother's bedroom door is closed. Through the partition, Emma listens carefully for tears and sobbing, but hears nothing.

The silence, on both sides, feels like hate. Maybe it was always like this, and she just didn't know it.

She gathers her books and drives herself to school in the car that her father left behind.

DWIGHT

A LITTLE AFTER TWO IN THE MORNING, I creep into his room to get my weights. Wired awake. Wanting to hurt and sweat myself into some purer condition—or, barring that, simply to pass out for the last few hours before sunrise.

The door to the room has a creak in it. I stand in the wake of that noise listening for his deep breathing. Sam still on his back on the bed, bare chest and cheekbones holding light that otherwise doesn't exist. On the floor, the dumbbells are low dense shadows like rooting animals underfoot. I feel for them in the gloom, and grip them by the necks, and two at a time carry them out of his room into mine. I'm leaving with the last pair when his sleep-fogged voice catches me.

"Mom?"

How do you answer? Except to say, No. You're mistaken. That's the other one. The one who raised and loved you right.

"It's just me."

But he's asleep again, and doesn't hear me.

SAM

IN THE DARK, just before sunrise, he comes awake in his father's strange coffin of a house. The bleached walls of the bare white room, and the morning dark somehow dishonest, permanently uncommitted, too much unearned daylight to follow.

He tries to roll over onto his back, but the bruise on his chest is still so deep the pain reaches through him to the bruise on the other side. He groans and lies motionless, breathing heavily.

Nonetheless: the hard-on he woke with stubbornly undimmed, an animate kickstand. The kind that weighs twelve pounds and hurts, has been attached to you for so long it's become your enemy and your soul. It defeats you in principle—there's nothing you can imagine wanting to do with it, other than to warehouse it somewhere, at low cost, by the month.

Once again, he's woken with Emma on his

tongue after some long, essentially plotless, mostly forgotten dream that sticks to him now like the spotted afterimage of camera flash in the eyes. A dream that's more than a dream because you know you're going to see it again, one of its hundred and sixty-seven variations. For two years that's been her presence in his life, no more and no less. And here he's crossed the entire country, trashed and ditched his future, wrecked the whole show, only to discover that she's followed him anyway. Followed him without really caring. He's given up trying to understand how it works: a single, almost wordless act that's held him prisoner ever since, free enough to pursue other girls and his life, but too emotionally shackled ever to really show up for the game.

With his hand now, he tries without much hope to free himself of her for the day. Using her all the way, of course. And gets what he came for. As if he ruled her, not the other way around.

Afterward, he curls up on his side. Sleep coming for him finally, lapping at his jagged edges.

RUTH

SHE STANDS AT THE STOVE the morning after Dwight's call, frying four pieces of bacon, mentally excavating the past twelve years, during which, for better or worse, she's been the

74

presiding parent to her son, the one holding the keys and laying down the law. (She cannot in all good faith include Norris in this regard; he's simply too much of a jellyfish.) With a fork, invisible droplets of hot grease spattering her fingers, she turns the fatty, half-browned strips one at a time and sees Sam graduating from high school. She drives him again, the car loaded to the roof, to his first day of college. She remembers him—this sequence mysteriously looming above the rest—two years ago, in the spring of his sophomore year, coming home for a weekend.

He arrived that Friday night just in time for dinner. By then she no longer bothered complaining about the infrequency of his visits, despite the nearness (a mere ninety-minute drive) of his college campus. Still, she had her arms around him practically before he stepped out of the car, the porch lights casting their briefly united shadow almost to the edge of the driveway. The clean-dirt baseball smell of his clothes penetrating her defenses as she noticed the touch of black greasepaint on his cheek that he'd missed in the shower after practice—this she wiped away with her finger, as if he was still ten years old; a maternally willful misconception that lasted, oh, about forty-two minutes, until the moment when, finishing the meal of pot roast, potatoes, and blackberry cobbler she'd prepared, he stood up from the table mumbling that he was going to "hang" with some friends from high school and not to wait up. She didn't set eyes on him again till he emerged from his room at eleven the next morning, at which point she fed him and did a load of his laundry and later, carrying the folded clothes back through the living room, found him sprawled on the couch watching the Red Sox.

Question: Was he already troubled then? Lying there all that day like a gorgeous lounge lizard, calling out at the TV, as a bunt was laid down by an opposing player, for the "wheel" play, whatever that is? Already troubled that second evening when, wolfing down his last bite of dessert, he once again jumped up from the table to go out, this time to a party in Falls Village? Bye, Mom—peck on cheek, brief hug, Don't wait up, out the door.

By ten, Norris was snoring. By midnight she, too, was unconscious. Was Sam, for Christ's sake, troubled then?

Which brings her to Sunday, waking that misty spring morning, Norris already out playing his usual eighteen at the country club. Rising, she went straight to the bedroom window to confirm that Norris's old car—a Honda Civic he'd agreed to let Sam use at college because of its Japanese reliability, admirable fuel efficiency, and impressively retained Blue Book value—was in the driveway. Wherever Sam had been the night before, he'd returned in one piece. And now they would have the day together before he went back to school.

She washed and dressed, taking her time, adding a touch of lavender water, appreciating the exceptional peace of the morning: her son, whether or not he chose to "hang" with her on a weekend night, asleep in his old room down the hall.

An hour later, she was frying bacon—frying it as she is today, with fork and grease-spattered fingers—sipping coffee, and scanning the newsless headlines in the Winsted *Register Citizen*, when she heard his footsteps on the linoleum behind her. The smile she turned on him then unfortunately misplaced; for he was wearing, she immediately saw, his jean jacket, the one with the beige corduroy collar, and carrying the UConn sports duffel he'd brought with him, the bag fully loaded, the zipper zipped. He was going back early, she understood, right that minute, taking with him the shirts and boxers she'd washed and folded, leaving her with half a pound of cooked bacon and too many eggs. He hadn't bothered to change his clothes from the night before. He hadn't even been home.

"You're going?" She was careful to drain the question of any note of accusation or feeling.

"I've got practice."

"But it's Sunday."

"Coach," he explained with a helpless shrug, as if he was a farmer and *coach* a euphemism for *hail* or *locusts*—which in its way, she could see, it was.

She studied him, certain he was lying, because he wouldn't look at her—at the floor, yes, the microwave, the sheets of paper towel on the counter already striped with pieces of crisp bacon, each in its own penumbra of grease.

She switched off the burner. "I'll walk you to the car."

Up close, he looked as if he hadn't slept. A raw streak like an unopened gash ran from his left ear to his jaw, but she wouldn't indulge herself or him by asking about it. He wanted to be such a grown-up, let him be a grown-up. She followed him out through the screen door. His work boots untied, though this she guessed was just a style, a way of moving through the world as if he didn't give a damn, dragging his feet—not unlike, it struck her, how he'd spent the weekend moving through the house. Just passing through, ma'am.

On the lawn a rabbit posed frozen, blurred in the sun-infused mist, its ears pinned to its back. Leaping into panicked flight when Sam popped the trunk.

"Well . . ." She was standing right next to him.

"Sorry, Mom." He still wasn't looking at her. The scale of her failure, which she couldn't yet grasp, threatened to blot out the day if she didn't cut this short.

"Call me next week, okay?"

She leaned forward and kissed him on the cheek. He smelled like someone else. Not her sandlot son, player of games, but a man, older and less wise than she knew what to do with. She stepped away before he could wrap her in his arms and make her disappear.

EMMA

SHE DOES NOT IMMEDIATELY RECOGNIZE Sam Arno leaning against the back wall in the living room of her classmate's house in Falls Village in the spring of 2004. She has not seen him in a couple of years, for one thing; for another, they haven't exchanged more than a casual hello since, with the hunched bolting of an escapee, he abandoned Wyndham Falls for Torrington High six years ago, willing to make the long commute just to get the hell away. Why he's crashing a senior high-school party when he's already a college baseball star (word has it) at UConn, she can't imagine. Though none of this, she viscerally understands, has anything to do with her level of shock at seeing him again.

He has changed. Grown and filled out; disposed of that small, weary boy with the traveling trumpet case. Become, as if reluctantly,

79

physically beautiful. His body long and muscular and lean, his hands large and thrillingly veined. His face marked by sharp memorable planes and just the right amount of natural punctuation. This Emma observes for herself when, after urgent navigation across the crowded, flailing room, she manages, through force of need, to take up the empty place on the wall beside him, turn and really look at him, and ask him what he's doing there. To which he stares back at her with green eyes flecked with splashes of gold, and gives some answer she instantly forgets. Because she has already reached the vanishing point, finding it hard to look at him head-on without looking past him, into the next moment and then the next, where in the context of private possibility all she can really imagine is him putting those strong hands on her, first roughly, then sweetly, then roughly, stripping her down layer by layer, till there's nothing left.

They leave after about twenty minutes. They are standing near each other; then she looks up and finds him staring at her with a ravenous intensity, as if he's just realized he is starving.

She follows him through the crowd. People make way for them. It never enters her mind not to go.

It is cold and poorly lit on the porch. The front door closes behind them and they are alone, the music and the shouting muted. She already knows they won't be returning to the party.

"I want to show you something," he says.

Half a mile up the dark country road is a house no one lives in. A working farm once, Sam tells her as they walk in the wash of moonlight at the edge of the road, twigs snapping under their feet, and then a kind of gentleman's farm, and then the widowed owner, learning that he was going to die of cancer and wanting to spare his family the trouble, got his papers in order and killed himself with a shotgun in his barn, and before they'd even buried him his kids started fighting over the property, greedy to carve it up and sell it off despite his stated wishes, and the lawyers were called in and the courts slapped a freeze on everything, and for years the farm has stood empty and half ruined. The widower's name was Carmody; Sam's father was his lawyer and, briefly, the executor of his estate.

Sam turns brooding after telling her all this, maybe regretting having mentioned the family connection. Emma doesn't confess that her parents are present too, in a way, a kind of pre-guilt already factored in, in spite or because of the warm liquid thrum between her legs every time her hip or arm touches his, her nipples erect in the night that is too cold for crickets, and the fact that she, who has never been especially keen on offering herself to the local boys, wants now, in

81

just a few minutes, to fuck this sad beautiful boy and be fucked by him, hard and permanently, with a raw need unlike anything she's known before, except maybe her unquenchable longing, during the total eclipse following his death, for the restoration of her brother to the world.

The house is locked and boarded up. Neither of them wants to go into the barn where the old guy blew his brains out, so they remain outside in the cold, pressed and heaving against a rusted feed trough. A few inches of rainwater pooled in the bottom—and in that water, she can't help noticing, the three-quarter moon hanging like a glass Christmas ornament; till their bodies set the trough to rocking, and the water ripples, breaking the moon apart.

Wet already as a licked kitten, she reaches down into his loose jeans. His gasp a small explosion in her ear. His grip suddenly fierce at her hips, hands pawing down her jeans: in the next moment she feels herself heaved up in his strong arms and fitted onto him like a missing part, a hovering sack of need. She cries out, imagining reaching into his chest and touching his beating heart. Her fingers accidentally rake the side of his face, though he seems oblivious of any pain, just repeats her name over and over under his breath, his half-closed eyes glazed with moonlight, right up to the second he bursts.

Afterward, he sets her down gingerly—as if, now that it's finished, she, like the moon, might break into pieces. In silence, they pull up and refasten their clothes. The left side of his jaw scarlet where she scratched him. She isn't sorry. She's swimming with him, leaking him into her underwear, smelling him with every breath, shaking so badly that Sam has to cover her with his body like a blanket. Not cold anymore, finally not anything. He lifts the hair that's fallen over her face and kisses her there between her eyes— such a tender, mature, manlike thing to do that she has to wonder who, by fucking each other, they've just become.

DWIGHT

SAM IS STILL CONKED OUT at eight the next morning as I stand in my kitchen, facing the open refrigerator. Food reserves totally inadequate for long-term occupancy, it must be said, or even guest residency by more than a single individual. Though I'm not thinking very straight about the matter, having been up since half past five, rattling around in my sun-filled cage like a lab hamster, waiting for my son to emerge from his room.

So that I might offer him what, exactly? A fatherly speech? A morning hug? A plan for living? Almost a relief that he continues to sleep—as tired, it seems, as if he walked all the way from Connecticut. And yet still the note I leave for him on the kitchen table rambles on too long about murky topics that have nothing to do, let's face it, with breakfast. Topics like family and the future. I give my cell number in case he has questions or simply wants to check in while I'm out (unlikely). Tell him that I'll be back in an hour and look forward to having breakfast together. That he should think of *mi casa* as *su casa* for as long as he feels like staying. Maybe we'll talk more over dinner about his plans, such as they are, though absolutely no pressure to cannonball into the familial deep end all at once if he's not in the mood. By now I'm on the back side of the page ripped from the SoCal memo pad, and it's time—even I can see—to bring this baby home. Keep the tone light and parent-friendly, but not too. After lengthy deliberations with myself, I sign the note "Dad," which is simple fact, but cautiously leave out "love": I don't want to antagonize my son or, in truth, to dredge up recollections (unwanted, I feel certain, by both of us) that might lead him to the judgment that I've yet again failed to earn something out. There'll be opportunity enough for that. My handwriting, jacked up on a second cup of black, is jittery, as if possessed.

Then, before leaving the house, I call my boss at home. An early riser, Tony will already have worked out in his home gym and be seated now in the family breakfast nook with the L.A. *Times*, a mug of coffee, and a bowl of Go Lean cereal with nonfat milk. (It's a depressing verity that every man of a certain age knows with self-absorbed precision the dreary, hope-to-live-forever routines of other men in middle life—hard-won knowledge, I might add, that gets us precisely nowhere.) On the wall above Tony's head are framed color photos (most professionally snapped) of the Lopez family at work and play, arranged in an artful mosaic. All in all, it's as pleasant a morning stage set as one could hope for.

One of the girls picks up and chirps "Hi" through a mouthful of something or other.

"Hey there. That Ruby?"

"It's Jade." Voice snippy: mixing up the twins is not the path to their hearts.

"Oh, right. Sorry. Hey, Jade, it's Dwight Arno."

"Dad! Dwight Arno!"

"*Mister* Arno, honey," I hear Tony murmur as the phone transfer gets made. "The store?" This to me, and all business.

"Morning, Tony."

"What's wrong?"

"Nothing. Everything's fine with the store."

"You sure?" I can hear his fingers drumming the table and Jodi telling one of the girls to clear her plate. "You know I get tense when I'm not expecting the call."

"Sorry. Everything's fine. Just calling 'cause I need the day off."

"You sick?"

"My son's here."

"Who?"

"My son. Sam. From Connecticut?"

"Yeah, yeah . . ." Tony's recall process virtually audible this morning. "Hold on—isn't he, like—?"

"He showed up at my house last night."

"Just showed up? Whoa, man—big surprise, no? He okay and everything?"

"He's okay. Thing is, he might be staying awhile. And I just, you know, I need to get him settled."

"I get it. Family, right?"

"Right. Family."

"You know me, I'm a family man, Dwight. So anyway, I was going in myself this morning. I'll open up."

"Thanks."

I hear him sip his coffee, turn a page of the paper. "See that piece on *Dateline* last night? East Coast parents all got kids learning squash so they can get 'em into the Ivy League?"

"Missed that."

"Something to think about—West Coast squash-clinic thing. Move some merchandise. Folks out here want Ivy League, too, right? Maybe build some courts. We'll talk about it."

"Okay."

"Okay. Later."

As usual after a conversation with Tony in which I've had to ask for a favor of some kind, I hang up feeling that I've somehow neglected to make some key point on behalf of my own dignity. What the point might have been, I can't figure. A gnatty cloud of frustration hovers over me. I sit with it for a time, then slip on my shades and exit the house. I lower the top of the Sebring and drive across town, my arm out and the sun on my face.

And the joggers jog, God bless them, and the sprinklers don't quit, and gulls fly over the marina and the beaches. And I go to the Vons at the shopping center like any red- or blue- or purple-blooded American. Get my four-wheeled cart and roll it down the bright six-foot-wide aisles, filling it with basics and sundries and the occasional frozen-dessert treat. Fill it right to the brim. Run my plastic quick and easy through the reader and clock my debt ($169.87) without so much as a flinch. Because this morning, with my son miraculously asleep in my house, my vision feels huge. Or I need it to be. I want to save my mind for the truly important questions. (Which are?) Refusing today to be brought down to the usual zero-sum state by the bad-news details of the everyday, the shocking price of milk or the one broken egg out of a brand-new dozen. These things happen; they don't have to be personal. Run your card and get on with it, man. Pay the minimum at the end of the month. This is our beautiful way of life.

And then a stop on the road home for gas. And—hell, why not?—I throw in another fifteen bucks for a car wash while I'm at it. (I'm just two full tanks short on my coupon card from a free wash 'n' wax. But today, I somehow understand, there can be no waiting, no deferment, and no deals.) I overtip the jumpsuited Mexicans who spot-towel my vehicle (tender as nursemaids, even with the paint-scratched rear-quarter panel), knowing that the only thing separating them from me is a green card; that they have better records, on the whole, than I will ever have again.

The rest of the way home is less than three miles. The car clean and fresh-smelling, the hood gleaming like a polished bowling ball. In the trunk, the fixings for breakfast and lunch and many more meals to come. A plan taking shape, or something like it. All I have to do now is stop myself from wondering if Sam will still be there when I arrive. If, sharp kid that he is, he might have reconsidered his situation overnight, changed his mind about his level of desperation. If I've already scared him away. If I'll get home and find the bed he slept in untouched and untraceable. If this is just memory busting me again, or for once the real thing.

SAM

CROSSING THE LIVING ROOM in his boxers, eyes crusted with bad sleep, he watches the front door swing open and a familiar, broad-shouldered man carrying two brown bags of groceries enter the house.

His father stops and stares: an apparition. "You're still here."

At the last second a kind of rictus grin added for effect, to mask the statement as a question, and the question as a joke. But the eyes appear strained, and there's nothing funny about the situation, really.

"I left you a note on the kitchen table."

"I saw it."

"We were a little low on food."

Sam nods. They stand staring at each other like strangers on opposite platforms of a commuter station.

"Hungry?"

He shrugs.

"Well, I'm going to make some breakfast for both of us." He moves toward the kitchen. "There are more groceries out in the car."

Sam walks to the bedroom and pulls on a pair of jeans. In daylight the room is almost unrecognizable, a holding pen with rubber matting and pairs of dumbbells on the floor. A place for desperate repetitions, not sleep. He pictures his father in a gray sweatshirt with the sleeves cut off and gym shorts too baggy for his age, doing curls and presses and squats by himself in the room every morning, sweating and grunting, pushing his thinning muscles till they can't lift a single pound more. A routine he himself often performed in the weight room of his dorm in Storrs, late into the night if he was feeling low, rep after rep, to the point where Jake sometimes wondered aloud what his problem was. *Why so intense?* Good question. Turns out he, too, knows how to punish himself without restraint, holding nothing back, half in love with the black curtain of manufactured pain.

Shirtless, he goes out of the house.

A few feet of grass; a couple of cement squares; his father's car, the ragtop that's seen better days but which, this morning, is reflective as if waxed by elves, filling the little rectangle of cement that constitutes a driveway. The trunk open, holding enough supplies for a visit that might never end. As if costly abundance alone can cover all blown bets, make everything square.

Picking up a brown bag and a twelve-pack of Diet Dr Pepper, he turns to go back inside, but freezes at the sight of an elderly Hispanic woman watching him from a window of the small beige house across the street, her hands pinning together the loose flaps of her peach-colored nightdress. She stands appraising his naked, bruised torso with a faraway half smile that doesn't seem to include him at all—as if he's marble and she's looking inward, toward some vision that's hers alone. He nods and smiles, but she turns away abruptly, and he's left greeting the empty street like an idiot.

In the kitchen, he sets the groceries down on the counter. There are glasses of orange juice laid out on the little table, a plate of toast, and the air smells fat with melted butter. His father at the stove, cracking eggs one-handed into a skillet that's already smoking.

"Still like your eggs sunny-side up?"

The smile cautious. Because there aren't any innocent questions anymore, haven't been for a very long time.

It's the word *still* that bothers him most. The word held over from the past as if from an archaeological dig. Unearth it if you want, dust it off and put it out for inspection, maybe even casually throw it into use again as in historical times when the word was once used. But that doesn't mean its value or meaning has survived. The value and meaning of the word will always reside with the original people in the original life. A boy and his dad. Folks as good as extinct now, or at best reduced to cheap replicas of themselves in foreign lands.

"I'm not hungry." He walks out.

RUTH

SHE DOESN'T SEE IT COMING, but Saturday opens into one of those days that seem to contain all the beauty and horror of living in the country. She wakes to an iconic New England spring, the ground well thawed, the flower beds smelling fertilely of mulch and compost, the daffodils that she planted along the front porch pushing up strong and bright.

She begins the morning with back-to-back piano lessons in her living room, the students both fourth graders—Carrie Lockhart, whose sight-reading is precocious but her fingering slow, and Adam Markowitz, whose skills run the other way—and then the time is her own and she loads a chair that needs recaning into the Subaru and drives it over to Great Barrington; then back through Canaan to the oblong, church-fronted green of Wyndham Falls, historic site of the American Revolution, bedecked today with balloons and checkered-cloth tables displaying many varieties of baked goods, wax-sealed jars of preserves and duck-liver paté and pickled vegetables, as well as stalls of arts-and-crafty-type things, kilned pots and beaded Indian belts and knitted sweatercoats with wooden buttons big as your thumb. A town fair, in other words, populated with neighbors, full-time and weekenders alike, from Goshen north to Ashley Falls.

She is in possession of a single secret goal, which is one of the turkey pies made by Lucinda Jarvis, wife of Andy and mother of her student Ben, to whom she teaches piano with a certain amount of irritation (her sympathy for his tin ear more than offset by his persistent, shin-kicking rudeness) on Tuesdays and Thursdays at school. The Jarvis family less than huggable but their pies sublime. She will take one home and, at six o'clock this evening with a glass of white wine (not approved by her doctor), pull it steaming out of the oven and devour exactly half, savoring every mouthful of the crimped buttery crust; and tomorrow night, with a second glass of wine from the same bottle, she'll eat the other half. And with that her weekend, recent chemo be damned, will be over.

Thus the beauty portion of the day, neatly encapsulated: an independent woman, personal and medical challenges for the moment denied, buying a turkey pie at a country fair. The horror is the complicated part, as it usually is.

She has the pie corralled and is waiting at the table for her change, Lucinda slowly counting out the bills while fishing in a roundabout way for Ruth's confirmation of her son's musical skills ("I heard Ben practicing the other day and he just sounded, I don't know, Ruth, so *mature* for his age"), and Ruth murmuring her noncommittal assent ("He does seem to have a strong sense of himself at the piano") when she feels a hand touch her shoulder. She turns and finds herself staring at Norris.

Typically for a weekend, he's colorfully dressed for golf, right down to the socks with little putters on them that she gave him for his forty-sixth birthday. He has less hair than just six weeks ago, she'd swear (but then, she reminds herself, so does she), and a few paces behind him stands a woman about her own age, not especially pretty, her face burdened with a look of anxious pedantry, as if in her life she's witnessed more than she thinks it proper to discuss in polite society, leaving her permanently betwixt and between. Next to the woman is a young girl in thick horn-rimmed glasses, her expression mirroring to an alarming degree her mother's.

"Can I have a word, Ruth?" Norris asks in a low voice.

Lucinda, suddenly all ears, places the bills in Ruth's distracted, outstretched hand but doesn't step away.

"I've got a lesson starting soon," Ruth lies, stuffing the loose money into her shoulder bag. "I need to be getting home."

"It'll only take a minute."

He seems to need her to follow him and, caught in an ebbing tide of passivity, hefting the turkey pie in its clear plastic wrap, she allows herself to be led.

Approaching the woman and her daughter, Norris stops and intones stiffly, "Ruth, I'd like you to meet Wanda Shoemaker and her daughter Celine."

There's no further information, but Ruth instantly calculates that the woman must be the widow of Ralph Shoemaker from Salisbury, who died falling through thin ice on the Housatonic last winter. (She further recalls that it's never been satisfactorily explained what the man was doing trying to walk across a frozen river in the middle of the night.) So, she thinks, Norris has found a widow to keep him company, and the widow has found him. Which is perfectly all right, though why the daughter should be named Celine when she clearly isn't the least bit French is beyond her. Ruth doesn't for a minute feel jealous, only shoved a level or two deeper into her isolation.

She and the woman nod to each other—with the turkey pie bobbing between them like a docking buoy, shaking hands would be too hazardous—and then Norris walks on and she follows.

It's all rather awkwardly handled, but that's Norris for you. He has an idea of things, but the idea never quite jibes with reality, and whatever he does or says usually ends up falling somewhere in no-man's-land, neither one thing nor the other, satisfying nobody. (Other than in the selling of insurance, for which he really does seem to have a knack.) They weave through clumps of people eating blueberry muffins and drinking cider and coffee out of paper cups and children playing tag, and recognitions are made, mostly silently, and various glances exchanged among the assembled adults, and Ruth sees it all and understands the range of implications and messages surrounding her and this man she once married but can no longer conceive of wanting.

Under the huge sugar maple at the east end of the green, Norris stops again and turns to wait for her. The heavy-limbed shade is a kind of privacy and seems to afford him some much-needed confidence, which in turn seems to infuse him with a dose of courage, and after a few false casts with his long, skinny arms his hands settle on his hips in a badly borrowed cowboy pose that throws into inadvertent relief the pink golf shirt and those socks with the little putters on them. Standing before him now, she doesn't come close to laughing at him. Wouldn't do such a thing in the first place, mockery being in her eyes the favored artillery of losers and cowards; and in the second place, though she can see what might be comical about the scene, it will never be funny to her. That's why she's divorcing him. There isn't a thing Norris can do or say that will ever be funny to her again, if it ever was, and for that she is truly sorry.

The surprising weight of the pie is making her arms hurt. She decides to dive in and get the conversation over with, whatever it's going to be.

"I guess you received the papers?"

"They'll be at your lawyer's by the end of the week," Norris responds, his words clipped.

"Thank you." She pauses, searching for an invisible plane of dignity on which to stand, not finding it. "I'm sorry about all this, Norris. But I'm glad to see you've found somebody nice to be with."

"Wanda and I found each other," Norris replies a bit too firmly.

Ruth is silent. She can feel the cool poultry insides of the pie through the aluminum plate and, ridiculously, her mouth begins to water. Had she known she was going to run into Norris she would have put off buying the pie until later, in fact would have skipped the fair altogether. No turkey pie, however perfect, can be worth this scene.

"I know about Sam leaving school," Norris says. And having delivered himself of his most dramatic line he rests, looking at her significantly, knowing he has her full attention now. But even his indignation, it strikes her, is like an old tire leaking air.

"Who told you?"

"Who is not important," uttered as though nothing in New England could be more so. "I happen to know someone at the university."

"Don't people have anything better to talk about than other people's kids?"

"Sam's my stepson and you should've told me."

"That would have been awkward."

"I don't care."

"I've been a little preoccupied, as you can imagine."

"I think he needs me, Ruthie. He sounds pretty confused, all right, just bolting school like that for no reason."

"Maybe he has his reasons."

"I want your permission to call and invite him to stay with me and Wanda."

She stares at him, honestly dumbfounded. "But Norris, Sam doesn't like you."

"That's exactly the kind of thing you would say. Look, I'm sorry you're sick, Ruth, but you really need to deal with the anger."

"I'm not angry with you. And my health has nothing to do with this. My doctor says my odds are terrific."

"I happen to know your doctor—Cusack at Yale–New Haven? Played golf with him last year."

"Stay out of my business, Norris. Jesus, one of these days I'm going to move out of this fishbowl into the biggest city I can find."

She's allowed herself to overheat, is speaking too loudly. Glancing out from under the burdensome limbs into the searing sunlight, she sees a few people turn their heads to avoid getting caught spying. Lucinda Jarvis, for one, will sell no more turkey pies until this puppet show is over.

"I need to get home, Norris."

"Will you at least tell Sam to call me? Tell him I'm here if he needs me. Tell him that."

"I'll tell him."

High on a limb overhead a squirrel jitters, pursuing its squirrel life, and a cracked branch falls through the leaf-dark air and lands inches from Norris's left foot. He flinches at the sound, then colors for having flinched.

Striding on trembling legs back across the green to where she's parked, her chin forced up, carrying that golden pie like a reward for being good, she is radioactive, her own little Chernobyl. People staring at her through their sunglasses.

But who, she desperately needs to know, will be there in the end to see her over to the other side?

She drives away wiping tears, unable to imagine dinner.

DWIGHT

THE WORKDAY PASSES. During my lunch break Sandra comes up and asks if she can talk to me alone. We go back to the mechanicals room, where she tells me that she doesn't care if he's, like, her cousin or whatever, she's sick to *here* of Evander stealing shit out of the store and selling it to kids behind the high school, and she isn't going to put up with it no more, okay? I calm her down and send her back to the registers with an order to keep it buttoned. Privately I check the books against our inventory, which confirms her account. Then there's nothing to do but wait for Tony to come back from lunch.

He doesn't accept the facts at first—"Family stealing from family? Fuck yourself, Dwight, okay!"—and comes awfully close to outright calling me a liar. My blood is up and we might be heading for trouble, but then Sandra barges into the office calling her cousin a motherfucking bodega thief (Evander, as usual, isn't around, having never shown up for work), and because she's family, and speaks with the imaginative conviction of a street poet, her uncle believes her. Tony says tightly that he'll deal with it himself, okay—family to family—and for the time being that's that.

The workday passes. That is all I know. As to

family, what do I really understand? My son doesn't see fit to call the cell number I gave him, and hasn't given me his, so I'm left to fester. At some point I cave and call my house in search of him, where I hear my own voice on the answering machine, a dislocating, even depressing, experience under the best of circumstances, and quickly hang up.

SAM

HE'S IN THE GUEST ROOM doing lat sets with his father's dumbbells when his cellphone vibrates that he has a message. He goes to voice mail.

"Sam, it's Jake. You need to get your ass back here. That guy you hit in the bar—Bellic? I just heard he's been moved back to the ICU. I don't know why, but he's not getting better. Listen, you better get back here, or you're going to be seriously fucked."

Sam listens to Jake's message a second time. Then he erases his friend's voice. Closing the phone, he sets it on the weight bench.

His face is dripping. The tendons in his wrists are trembling strangely.

He gets up and walks through his father's house to the kitchen. He pulls a beer from the fridge and twists off the cap and drinks until the bottle is empty.

It is late afternoon in California. In Connecticut, he thinks, the sun will be going down.

He turns and vomits into the stainless-steel sink.

PENNY

HER WARDROBE ISN'T EXPANSIVE ENOUGH that it should take her this long to get dressed for a date with a man whose personal style, based on her four months of fairly close but intermittent observation, could best be described as "casual amateur athletic." And yet, after twenty minutes and three full outfit changes, her bed strewn with decided noes and possible yeses (the sequin shimmy thing just now demoted because she is not, and never has been, a twenty-year-old country-and-western singer from the Blue Ridge Mountains who looks great in cowboy hats), she's still at it, sideways to the full-length mirror that she can see from her closet only with the bathroom door all the way open, a hangered dress pressed over her bra and panties and a pair of low-heeled sandals not quite doing the trick. These accoutrements, too, soon tossed on the bed, leaving her mostly naked before the ruthless glass, with nowhere to hide from the truth of her post-forty body: disturbing lines turning her neck into a segmented rather than a fluid object, the soft oblongs of flesh above her hips beginning to do double duty, during her baths, as personal flotation devices, and her legs, which might once have inspired a sonnet or two, now looking weirdly Japanese (too much tennis!), hardly worth a haiku from a visiting Buddhist scholar.

Ali, wearing iPod earbuds and sexy Lolita overalls, appears behind her in the looking glass: some sort of visual genetic extrapolation, it seems to her mother, here run cruelly amok.

Penny hesitates, steeling herself. "Any advice?"

Frowning at the inconvenience of being asked a live interactive question, the girl extracts the earbuds. "What?"

"Never mind."

"Mom, we have totally different styles, you know?"

"This is an emergency, Ali. I'm having some kind of sartorial-aesthetic breakdown."

The girl is silent, sizing her up. Finally, a nod: "I'd go sleeveless."

Penny is horrified. "Sleeveless?"

"You have really sexy arms, Mom."

"I do?"

"Yeah, and a skirt, nothing lower than the knee—you've got those killer legs. And heels, duh."

Ali replaces the earbuds and goes out. Penny stands staring after her.

DWIGHT

SAM ISN'T THERE when I return home around
six. And he's still gone while I shower and shave
and put the coals to heat in the grill out back.
There's no sign of him while I dress in clean
chinos and a white button-down shirt and drink a
first beer and salt the steaks I picked up at Vons,
and slice some beefsteak tomatoes and stick a
couple of baking spuds in the oven at 400
degrees. Then it's five past seven and my doorbell
chimes and I think it might be him but it isn't, it's
Penny, in a sleeveless top, knee-length skirt, and
open-toed sandals, with her hair pulled back tight
as a pearl diver's from her face and her nails
unpainted. She strikes me at that moment, in a
place beyond speech, as the ideal respite from the
guilty, hopeful, almost unbearable pressure that
my son's reappearance has brought to my
carefully tamped-down California existence, and
my sudden physical need for her is overpowering,
virtually narcotic. I kiss her long and hard in the
doorway and, a minute later, in my bedroom
while undressing her, having lost all track of
everything else.

It is possible to carry on several lives at once,
skillfully keeping them from intersecting, and
this is something that a certain kind of person, if
properly seasoned and trained, can go on doing

for quite some time. I have done it myself, though not always on purpose. There's a kind of ironic innocence involved, and it stems from genuine hope. The hope being that when judgment finally comes, if it does (and I'm not talking about the law here—that already happened—or about God, either), good intentions might actually count for something concrete, or at least there might be an understanding by someone who matters that bad intentions were not originally present, but rather appeared unexpectedly at some horrible juncture, and somehow took root, and only then ruined everything. What I'm getting at here, on a minor level, has to do with Penny showing up in my house this evening and my son not being there, the two of them, like parallel lines, knowing next to nothing about each other, and my continued reticence on the matter. Maybe, having done so much harm in my life and having received in the aftermath of a just punishment some decent luck that I know I haven't earned, I simply don't want to make a stupid mistake that will set any of it back, make it disappear. A matter of protective habit, I've grown used to saying as little as possible to anyone about my situation, past or future, including and especially the one or two people I hope to be closest to. It's almost always safer to ask questions than to try to give answers anyway, I've found. This is considered good manners, of course, but I also can't help but recognize it as a cagey, instinctive form of playing not to lose, a strategy that all losers know in their secret hearts, until you wake up one day and realize that you can no longer remember the other kind of playing, because it is gone.

PENNY

SHE ARRIVES bearing a bottle of Chardonnay, and this he takes from her hand at the door while kissing her, and it's only later, after she's walked out on him midway through the evening and returned home, that she recalls thinking fervently in his arms, her lips locked on his, that should she never see that bottle of wine again and never drink from it, it will be no loss, because she'll have had her fill anyway.

And she can be called many things, but not a fabulist; for all of this actually happens. In his bedroom, as sparsely furnished as a frat boy's fridge, where they somehow land breathless mere seconds after her arrival, he unzips her skirt with one hand while the other, each finger pulsing as if it contains its own heart, breaks the seal of her panties and enters her. A warm-up that just about finishes her off. She literally throws her head back: *I laughed, I cried.* That's right. You think when you're younger that to do this—to fuck when and whom you want—in middle age will somehow be disgraceful, or a waste, not even worth counting in the annual survey, or just another cliché—but, honey, it ain't necessarily so. She releases him and his penis leaps into both her hands. A big man, which she loves, requiring all of her. Then he's on top of her, spreading her across the bed, covering every inch of her exposed flesh, burrowing. Not the first time, certainly. But what presses out of him tonight is a surprising kind of need, she senses, hard to explain—as if in his previous life, however it was, he set some of the years aside unlived, put up on a shelf till now, saving or watching or hiding from himself while the real stuff passed him by.

But this isn't passing; it's here, nothing kept in reserve or at bay. The expression of him entirely physical, almost animal, which, after all the talking and talking and talking she's done and listened to in her days (Christ, the academic declaiming and posing, with so many people she's never wanted to understand or reach), she receives like a gift, with inordinate pleasure and relief.

She decides she wants that wine after all. Grapes after sex is poetry, said the Greeks, or can be. Anything can be poetry—isn't that her mantra in class: *Open your senses! Use form and language to investigate every aspect of the human! Don't be scared to see! Swallow everything!* Now, happily fucked and half dressed in her lover's house, twisting her skirt right way round as she meanders from bedroom to kitchen, one mental eye on that uncooked steak, she thinks she can finally see her own point—

She stops dead in the living room, and covers her naked breasts with her hands.

A young man is standing by the front door. He is tall, good-looking, and shabbily dressed. His shock at finding her here appears even greater than her own—he looks angry. His arms and chest are strong, and instinctively she feels afraid of him.

They stand staring at each other. Till he wheels round and, grabbing Dwight's car keys off the table by the door, strides out of the house.

"Hey!" she calls after him—a coward's *Stop thief!*—never moving her feet.

"Let him go."

She turns: Dwight behind her, still naked. Though the expression of the triumphant sex stud he was wearing a few minutes earlier is gone. He is defeated, she sees. He has now the face of the caught-out liar.

SAM

HE DRIVES his father's car in the only direction he can think of in this country not his own, fifteen minutes south. No plans on a Saturday night, no road map, *nada*. Missing especially at this moment, blindly crossing out of the unincorporated township of Arenas and into the city of Santa Barbara, the green road signs with the little maps outlined in white that mark the Northwest Corner like so many coming-home flags, telling you which town you've just left and which you've just entered: Salisbury, Box Corner, Canaan, Wyndham Falls, Bow Mills . . .

Native tattoos under his skin that he's never felt compelled to acknowledge till now, probably because he's never felt so far from home.

He parks on the main drag, if that's what it is, not far from the marina. Sounds of voices and music from restaurants and bars down the street, storefronts open to the balmy weather like undefended faces—and so, again, nothing like home. He turns the other way and walks across a thin strip of park toward the piers. High up in the palms a breeze rustles, a whisper too exotic to be true; and ahead, keeping their own rhythm, beneath anchor lights dotting the near horizon like roped constellations, halyards bang with faint urgency against a hundred masts or more.

All this he can hear, but not believe in. Pictures and sounds will never be enough; he must always come armed with his own theory of emotional relativity, awaiting impossible confirmation. He can't remember a time, for instance, when it didn't seem to him, down deep, a factual certainty that his father's fist once struck his five-year-old face simply because, at a precocious age, for some reason not of his understanding, his face, needing to meet that fist, arranged for it to happen. That he will never be able to prove this does not make it false.

He walks the piers, one after the other. Some boats are party boats with convivial gatherings on deck, coolers of beer, here and there a blender coughing up daiquiris and margaritas. He is a sentry or night watchman or resident Batman: the drunk look at him soberly as he passes. Other boats are dark. He stands by the dark ones, peering into their lightless cabins, the vessels shifting restlessly on the invisible tide. A hundred feet behind him, above the marine shop, a bar-and-clam shack spills life over the docks, the yellow light catching in acid-colored pools on the oil-slicked surface of the water. It is beautiful, and it makes him close to seasick. He feels the need to sit down. Near the chest-high metal gate that separates the nautical or would-be nautical population from the rest, under a low-wattage municipal light peppered with suicidal moths, he finds a bench partially occupied by an old man in a crushed captain's hat and dirty Bermuda shorts. The man nods at him blurrily, drinking a pint of something from a brown paper bag. Sam sits down, leaving some space between them. He can smell what's in the bottle now, or maybe it's the man's breath: Jack Daniel's. *With a shot of J.D.*

this time, he thinks. And Nic Bellic lies slumped on the filthy floor of O'Doul's; and Nic Bellic rises again like Lazarus or Frankenstein; and Sam watches with lacerating clarity as a gleaming scalpel blade trails a ruby cut line across the fish-white belly of a man named Nic Bellic. And he says good night to his seated American neighbor, the man in the crushed hat, and gets up and walks toward the marine shop, which is closed, and the wooden stairs that lead up to Captain Cook's, which beckon infinitely. In a minute he will climb those stairs, and take a seat at the bar, where no one will know him and there will be everything visible to remind him of where he's been.

DWIGHT

"IT COMES DOWN TO TRUST," Penny says, not meeting my eyes as she sets a mug of coffee—my fourth of the morning—in front of me. She's looking pretty and fit in tennis whites, but otherwise as hard and cool as a Greek statue. I'm seated at what used to be her former husband Darryl's place at the kitchen counter, precariously perched on a high stool, no more in control of the situation than a man trying to ride an emu.

"I agree with you, Pen."

"I was looking at him last night, the son you almost never mention and who I had no reason whatever to believe was in town. In your house.

111

A lot of history there—I could feel it without any help from you. And you know what? You're hardly better than a liar. I've realized that I don't really know you at all."

"That's not true. You know more about me than anybody else around here."

"Which isn't saying a whole lot."

"I don't know, but if you were me—"

"If I were *you?*" Penny leans into the counter till she's inches from my face, her hazel eyes moist but on fire. "If I were you, we wouldn't be having this conversation. I wouldn't be committed enough or brave enough or engaged enough to actually tell you, another person with another person's needs and feelings, what I really think. What I care about. What the real story is. What I'm just willing to—just to, to bring to the fucking table of human relations."

"Point taken."

"It isn't a point, you asshole." Her eyes well up and she pivots and walks to the sink, where a pile of dirty breakfast dishes can be seen tilting toward the coast. I think she's going to say more, but instead she turns on the faucet. A squirt of soap on a sponge, and she begins to scrub plates and load the dishwasher.

I've been gripping my mug too tightly, and I see now that I've spilled some coffee on the counter: another stain.

I set the mug down, get up and go to the sink,

and put my arms around her from behind. I can feel myself getting hard before I even touch her.

"I'm sorry," I murmur in her ear.

She smacks the single-lever faucet and the water shuts off. "Move."

I step well back as she transfers a heavy skillet from sink to dishwasher. Historically, pots and pans in the hands of aggrieved women are not my friends, and by the time Penny's added detergent and switched on the machine my nascent erection isn't even a memory.

She turns to face me, drying her hands on a dish towel. Her eyes are no longer moist. It is in fact hard to imagine that we've ever fucked or had coffee in the mornings like a couple that doesn't need language to know a few important things about each other.

"Pen, listen—"

"I think you've got the wrong idea about me, Dwight. Probably had me wrong from the start."

Her tone is so realized and final it's hard to recover. The dishwasher kicks into a higher gear, then turns eerily hushed. Just to have something to do, I retreat back to the counter and my abandoned coffee mug—but, even as I move, a small sac of despair is leaking inside my chest, which mystifies and frightens me. It's unclear whether this feeling has to do with Penny, or with myself, or with this sunny California morning that seems already to presage another dead-end journey.

"What happened to you?" she demands. "That's what I woke up this morning asking myself. Why the hell are you like this?"

I taste the coffee again and it's cold. I carry the mug to the sink and rinse it out.

PENNY

SHE DRAGS HER HEART with her onto the tennis court, the UCSB courts, which it is her privilege as faculty to use when she's so inclined—her daughter, too, when the little tart-tongued sprite can be bothered. And there, if you've nothing better to do on a Sunday morning, you might observe her taking her romantic frustrations out on her own flesh and blood, whipping forehands and two-fisted backhands from corner to corner, dropping Wimbledonian touch shots just over the net, wristing ungettable topspin lobs over the head of the strong-willed but vertically challenged juvenile whenever the impulse strikes. Honestly, where is Child Services? Are there no protections for the young? She should be hauled in and booked, fitted with one of those white-collar security anklets.

Ali watches another lob arc over her head, land fair, and, torqued with spin, rocket beyond reach. Her feet never move.

Game, set, match.

Congratulations, Professor Jacobs! You've just

demolished your adolescent child, whose proper idea of sport is throwing herself into the Columbus Day sale at Abercrombie & Fitch.

Mother and daughter stand on the court regarding each other. Mother already beginning to look a bit sheepish.

Let's go to the videotape, shall we: mother mumbles generic apology for deranged on-court behavior, which said apology daughter chooses to ignore; daughter walks to sideline, takes paperback of Philip Pullman's *His Dark Materials* trilogy out of backpack, sits down on the hard ground, and begins to read.

Take that, Mom, you bitch.

Mom stands wiping perspiration from face with towel, watching daughter immediately sucked into better, fuller alternative universe, to which Mom herself wouldn't mind being transported, though she knows she wouldn't deserve the pleasure. Which leads her to the sadly inevitable conclusion that, despite the impressive plaque on her office door, she is an authority on precisely nothing. Leads her to consider possible means of escape. Leads her to say aloud to daughter, "Will you be okay alone for fifteen minutes? I need to check my office for something." Though this is quite baldly a fiction; there is no something awaiting her, only silence, that simulacrum of peace. Daughter, in any case, doesn't bother to respond.

Mom hesitates, then begins walking away from maternal crime scene, thinking, in clichéd aphoristic fashion that ultimately depresses her further for its lack of originality: *Another day, another disaster.*

Thinking: *I hate you, Mr. Pullman. Thank you, Mr. Pullman.*

Thinking: *My heart is sore and frightened because of a man who is a man who is a man.*

EMMA

THIS SHE REMEMBERS EXACTLY: on freshman moving-in day at Yale, her father waiting for her outside Durfee, on Old Campus.

She has seen him only once since his move to Chicago, a weekend visit to his new city that, they both afterward agreed, though it had been a while in coming, had yet somehow arrived too soon. They were not ready. Now she embraces him carefully, not sure what she will feel. This is habitual, but also encouraged by his appearance. He has lost weight, is slender as an immigrant. His beard is gone, his thick salt-and-pepper hair shaved close to the head. His glasses are different—severe black frames, in the manner of the Jewish intellectuals of his parents' generation, whom he once told his daughter he had turned his back on.

116

He smiles tightly, opens his arms. "You didn't think I was going to let you do this all by yourself, did you?"

He is speaking to her, but he might just as easily be speaking to her mother, who has stopped, in rebellion or shock, a few yards from the car, a box of books in her arms.

"Hello, Grace."

"Ethan. I had no idea you were coming." A sharp look at Emma. "Did you invite him?"

The answer is negative, but Emma says nothing, neither nods nor shakes her head.

Her mother marches forward slowly, eyes on the ground, as if suddenly mistrustful of her footing. She lightly bumps Emma's father in the chest with the box of books, holds it there until he takes the weight from her.

"Since you're here," she says, and returns to the car for another load.

At Frank Pepe Pizzeria, crowded in by other freshmen and their families, the three of them share a large vegetarian pie and a carafe of the house red. The lunch, ostensibly celebratory, is laborious to the point of absurdity. Her mother's manners are too perfect, sharp as the saw-wheeled pizza cutter that rests on their table like the symbol of an amputation none of them dare acknowledge.

"Another piece, Ethan . . . ?"

Her father has drunk most of the wine. He cleans his glasses with his napkin too many times, and he begins to perspire.

"I'm afraid I'd better start thinking about getting to the airport."

Emma looks from one parent to the other, a sickness rising in her throat. This is what it is like to know you are not forgiven.

DWIGHT

"SO?" I SAY.

Sam and I two beers deep apiece at Loney's, a pubby sort of eatery I frequent largely because, with its satellite-TV subscription to Red Sox Nation, it reminds me a little of home. Not that this is necessarily a plus; but it needn't be damning, either. It was my hope that Sam might appreciate it, too, for not dissimilar reasons.

Unfortunately, with the Sox-Angels game already started on the wide-screen above the bar, and the room three-quarters empty, the ambience seems instead to have raised up our ghosts, the lost years and meals and the rest, the evenings not like this one.

"So?" Sam repeats.

"Do you have a problem with anger?"

"Do I have a problem with anger?" A rippling smirk breaks the surface—my son, like his old man, no rank amateur: he can tell his mimic job is starting to get under my skin. "A problem like yours, you mean?"

"I don't have that problem anymore, Sam. I have other problems now, which we can talk about later, if you're really interested. How about right now you just answer the question."

"I'll answer it after you, *Dad*."

"Okay. I don't have a clue. Last time I saw you, you were this little muffin of a kid struggling under a whole lot of stuff no kid should ever have to deal with. A pretty gutsy kid, in my opinion— a good kid. You'd had some tough luck in the old man department, okay, but you weren't clubbing anybody with a baseball bat."

"Everybody grows up eventually," Sam mutters darkly, eyes glued to the TV above my shoulder.

The quiet bitterness of this remark sets me back in my chair. I reach for my glass, but it's empty.

And time seems to stop then, or even goes into reverse, as I look at the angry young man sitting across from me, unable, however I study him, to find evidence of the thin white scar that I know runs along the line of his left jaw: the scar made by my fist when, five years old, he jumped into the middle of a drunken fight I was having with Ruth on the night our marriage went bust. Every single second of that night was, for all of us, an accident of the worst kind. Just like that, because of me, his life—and mine—swerved off course. Though the still worse turns that were to follow didn't immediately make themselves known—as, of course, they never do, until it's too late.

I've heard it said, and am here to affirm it myself, that if you turn yourself in for a crime you will earn yourself a shot at redemption. But there's a statute of limitations on that one, I believe, though it's not much mentioned by the moral philosophers of the day. Wait too long to speak up and you might just miss your shot. You may do your time, but you will never really get out.

"You guys doing all right?"

Our blond waitress, half my age, with the surfer's wide shoulders and the blazing California smile: a veritable fun house of sun and salt packed into tight chinos and a blue oxford. My jack-o'-lantern grin seems to startle her, leading her to rear back slightly.

"Doing great, thanks," I answer, meaning possibly the opposite. It's hard to tell anymore, so beset am I by memory, and now suddenly, incongruously wistful for all the waitresses I ever knew in the Northwest Corner, never as young as here but undiscovered stars every one of them, with their dark-polish nails and winter-colored hair and crow's-feet around their eyes, and those lived-in smiles that draw you closer.

"Just let me know if I can get you anything else?" This directed meaningfully at my son, whose handsome slouched fury she can't take her eyes from.

"Will do." I grin tiredly at her again as she walks away. "Keep ignoring her like that," I say to Sam, winking, "and she just might follow you home."

"Whatever."

We fall silent.

At the start of the evening—with the sun still lingering in the sky and the dinner still just an idea in the making—it had been my sincere intention to try to persuade my son to return to school. *Get your diploma first,* I'd been going to exhort him, *just get the goddamn thing and stick it in your pocket and that, at least, no matter what else comes to pass, they'll never be able to take from you. . . .*

But the right time to have that pep talk somehow never seemed to arise; or maybe, rather, I just didn't have the stomach to send him back East once he was finally here.

I follow Sam's gaze to the wide-screen above the bar. The game is in the eighth inning and the Sox, with a runner on second, are trying to fight their way out of a two-run hole. The base runner is Coco Crisp, I see, and in the batter's box Big Papi's stamping around, bat handle propped against his crotch, spitting into his massive palms and clapping like a circus strongman let loose from his cage.

"Here we go!" cheers the Boston announcer, practically pissing himself with excitement. "All right, folks, here we go!"

I turn back to my son, who's no longer watching the game, or anything. A muscle twitching in his jaw, biting down furiously on all the words he'll never say.

I reach out and squeeze his arm. My voice thick and unfamiliar to us both. "Whatever the situation is, Sam, whatever happens with this, we'll face it together."

His expression then declares that he can't, or won't, believe me.

And in this, at least, we are the same.

PENNY

LETTING GO IS EASIEST. It would be by far the easier thing to do, and the smarter thing. She likes to think of herself as an intelligent woman of independent mind. She could just let Dwight Arno go back to wherever it is he came from.

She could do that.

The door to her office is closed. It is three-fifty in the afternoon, which leaves ten minutes before the start of office hours. In this circumscribed shelter she sits. Her box of Kleenex ready, next to her dog-eared copy of *The Rattle Bag*.

Ten minutes: she could pick up the phone now and call him.

Her office phone is black and old-fashioned. Bought at an antiques store, it is not retro but original; it refuses to indulge in the idea of change for change's sake. It weighs about three pounds. With it, she likes to think, she could sink a dinghy; or call the president of the United States (no thanks); or, with a modicum of chutzpah, knock a broad-shouldered man unconscious.

DWIGHT

TONY LOPEZ, avowed family man and shrewd small-business operator, has offered my son the stockroom and cashiering duties previously performed by his nephew. Despite his misdemeanors, Evander will continue to receive his more than generous paycheck, but will henceforth be ghosted out of the store, made an employee in name only, free to skate and smoke his days into contented oblivion. Sam, on the other hand, not being family, will be paid a buck above minimum wage and embark on a trial period until Tony's comfortable with the situation on a long-term basis, at which point opportunities for promotion may be explored.

"Maybe take your old man's job," Tony says to him with a grin that can only be described as sly.

The three of us are gathered at Mama's Taqueria on a Tuesday evening. The workday done, the oiled-cheese scent of nachos in the air.

I sip my Dos Equis and think about how all this might appear to Ruth—the paltry back-room starter job for our messed-up son—and feel a stirring of shame at not being able to do more for him. And yet, simultaneously, I am guiltily heartened by the prospect of commuting to work with him each morning, returning home each evening, the wordless camaraderie this would seem to promise, the intimate, meaningless chatter. The truth is I can hardly wait for it to begin.

Tony sets down his mineral water with lime and leans across the table. "One thing we gotta get clear, Sam, okay? Whatever problems you had at school? Your dad here"—reaching out and pincer-gripping my forearm—"he'll tell you straight out, I don't put up with no shit in my business. You understand what I'm saying to you? Not in my business."

"He understands, Tony," I say.

Tony frowns at me without taking his eyes off Sam.

"I understand, Mr. Lopez."

Tony sits contemplating the young man. What he reads there is anyone's guess. Finished, he checks his gold Rolex, pushes back his chair, and stands up. It's seven past seven, which makes him seven minutes late for his regular sit-down dinner with Jodi and the girls. He is a family man, by God, and there are demands.

"We got ourselves a little weekend softball league," he says. "Hear you play some real ball—varsity third base?"

"Till a couple weeks ago." Sam's face has begun to flush.

"Me, I was center field, way back. Brother Jorge played catcher—like Posada with the Yankees. Man, I tell you? Jorge could swing the fucking lumber. Made it to Cape Cod summer league 'fore he blew out his knee."

"You should see Sam hit. The kid can smack it."

Sam turns and stares at me, the color vanished from his cheeks and his eyes dimmed by some internal judgment that I've just failed.

"All right . . ." Tony's already on his way to the door. "Just make sure you come out to the park with your old man this Sunday. We could use some pop in the lineup." He pauses to grin over his shoulder at us, then he's gone.

Outside, the evening has turned California cool. Sam and I stand like tourists at an auto show, watching Tony guide his Mercedes out of the lot. Then we climb into my own car, the treated canvas top raised against the surprising springtime chill, and start for home.

Neither of us speaks. Sam tries out a couple of my CDs, dismisses them with grimaces as geriatric bluegrass crap, and punches off the stereo. We make our way in silence through the night-shadowed, seemingly abandoned town, as if it isn't the right town but some other. My son beside me yet miles distant, I have little choice at this moment but to acknowledge that I might be lacking some of the necessary tools for what I hope to do in the here and now. To build a solid, lasting bridge between two people, let alone a father and son with a history like ours, is a mighty human endeavor, and to sit here and think I might be able to accomplish it alone, with no previous success to my credit (indeed, failures too numerous to catalog), a tube of glue, a few pickup sticks, and a dollop of spit, is nothing short of hubris. And hubris, the Greeks tell us, will see you dead. The robed chorus chanting your name until, in the last act, they bury and forget you.

I lower my window, suddenly needing to smell the ocean, to know where the hell I am. But the ocean is not to be located. What I get instead, crossing the 101, is the vehicular exhaust of other capsuled, weary dreamers shooting up and down the coast, their passage sounding to my estranged ears like blood rushing through a tunnel.

Five minutes later, I pull into my driveway and cut the engine.

"Work tomorrow," I say. "Might as well turn in early."

Sam doesn't respond. We enter the house and I go to the kitchen for a glass of water. I can feel a headache coming on. When I come out, he's already in his room with the door closed. I sit down on a chair facing the TV. But I don't turn the set on, or drink the water, or do anything but think about the fact that, as my son so clearly registered—though admirably didn't say aloud to a third party—I have never really seen him play ball. For three years, while he was between the ages of seven and a half and ten and a half, we occasionally played catch together on my rented lawn in Box Corner. Which at the time meant a lot to me; I won't say it didn't. My sense of things then was of an extended warm-up between two teammates old and young, the sweet early innings of what would eventually become a long, meaningful game stretching through the afternoon hours and into the starlit evening of our lives. A game whose memory we would both always cherish.

Of course, for many reasons, things did not turn out that way.

RUTH

WHEN THE CALL COMES, late afternoon on a Friday in May, she is sitting at the upright piano in her living room, a mug of steaming green tea on a coaster, playing a song that Sam loved as a baby, before he ever had language. Her memory not so much the proverbial sieve as an increasingly rusty grater, shredding little shards and slivers from the original whole. Sometimes you can tell where a piece came from, but often not. Giggling at dust in a sunbeam? A suddenly curled fist? A squeak like a rubbed balloon? Sam's infant joy might have shown in anything. In lieu of being certain, she can just sit here and play the song, an American classic older than her grandparents, that gives rise, for her, to nostalgic images of wheat fields and haystacks, clean rivers and log fires. All of which, without lyrics to accompany the notes, maybe makes no sense, yet isn't meaningless. It doesn't matter that she never grew up with any of these iconic things herself. A loss of memory she can live with, but not a loss of feeling.

She plays three successive chords and breathes. She plays three more. She begins to hum, remembering her baby in her own way.

The cordless phone rings, and she reaches for it.

On the line, an official-sounding man introduces himself as Sam's dean.

Correction. What he actually says is:

"Mrs. Wheldon, my name is Chas Burris. I'm dean of students at the University of Connecticut. Is Sam there?"

"No, Sam's not here."

Her voice eminently reasonable, she believes. But her hands have already fled the piano keys, become fists in her lap. She scrapes the bench away from the instrument, distancing herself:

there is hot tea there to be spilled, there is music.

"Do you know where he is, Mrs. Wheldon? It's very important that I speak with him."

"Has something happened?"

"Mrs. Wheldon, do you have a cellphone number for your son? Any way of reaching him immediately?"

The man's insistent use of her name, she understands, is the most dangerous thing about him.

"Not until you tell me what this is about."

"Mrs. Wheldon, we would have contacted you sooner, but the facts were slow in reaching my office. Your son's roommate has not been cooperative."

"What are you talking about?"

"Mrs. Wheldon, your son, Sam Arno, has officially been expelled from the University of Connecticut. He won't be receiving his diploma, now or ever. In fact, that may be the least of his problems."

Ruth tries to speak, but fear constricts her throat.

"There was a violent incident in a bar off campus. You may know about that already. Immediately afterward Sam seems to have disappeared from campus, leaving behind many of his belongings. He's been absent from his classes for nine days. You may be aware of that, too. Unfortunately, as I've said, the cumulative facts were slow to reach me. So I must ask you again, Mrs. Wheldon, with urgency: Do you know where your son is at this time?"

"No, I do not."

"Very well. But, Mrs. Wheldon, you should be aware that the situation has progressed. As we speak, a young man is lying in the hospital in very critical condition. Legally, your son is an adult. It's important that you and your family understand this and prepare accordingly. I imagine you'll want to hire a lawyer, if you haven't already. And wherever Sam is now, he should remain in the state of Connecticut."

"Legally?"

She can hear herself, faintly, over the phone, in the empty house, holding their lives together with a single question mark; but it is borrowed dialogue. The whole day, suddenly, cut off from the time within it. The music dead. The wheat fields burned.

DWIGHT

I'LL SAY HERE STRAIGHT OUT that I believe there's a legitimate case to be made for softball as the true American pastime. The dowdy, smaller-than-regulation, always a little unkempt plots of dirt and sparse grass tucked away in city parks and derelict sandlot zones all across this land of ours: these are the fields of dreams for your average citizen.

Dirty-faced kids wearing their older brothers' hand-me-downs; divorced dads with abdominal six-packs more pale ale than muscle. The ball swollen yet embarrassingly unhefty; the bat light as a wand yet boasting an extra-large aluminum sweet spot. The pitching tends to be fat city, a perpetual home-run derby set up to make the hoi polloi feel like Barry Bonds. You gaze at that huge ball arcing toward you, tossed by friend or colleague or crazy-ass uncle, and it can only seem like the best moment of your week.

My son, quite naturally, doesn't see it this way. When Sunday rolls around and I venture into his cave den—covered in dirty sweats and T-shirts and jeans, the guest bedroom has become a rogue state in the act of seceding from the rest of the house—to wake him at nine, he expresses in foul terms his disinclination to join me. It's only when I explain that in all likelihood he'll get his ass fired if he doesn't play ball—he's only worked three days so far, earning a whopping $146 after taxes—that he grudgingly pulls on some rank UConn athletic clothing and an old pair of sneakers, sucks down the mug of coffee I stick in his hand, and follows me out to the car.

Most of the assembled twenty-odd people who show up at Arenas Municipal Recreation Park this morning are either SoCal employees or Lopez blood relations, or both. Mostly male bodies in various states of gravitational and pharmacological crisis. Uniforms homegrown and haphazard. Coolers of Powerade, Red Bull, and Tecate thoughtfully set out behind home plate for constant rehydration, revivification, and general watercooler-like conviviality. I greet the others with clunky fist bumps and even, here and there, quick back-slappy hugs, and introduce Sam all around. The weather is typically fine, the grass in our relatively prosperous township green and neatly trimmed, the recently rolled lines gleaming like fresh deck paint. Beyond the fenceless outfield ringed by half a dozen tall, lithely swaying palm trees are two municipal tennis courts, and in between our jovial beer-infused chants of "No batter!" and "He's a chump!" and "You call that a swing?!" (and we haven't even started playing yet) can be heard the distant hollow *thwock* of tennis balls being struck, which for some reason my ears always interpret as hauntingly inverse, like echoes before sound.

To all this Tony brings a high seriousness that might be comical if it weren't underwritten by native competitive menace. One need only study his high-school sports trophies displayed in the window of the store to know that he's a man used to winning and who, beyond that, hates to lose. When Tony takes the field against you, he wants to grind you into the dirt and, for good measure, kick you in the back of the head and steal your teeth. This is one of the reasons, I suppose, that I feel comfortable around him. The fact that we aren't really a softball league, more a loose federation of Roman slaves gathered to fight the lions under the gaze of the emperor, doesn't in any way diminish his vision of the game as a microcosm of everything we're meant to achieve on behalf of his business interests. Teams are chosen the good old feudal way, which is to say that Tony acts as one captain and I, technically the next man down the SoCal totem pole, stand in as the other. Tony, of course, Big Chief and Grand Pooh-Bah, picks first from the pool of assembled talent—which on certain weekends, depending on attendance, can seem as pointless as picking dead horseflies out of a swimming pool with a long, droopy net.

With Sam added to the mix for the first time, however, a new level of excitement is palpable as we divvy up players. Rumors of his prowess on the college diamonds of the East Coast have already spread through SoCal and the large extended Lopez clan, and now, as Tony nods proprietarily at my son, drafting him first, a murmur of baseball-fantasy appreciation rises from those still waiting to be noticed. Like all true athletes, Sam seems to accept this awareness of his talents as his due, indeed to grow more relaxed amid the incipient admiration, unbuckling his shoulders and easing himself loose-limbed across the invisible line into Tony's stable, like the prize thoroughbred he is.

My turn next, I pick Derek, who, bong habit and lack of social affect notwithstanding, actually hits for decent average and plays a nice, tight second base. And so the process goes, ending only with my final pick of Sandra to play catcher. We break huddle and I lead my gang over to the chain-link backstop to ready ourselves for our first at-bats. Overall, despite having lost Sam to the competition, I'm feeling reasonably satisfied with my roster. We've gained some small but decided advantages. Sandra's lower-back tattoo of a naked angel that peeks into view whenever she crouches down behind the plate or swings gustily for the palms, for example, makes her presence on our team an unequivocal plus for morale, if not necessarily for the virtue of old men.

Batting in the third with two men on, Sam slugs a ball so high and far it clears the forty-foot-tall palms at the back of the outfield and lands on the farthest of the two tennis courts, about a yard from a bald dentist just making his approach to the net. The dentist gives a shout of alarm that can be heard in every corner of the park, and the falling meteor, propelled by its contact with the hard earth, takes flight again, eventually coming to rest in a sandbox some twenty yards distant.

Thankfully the sandbox is empty and no one gets hurt. Save for my son, who can be seen humbly rounding the bases, the entire park appears to have come to a standstill, in a state of communal awe. The dentist is leaning on the net, too unnerved to continue.

Tony is first in line to greet the hero at home plate. The Captain is beaming, left fist pumping the air in unbridled joy, eyes wide with *did-you-fucking-see-that?* wonderment, right hand reaching to clasp Sam's hand in a vertical amigo handshake, thumbs up and palms cupped, the grip that ends naturally in a kind of chest-bump hug— reserved, in Tony's unwritten book of code, for family and superstars.

I myself am thrilled for Sam for my own reasons, and profoundly impressed with his physical abilities (that body that in part came from me, even if I can't at present perceive the connection), standing at first base oohing along with the rest of the crowd. There's only one thing I genuinely need at this moment, and that is to make eye contact with my son. Just a glance, a privately enacted moment between us. Though I can't but be aware that this is a selfish and sentimental impulse, not in fact a passing of the paternal torch (I'm no Athenian) but rather a childish yearning to bask in the warmth of his brightly burning flame as he runs by on his way to some other, more glorious Olympics. Maybe it should come as no surprise, then, that my look never lands and my glance goes unmet, but the surprise is there anyway (as it always will be on the parental end), along with a sting that's slow to bloom and long in fading. And then the next batter's coming up and it's time to get back in position.

And that, more or less, is all I'm conscious of till the seventh, when once again Sam strides to the plate, this time with nobody on and his team ahead by a good five runs. A game situation without interest whatever if not for the young god at the plate, who, with one epic swing and a couple of nifty plays in the field, has already made groupies of us all, including his old man.

Now we watch him let the first three pitches go by, none of them quite right. The pitcher—Tony's accountant and "numbers guy," Brew Donadio, relegated to light field duty by an arthritic hip—finally turns up his palms in mock frustration, as if to say, *Whaddya want?* And someone on the sidelines starts chanting, "Lo-ser bat-ter!," drawing ironic chuckles from the crowd, though Sam himself remains unsmiling at the plate, calm as a sniper. Then the next pitch is on its way, underhanded and right down the pipe, and Sam steps into it with a long stride of his left leg and swings smoothly from his hips, rifling the ball on the fly into the gap between right (Tony's cousin Chuckie) and center (Chang Sook Oh). As soon as I see the ball's flight—a classic inside-the-parker—I start jogging for home to back up Sandra at catcher. Sam, reaching full speed after just a couple of strides, flies by me heading for first. He's rounding second when the ball strikes one of the outfield palms and ricochets back onto the field, allowing Chang to scoop it up rabbit-quick and fire to the cutoff man Derek, who turns and hurls a strike to me at the plate, bypassing Sandra, who's stepped out of the way.

The ball smacks into my glove with Sam just a few strides past third and coming hard. I look up the line at my son pounding toward me and grin at him—as if to say, all in good fun, *Hey, look what just landed in my mitt! I'm going to tag you out, sport!* I stand and wait, glove and ball on prominent display, for him to concede, downshift his headlong sprint for glory into a trot acknowledging that I've got him dead to rights.

But he does not slow down. If anything, he runs harder. I watch him with a kind of numb astonishment. And then, a moment before impact, I see him lower his shoulder.

Of the actual collision at the plate I remember nothing. I am a relatively big man, heavy-chested, bearing a certain amount of muscled bulk. And my son, too, is good-sized, though sleeker and faster than me, befitting his mother's more refined genes. What Sam possesses, though, and of which maybe I've never had enough, is sheer will. He wants to make it safely home, and, maybe more than anything, he wants to run through me to get there. It is, in a sense, not complicated at all.

Someone helps me to my feet. I don't remember who. I don't remember anything about those seconds but the ball lying off to the side, where it's rolled after being violently dislodged from my glove. And the dust on my tongue. And the pain in the center of my chest where his shoulder struck me. And my tall, beautiful son, having picked himself off the ground and been called safe at home, standing among his new teammates and receiving their shouts of congratulation, their wild slaps on the back, looking every minute as if he hates his own guts.

PART TWO

RUTH

HER FLIGHT LANDS in Los Angeles at two-thirty. She rents a car and drives two hours up the coast, following directions printed off Google. Even in the middle of the afternoon the freeway traffic confounding, claustrophobic: briefly it speeds up, only to come inexplicably to a slamming halt. She keeps her windows closed and the air-conditioning on high, taking small sips from a bottle of water she cadged on the plane.

After an hour of stop-and-go riding in her chilled little econobox, she begins to shiver. She turns off the air-conditioning but keeps the windows closed. Her body is still unnaturally thin; maybe it always will be. Although she has recently vowed to herself to give up the word *always,* because it is fraudulent. There is only now; there is only this. She drives toward her son, eyes darting between the small, carefully positioned mirrors and seeing nothing but other cars, behind and around and in front of her, more and more of them, as if no one in this strange, disconnected country ever finds where they're going.

She didn't want to tell Dwight the full news about Sam over the phone; she would prefer, in fact, to tell him as little as possible about the situation. She doesn't trust him not to take the bad news and immediately make things even worse. She needs to be there in person to intervene between father and son, mediate, lead, regroup. A plan that struck her as sound enough while she was on the plane, when it was still just thoughts in her head.

But turning into the parking lot of the sporting-goods store now and seeing her ex-husband waiting for her, brooding over a cigarette, comes as an old-time shock: solid as a New England drystone wall, a little gray dusting his short brown hair, the masculine and unrepentant physicality of him looming as something more than the mere representation of her former life. Which instantly makes her angry in some way— with him, with herself; but then so, too, does the way he's staring at her, that critically clueless expression of the arrogant cook at the farmers' market holding up the scrawny wartime chicken and demanding to know why it isn't the glorious pheasant of the salad days. She thinks she won't deign to remind him, because he knows it perfectly well, that there weren't any salad days. The promises they once made to each other were hastily scribbled IOUs, and the two faintly familiar bodies standing here, for better and mostly worse, are undeniably honest products of their times.

He drops the cigarette, grinding it out with the toe of his age-inappropriate sneakers.

"Well." He dips his large, lived-in head—

almost humbly, she thinks—then tries on a half smile and spreads his arms to embrace his mock kingdom. "Welcome to California, Ruth."

"Sporting goods?"

"You name it, we sell it. Need anything?"

"I need to see Sam."

After what seems like ages, staring at her as if she's crossed the country just to be near him, he replies, "I'll get my stuff and be right out."

Through the plate-glass window she watches him talking to a pretty young Latina behind the register. Leave it to Dwight, she thinks, to find his livelihood (if that isn't too grand a word for it) in a business that manages to combine his boyish passion for sports with the fig-leaf ambience of Hooters.

But, to be fair, he seems to be doing all right. He is decently clothed and well enough fed. He doesn't look broken or unhinged or permanently scarred, isn't covered with the ugly ghosts of removed tattoos or missing an arm. Beyond that, she assures herself, she doesn't care to know. She hasn't come all this way to exchange personal information. He isn't a prospective anything but the opposite—an island she's already visited, lived on, explored, and forcibly quit. She knows every inch of that terrain and wouldn't believe in its reinvention as a luxury resort if the Four Seasons itself vouchsafed it.

The fact is you can put up palm trees where

once there were elms ravaged by beetles, shine the sun all day and banish winter, bronze your skin and whiten your teeth; and still the pale depressed people who stayed behind will go on telling their pitiable or outraged stories of the old days. Because the place where they live isn't in the end some artificial stage set that can be struck down after the show's disastrous run, not just home but a constant reminder; because every dead tree and every endless winter are headstones beneath which lie the long-buried memories that no one, anymore, wants to hear.

DWIGHT

Got a ride to L.A. Back tomorrow.

These unfortunate exit lines Sam has scribbled on the back of the morning note I left him the previous weekend—which he's either been saving as some sort of voodoo memento or has simply forgotten to throw out. In any case, Ruth is standing in the kitchen reading and rereading his words as if they were clues to a tragic treasure map, the edges of the paper vibrating in her hands, while all I can do is stare at my own handiwork on the reverse side:

Okay, so Solvang's kind of a ridiculous tourist trap. But trust me, Sport, those Danish *waitresses in the pancake house across from the Best Western are worth the trip anyway. Don't forget the bus map. We'll talk about car and $$ situation when I get home. Call you later. Dad.*

My note, I must say, seems more egregiously idiotic the second time around.

Slowly, Ruth lowers the paper. Her green eyes have turned the color of smoke. Sensing where her accusations might be headed, I quickly explain that Monday is Sam's day off at the store and that he announced zero of his plans to me when I left the house this morning. I got his voice mail during the day, but nothing unusual about that. He could easily have caught a ride from one of the various members of Tony's extended family who are always shuttling back and forth between Arenas and L.A., I say, and, whatever the individual deficiencies of some of the Lopez clan, they have a strong family sense and, I feel confident, will look after Sam just fine. He'll certainly be back in time for work tomorrow morning.

When I've finished all this, Ruth takes a few seconds to stare at me. Her look and what it says about my judgment are eloquently familiar from our marriage. Then her eyes fix on the wall and she flips open her cellphone. Soon the automated message on Sam's line that I heard earlier spills tinnily out of her earpiece. After dialing twice more with the same result, she sinks wordlessly onto a chair.

Her purse is lying on the table; now she opens it and starts fumbling through a heap of feminine junk. Whatever she's looking for in such a desperate manner is her own business, but inevitably I find that just the sound of her trinkets being pawed through takes me back to a place I don't wish to go. That first day in Somers, I emptied my pockets and removed my watch, and a man in uniform sorted and bagged it all, keys and coins and money clip grating against the metal table, till all of it was gone. And then, thirty months later, the same junk was returned to me, only it wasn't the same, it was invisibly tainted and always would be, and I threw every last item, except for the money, into the trash.

"I thought I had the number for a school friend of his on a piece of scrap paper," Ruth says miserably. "But I can't find it."

I pull a bottle of Chardonnay from the fridge—it's the bottle Penny brought me, I realize just after I've opened it—and pour a glass and set it on the table in front of her.

Ruth shakes her head.

"Come on, Ruth. It'll do you good."

"I'm not drinking these days."

"Suit yourself."

I take the glass back and sit down across from

her. We stay like this for a while, me drinking the wine I poured for her. The kitchen is bright like any kitchen, and in its harsh light now it's clear how thin she is. Her blond hair, though neat and pretty enough, looks dry and coarse in the light.

I sit looking at her.

"He's my only child," she says, after a long silence.

"I know."

We met while I was at UConn law school in Hartford and she was an undergrad in music on the Storrs campus. She came to Hartford to visit a classmate of mine named Donald for the weekend. He was her boyfriend, lover, what have you, and I was just a stranger. She was standing at the jukebox in the corner of my regular bar one Friday night, tapping a quarter against the domed glass and trying to decide which song to play, when I turned and saw her from behind: sand-colored ponytail, faded old Levi's.

The song she ended up choosing was "You Can't Always Get What You Want." I never did learn what happened to poor Donald.

We moved her piano into our first apartment. A Yamaha upright, well-used but gleaming black; she used to polish it with a chamois cloth. It followed us around during those early years of promise and undone deeds, always taking up half the living room. I never so much as touched those keys, but I used to look at the hulking pretty instrument and admire it, thinking about my old man and what he might have said had he been alive.

The movers set it up that first day and left. Ruth sat down on the bench, half-emptied boxes and yards of torn wrapping all around her, and started to play some old song I didn't know. An initiation was what it felt like, or a welcoming. It was a slow song, and I sat on the futon sofa behind her and watched her arms and hands gracefully moving, the graceful curve of her neck, the window light on her hair. The people I came from, my father's line especially, had been bitter, crimped survivors of the failed textile mills in Lawrence and Fall River, with no appreciation of music or beauty. Growing up, it had never occurred to me that one day in my life I would live in a house with a piano, or watch a beautiful woman with sand-colored hair play that piano for me.

"You look sad," Ruth said. I thought she was still playing, but she'd stopped and turned to face me.

She patted the seat beside her. "Come sit with me while I play."

I did, and it was the only time I can remember doing that, before we became parents and all the rest.

Somewhere near the end of the Chardonnay, Ruth tells me about the call she received from the UConn dean. She tells me what she knows, which isn't a lot, and yet is more than my son confessed to me, and is enough to cast our scattered family at once forward and backward in time, into a shadowed, threatened place of suddenly diminished hope that is too familiar, I can't help feeling in my gut, to be merely an accident of fate.

I start in on the only other wine in the house, Merlot in a box. We move from the kitchen to the living room, and there we sit wordless for long stretches, two people who know the worst about each other and, if need be, are still alive to prove it in court. The TV's on, CNN on mute, as if information about Sam's whereabouts and well-being and prospects for his life and his victim's might at any moment appear in the ticker running beneath the talking heads.

Finally, Ruth gets to her feet.

"I have a headache and I'm tired. I'm going to get a glass of water now and go to my hotel."

"Let me get it."

"No, I'll do it."

She goes into the kitchen, and I sit listening to the cupboard opening and the faucet filling a glass. The silence afterward, I guess, is her drinking the water.

The day has faded out, and the lights are off, all except the voiceless TV. And maybe it's no more than Ruth's presence in my house, but the moment feels to me more like Connecticut than California; it feels like the past.

I know her sounds and habits, the warm sour-sweet smell of her skin in the morning bed. How, coming out of the shower, she dips at the waist like a Russian dancer to wrap her wet hair in a towel. How she warms her coffee mug by running hot tap water into it first. How she slices cucumbers with her pinkie sticking in the air like an old Boston lady drinking tea. How centipedes and bats make her shiver uncontrollably, but how she can use a wrench and fix a toilet as well as any man. How she, not I, was the one to teach Sam to build sandcastles and fly paper airplanes. I know how she communes with a piano before playing or giving some kid a lesson, the first two fingers of her right hand running a simple back-and-forth over the center keys while her left palm presses against the face of the black box, feeling for the music to come. I know how, back in the days of our love, she would hook her thumbs over the waist of my jeans and pull me closer, and the little arching gasp of surprise she made when I touched a certain spot in the small of her back.

I hear her place the empty water glass on the counter.

Coming back into the living room, she says in a threadbare voice, "Call me if you hear from him. Otherwise I'll call you tomorrow." She slips her purse over her shoulder and walks to the front door.

I haven't moved, am still looking at her. She is still beautiful, I see, but her beauty is under some kind of assault; it's there in her face.

I say her name. She turns and looks at me: my ex-wife. I have no plan, just a host of feelings I'll never be able to find words for.

Ruth puts her hand on the knob. "I hope you're not thinking about trying to hug me or anything like that. I don't think I could deal with that right now."

My arms dangle by my sides. "Are you sick?"

She starts to cross her arms over her chest but stops herself. "I found a lump in my breast last winter."

"Jesus."

"My surgeon said they got all of it. No lymph nodes. There was six weeks of radiation, and I've just finished my last cycle of chemo. That's really the whole story at this point."

"I'm sorry, Ruth."

"It could be worse." She opens the door and stands there, a hand rising up to touch her head. "And just for the record? This isn't my hair."

"I kind of figured that."

"Okay. Well, good night."

"Night, Ruth. It's good to see you. I'm just sorry the circumstances aren't better."

The ghost of a tired, complicit smile on her face. "Were they ever?"

SAM

COMING AWAKE in the reclined front seat of a parked car:

He sits groaning softly and blinking. His head the flattened roof of a hammered nail.

A night has somehow passed; it would seem to be Tuesday morning.

He finds himself in a black Mazda hatchback. On a quiet, semi-industrial side street. Somewhere near Venice Beach.

There is no evidence of Evander, whose car it is.

On the car floor: a greasy wad of burrito wrappers and four empty Corona bottles.

An exact replica of the Mountain Dew sign above the drinks cooler in the Cal-Mex take-out joint on Abbot Kinney suddenly appears naked before his awareness: the image mentally snapped during some blurred period of time following a late show of *X-Men 3* with Evander; yet prior to another blurred period of time during which they met up with some girls at the bungalow of some guy Evander regularly sells coke to.

One of the girls, blond with dark roots, called herself . . .

What he remembers instead of her name: under tight jeans, the triangle of black thong printed with vibrant red cherries—"bing" cherries, she enigmatically insisted, right before she knelt in front of him. . . .

Sitting bolt upright in the car, Sam cricks his neck left then right, shooting stars of inconsolable pain into his head, and mind. He left the car windows open overnight. The inside of the windshield is opalescent with ocean humidity—a pearled, deadly mirror of nothing.

He can't remember what the point was, tearing off down the coast with Evander as if he had somewhere to go. The fear of himself remains, and the need to run that he's always known; but also the bittersweet sense that another desperate experiment has failed and now there are no more decisions to make.

With the sleeve of his hoodie he rubs a small aperture, about the size of a plum. Through it he can see a lone figure at the end of the street. A man walking a small dog. The man's head is down. His shoulders are pressed up by his ears.

The walking of this dog down this same street every morning, afternoon, and evening, it seems absolutely clear to Sam, the same steps along the same path, is the one thing that this lost man can still do with his life.

DWIGHT

"COME HERE A LOT?"

"Almost never."

Ruth nods as if mine is a telling response, some sort of pocket metaphor, when in fact I don't mean it as much of anything. I take the fishing rod from her—the starter spin kit I borrowed from work for my lunch hour, thinking that a little pier fishing down at the marina might be something to carry us through the difficult Tuesday doldrums while we continue to wait for some word or sign from our AWOL son who—maybe predictably—failed to show up for work this morning. (I told Tony that Sam's recovering from a bout of food poisoning, and he seemed to believe me.)

"Is this your community?" Ruth asks.

I look at her, my sarcasm meter touching red, but her dark sunglasses give away nothing. "Pier fishing?"

"The marina. This whole shaggy California scene. Long-in-the-tooth beach boys chugging Cape Codders at the clam bar all day."

"Sea breezes," I correct her. "And no, Ruth, this isn't my community. I actually work for a living. But thanks for including me in your heartfelt democratic vision." I'm annoyed by what seems her persistent downsizing of my prospects, to say nothing of her knee-jerk stereotyping of my adopted home. But then she offers a self-deprecating little smile, and I briefly forgive her everything.

We go on fishing. The sun-pruned old local next to us reels in his Day-Glo rubber worm and leaves, muttering to himself like an amnesiac. No doubt he'll settle himself at the bar at Captain Cook's, up to his soggy gills in sea breezes and invented maritime escapades: the thousand-pound marlin that stared him in the eye and spit the hook.

"You used to be quite a fisherman," Ruth muses.

"I wasn't so good. But I liked doing it."

"We took some nice trips, didn't we?"

Her tone is sincere and I fall silent, calling up, in my own version, what it is I imagine she's talking about.

The car we're driving is a Ford pickup, circa mid-eighties, with a camper rig battened over the flatbed. Duffel bags and sleeping and fishing gear piled in back, as well as two rods and two pairs of waders and two pairs of felt-bottom boots, a large of everything for me and kiddie size for Sam. The big-volume item a fisherman's float like the kind of inner tube I used to frolic with in the North Haven public pool as a kid, but this one fitted out with leg holes and a nylon skirt.

Sam, five years old and small for his age, sits low on the bench seat between Ruth and me, knees up and Converses resting on the wheel well. He's wearing a Red Sox cap and a Freddie Lynn jersey that reaches mid-thigh, the bill of the cap brushing against my right arm whenever he turns to ask me a question about something he's seen out the window or just something he's been thinking about.

Does it ever rain here?

I tell him that it rains sometimes, but mostly out West what you get is snow. Tons of snow in the winter. Otherwise it's pretty dry country. Except for the rivers, which are fed each spring by the snow melting up in the mountains.

Is that cactus?

No, sagebrush.

How tall's that mountain?

Tall. Very tall.

Why's Idaho called Idaho?

That's a damn good question.

Ruth reaches across him and turns up the volume on the radio—Johnny Cash singing "A Boy Named Sue." We listen to the song and Ruth and I smile at some of the lines, which makes Sam smile, too, though parts of the musical tall tale aren't exactly clear to him. A son trying to kill his father? A father trying to kill his son? Reconciliation that still sounds a little like hate? And all because some kid was given a girl's name? It seems simple but isn't. For no declared reason, Ruth leans over and plants a kiss on top of his head. Her throat and collarbones above her white V-neck are brown from the sun, and so are her arms and her legs beneath the cutoff jeans. She's kicked off her hiking boots and her feet are bare. Her hair's held back in a ponytail by a red rubber band that's been with her since we left Connecticut a week ago. She smells of suntan lotion and mint.

Then it's later, don't know when, somewhere north of Salmon, deep in crazy-militiaman country, but oh the fishing is sweet. The gravel beds in the shallow rivers gleam white under a sun that knows nothing but clean. The water glints and ripples. Wild trout are mere shadows in the light patches, then gone. Cicadas make the world sound electrified.

Sam, I say, eagle.

He follows my finger and it's true and he smiles. The majestic creature circles for a while, just for us, like some little man in an eagle suit, rented by the hour.

Time up, the bird catches a tailwind and soars away.

We go back to fishing. The water in which we stand is a foot and a half deep, fast-running, a rubberized mountain cold pressing on our waders. The heavy flat stones slippery beneath our felt-soled boots. We've been working on the cast. I count one-two, one-two like a human metronome on Sam's take-back-and-release, trying to teach him the rhythm that I myself have never come close to perfecting. Though he doesn't know this yet, bless him. He is enamored not so much of me as of the showboat side of the sport, the mostly unnecessary loading and unloading of the rod as the weighted and coated tangerine-colored line unfurls behind him and then furls forward again, hissing by his ear and mine as it plays out straight and soft, directed at a spot underneath a hanging branch some twenty-five feet away.

Of course, being small, buffeted somewhat by the onrushing water, his feet grasping for purchase, his short arm firing too quickly in his zeal to win the national fly-fishing title and bring home the forty-pound rainbow that doesn't exist, Sam doesn't entirely pull it off. The line gets caught in a stand of brush on the bank behind us. He tugs at it, getting frustrated, making things worse till I tell him to stop. I trudge out of the water and up onto the bank and spend close to twenty minutes extracting the line from the brush, detangling the leader. I think about changing the fly for better luck, but the truth's that, with my meaty fingers, the delicate, almost surgical fly knots are a little out of my small-motor league. Nothing's easy, is what I mean, so I decide to just stick with what we've got on. I carry his cleared line back into the river and tell him to reel in a few feet. He does this, in the process burying the tiny stone-honed barb of the fly into the tender skin between my thumb and palm.

My shout of *Fuck!* echoes briefly through the Salmon River Canyon before disappearing.

At this point in his life, Sam isn't scared of my temper as some kids might be. He actually thinks I'm funny, and stands laughing in the flowing river while I extract the hook and suck the blood from my hand, laughing too.

On the pier, in the astounding coastal light, I stand dazzled and bereft. My ex-wife beside me. Fishing, or so we call it. Observing now a large white sailboat as it enters the mouth of the harbor and approaches slowly under power, the halyard making a hollow *clang-thwack* against the aluminum mast. Dad at the helm, mom and two teenage sons readying the dock lines and fenders. "Tommy, make sure you run the bowline *under* the bowsprit and through the chock!" And curly-haired Tommy, as if he's heard the same directive a hundred times before: "I've *got* it, Dad!" Dad slows the engine still more, cuts the wheel hard, and the long beautiful yacht—my God, half a million easy—swings gracefully into the empty berth and is docked.

"Ruth, what happened with Norris?"

"Oh, please let's not."

"Do you still love him?"

Ruth sighs. "I've begun to think recently that maybe right from the beginning what I loved most about Norris was how he wasn't anything like you. He was so anti-you it was almost funny. On the wrong day, being with Norris could be like running a knife through left-out butter. You've got a lot of things wrong with you, but a lack of resistance isn't one of them."

This is amusing to me, or almost. I chuckle for a while, the fishing rod twitching in my hands.

"Laugh all you want," Ruth says calmly.

Stepping off his yacht onto the pier, Dad throws an arm around each of his sons, ruffling hair, and the family makes its way toward Captain Cook's and the parking lot. Screaming gulls follow them, hovering, stiffly inhabiting the sky like birds on a mobile.

"I miss you, Ruth." My ambivalent chuckle has died in my throat.

Ruth turns and studies me. I can't see her eyes behind the sunglasses, but I can tell by the way she's holding her head that her perspective is steady, neither sentimental nor aggrieved, just watchful and knowing. She takes the rod from my hands and slowly begins reeling in.

"Dammit, it's the truth."

"*A* truth, you mean. If it's even true, which I sincerely doubt."

"Which leaves us where?"

The plastic bobber reaches the tip ring and stops there. She takes hold of the purple rubber worm without distaste and hooks it to one of the lower guides.

"You know, that's the same thing I asked my oncologist when it all went south," she says. "He's older, not one of those cocky hotshots. This really sad face. Lost his own wife to cancer. I was sitting in his office right after he delivered the bad news, about to fall off my chair or throw up, and I said, I asked him, 'So where's that leave us?' And know what he answered?" Ruth's eyes are hidden from me, but I can hear the tears rising through her voice. "My doctor said, 'My dear, that leaves us *alive.*'"

She leans over and gives me a peck on the cheek. As she does, her arm with the rod comes forward and the rubber worm brushes my ear, causing me to shudder.

RUTH

DWIGHT INSISTS on driving her back to her motel to rest. Surprisingly the time with him, however weird, wasn't awful. Yet watching his car pull away, taking him back to work, she feels the old sense of relief. Her very bones are tired. Like spending the day on one of those moving airport walkways and only now, stepping onto solid ground, do you realize how hard it is to walk unaided on your own two feet; hard, but still easier than being with someone else.

The endless sunlight pours through the flat square windows of the motel room. Tiny flotsam of industrial carpet in the air. She draws the blinds and the room darkens, the air disappears. She sits down on the edge of the bed, her hands in her lap. A minute passes like this: for once, she isn't aware of thinking. She lies back and rests her head on the thin pillow. To hell with the wig, she thinks. She closes her eyes.

When she wakes, the sun is pressing around the blinds at a dying angle. It's past five o'clock. She feels as though she's been sleeping for days, as though a solid chunk of her life has fallen off and disintegrated while she slept. One moment you're standing on a pier like some jaded high-school heartbreaker; the next you're as good as ninety. One morning your child is in your womb; by evening he is forever outside you. And still the sun rises and falls.

On the cheap bedside table, her cellphone lies blank; no one has called while she slept. And it is the same day, Tuesday. She will have to find Sam soon, tonight or tomorrow, and take him back home, or the whole rickety scaffolding is going to collapse for good. Even so, she can't imagine how she might protect him. Her son. He is unprotectable, and still she will have to figure a way. This is her job in life, or there is no job at all. A small hope breathes inside her that Dwight might be of some help, but it's nothing she can count on.

Carefully, she gets to her feet. She goes into the bathroom and splashes water on her face and brushes her teeth. Looks at herself long and hard. Tries to arrange the borrowed hair where it sticks out awkwardly from her head, but soon gives up.

SAM

HE STANDS BY THE WINDOW in his father's living room watching his mother step out of the rental car. Both of them far from home, on the backside of lost. He angles himself to one side to make sure she won't spot him, and to give himself a moment to adjust to what he's seeing. The wig he can deal with—he knew it was coming, figures it's better than nothing at all— and the starkness of her cheekbones in the blue falling light; but her physical tentativeness sounds an internal alarm, the way her feet walk the cement blocks to his dad's front door as if following some invisible Seeing Eye dog.

He understands too well, which is what frightens him.

He lets her ring the bell. Even then, doesn't rush to greet her. Knowing that once he lets her in and she reaches out to hug him and tries to peer into his eyes to read him, as if that was possible, they'll already be into the next frame, whatever it is, and the story will go on. And he's reached that point in the story where he doesn't want to know the rest. He's sick and tired of his own story and would just prefer not to.

"Where have you been, Sam?"

Her face an involuntary flip book of the human register: shock, anger, love, terror.

"L.A. Like my note said."

"What were you doing there? Why haven't you answered any of my calls?"

Tender as a sunburn victim, he turns back into the room before she can try to touch him.

"Do you have any idea what's happened since you ran away?" she demands to his back. "Do you know what you've done, and what you're accused of?"

His throat, physically, will not allow him to acknowledge the truth.

"Get your stuff. I'm taking you home to Connecticut tonight."

In the end, his mother puts her arms around him.

For a full minute, she cradles him. Their reunion lingers indefinitely, carving its own warped dimensions, till his feet begin to shuffle in her longing, inconsolable embrace.

And still he's painfully aware, deep down at the level of the soul, how he presses back, towering over her, his head tucked low so that he might fit once again into the crook of her neck: that uncataloged place on her body where, in another life that he can't quite remember or get back to, he knows he once felt safe.

DWIGHT

IT'S EARLY EVENING when I return from work and find Ruth's rental parked outside my house.

I stand for a while on the quiet empty street, in the imperceptibly darkening air, thinking about my ex-wife sitting in my house at this moment, and my son maybe with her—maybe Sam has returned of his own free will, I think, maybe he's done that. It's possible. The two of them together, in my house. And that is all. I don't travel so far as to mentally investigate their conversation, difficult as it no doubt will be, or their states of mind, or the fragility of their individual futures. It's just their combined presence that absorbs me, their being in my house, the miraculous nature of this, the sheer cosmic improbability when you consider the torn and poorly drawn road map that's led me to this place over time, to this street and this house and this half-lived life. A simple thing in the big picture, maybe. And yet this evening I can't seem to get over it. It almost brings me to my knees in gratitude, here in the street, this unexpected suggestion that my family was once more than just ruin.

In my living room, they stand literally wrapped in each other—an image so old and storybook it feels iconic to me, bigger than all of us, a tattered flag flying over our tiny burned-out village long after the war has ended. I stand watching them in silent awe. And then they break apart, and without looking at me Sam goes down the hall to his room, and Ruth turns to me and says, quietly and firmly, "We've got to get going."

I drop my keys on the table by the door. They make a clatter, which seems to move reality along a little.

"Maybe I should go with you." The thought occurs to me only as I speak it aloud.

Nor, apparently, did it occur to Ruth; the surprise on her face is its own rebuke. "I don't think that would be a good idea."

"I used to be a lawyer, Ruth."

"I have the names of some people to call," she replies warily. "But thanks, anyway."

Nothing more to say after that. We fall silent till Sam comes back into the room.

He sets down his UConn duffel and, looking at the floor between us, formally thanks me for letting him stay.

"Don't thank me. You're my son."

And that's it, our big conversation.

You can do all the planning you want, or you can do none: once their bags are packed, people leave.

・ ・ ・

I walk them outside. The street still deserted, on the verge of another perfect dusk.

"You know the way?"

"I'll follow the signs," Ruth says.

"I could make you some coffee for the road."

She stops and puts a hand on my arm and looks me in the eye, some kind of tenderness there.

"We can't wait."

I hold the car door for her, seal her in. And then there's just Sam, standing by the hood.

"Bye," he mumbles.

"I'm glad you came. You take care of yourself."

He nods. Mumbles something else—I think it's "Sorry"—and ducks into the passenger seat.

Ruth starts the engine. I can't bring myself to step away.

Words leave me then. You spend them carelessly, flagrantly, and the next thing you know they're gone.

EMMA

FROM NEW HAVEN to Wyndham Falls is sixty-one miles, a distance that for two years has represented a protective and largely metaphorical moat separating her Gothic Ivy League fortress from her mother's creepy cottage in the dark northern forest. So very Hansel and Gretel: her mother the old crone who boils kids for supper, and she the silly frightened girl who, following her brother, will never more than half believe in the power of breadcrumbs to lead her back to safety. That there's no brother anymore just makes the journey that much more pathetic.

She takes Route 8, her mother's old Volvo wagon with 134,000 miles carrying her and the sum of her college belongings north through Waterbury, past the Mattatuck State Forest, through Torrington to Winsted. Not for the most part the glossy verdant Connecticut of second homes and country clubs and famous writers and movie stars but the working-class state that's produced, all by itself, some of the most unappealing cities in the country, among them Hartford and New Haven.

She drives, imagining turning west and not stopping; imagining being like that. All spring for American Studies she's been reading firsthand accounts of women—pioneers, freed slaves, Native Americans, line cooks, horse breakers, prostitutes, factory workers, Civil War nurses, even a midget in an early American circus—who for one reason or another set out westward into the American unknown. And in most cases it was only after this radical displacement that they found voices with which to speak of what had happened to them. And the difference, the enormous gulf in meaning and actuality, between these voices and the historical silence that they otherwise inhabited is what moves her most keenly; how what made their lives bearable lay not so much in their surviving their literal experiences, however brutal or good, or in the stories they eventually came to tell (if they were lucky), as in their somehow learning to navigate the terrible isolation before and after the telling, the unspeakable, ingrown silence. It's so easy to get swallowed up by the life you never expected to have. To just disappear. To live inside this great white whale of yourself and never have a vision of where you might be going, or where you've already been, or why.

She comes back to reality just as the car is entering Winsted. Not a long journey after all, not as she hoped it would be. A Chevy dealership and a Sunoco station and a diner with a HELP WANTED sign posted on the glass door. A mother with dark-red hair and pale unhealthy skin pushing her baby in a stroller with a loose front wheel: the stroller wobbles and swerves, wobbles and swerves, and the mother does not stop.

A streetlight, and Emma turns northwest, onto Route 44. Soon enough, on the left, a sign for Rugg Brook Reservoir. Then the sign is a disappearing eye chart in her mirror and she's driving on, her body but not her mind—her mind stuck back in a morning walking around that reservoir with her father and brother. Josh in the lead playing Indian scout, having discovered a deer floating on its side at the water's edge, its abdomen a swallowed brown globe. Hideous and gross, but he was thrilled, his narrow shoulders quivering with fascination. He was poking the bloated carcass with a long sharp stick, probing and investigating, trying to make it bleed, when their father, roaring up from behind, tore the stick out of his hands, shouting, *Don't touch it! Leave the dead in peace!*

A disturbingly uncontrolled reaction coming from an adult, a father, it strikes her now, something too desperate already there, adrift and fearful, excruciatingly prescient. Nothing she wants to remember, driving past the sign for Millbrook Road and pushing on, going inexorably home.

And the memory, and her failed attempt to escape it, leads to another recollection, as she continues along 44, seeing more and more signs of the familiar, the protective moat of distance between her and her mother good and breached now: walking into Josh's room one afternoon and finding him cradling one of his most prized possessions, an antique bowl-shaped gold pan, the gift of an eccentric uncle. He used to keep it in a silk-lined box on the shelf above his bed. The bowl made not of metal, as one might have expected, but of some low-grade ceramic, with distinctive grooves and runnels to allow the gravel and silt to sluice off, leaving the gold nuggets and the dust behind. And Josh, thorough and secretive as ever, had done his homework. At the age of ten, he could tell you all about the gold rush and the lives of the prospectors and the harsh anarchic conditions in the mining towns of Northern California. He knew enough about that lost world to invent a future for himself in which one day, on a break while touring San Francisco with the New York Philharmonic, he would drive inland and visit one of the original mining ghost towns and, pulling his antique miner's bowl out of his authentic turn-of-the-century miner's rucksack, do a little panning himself. Because there was still gold to be found coming out of that earth, he was sure of it. You could not convince him otherwise.

And this, thinks Emma—entering now, slow as she can go, the town of Wyndham Falls and circling the green—is what happens when your life is taken before your eleventh birthday. No one can argue with you anymore, or prove you wrong, or celebrate your genius, or love your imagination more than you do, or make there be gold where there isn't any, or discover that gold, or be with you as you look for it full of hope, on your knees, panning in that wide, rushing river that still runs out of the mountains.

SAM

IN THE AIRPLANE CABIN, the lights are off. His mother's eyes are closed. He thinks she's asleep until, in a soft, middle-of-the-night voice, her eyes flutteringly sealed, she begins to talk.

"I've been sitting here wondering what you could have been thinking when you hurt that other boy. The violence of it still shocks me. That you could do something like that. But I don't believe you're a person who would ever want to hurt someone else. I don't believe that. I know you, Sam, and that's not you. You're not a person who would ever want to hurt another person. I've never believed that about you, and I'm never going to."

Sam watches his mother's eyes peel open in the dimly glowing darkness. From two feet away, he can see the whites of her eyes shining like lights across a river at night.

"So you can talk to me or not talk to me. It's been a long time, and I guess I doubt you're going to start now. You can let me in or you can keep sitting there in silence, hour after hour. But one way or another, Sam, you're going to need me. Because I'm here. I've always been here. It's the one thing I'm probably any good at, just being here for you and loving you a whole lot. I'm good at it. I'll be here for you, and I'll love you, Sam, whether you decide to talk to me or not."

172

RUTH

IT'S MIDDAY when they drive up to the house. The sun floats high and bright over the trees. Door to door, between car and plane, the overnight journey from California has taken fourteen hours.

She gets out of the car, and then Sam does. Wordlessly he lifts his duffel and her carry-on from the trunk and walks to the front porch. She follows, her head gauzed with exhaustion yet still somehow perceiving the lawn's emerald-green depth, from recent rain or heavy dewfall, and the scattering of rabbit pellets by the three wooden stairs, and the deer trace of rubbed-off bark on the taller of the two oaks separating her property from the Newmans' next door. A clinging scent in the air of sunbaked compost. The newspaper in its clear Baggie sleeve lying in the gravel driveway. The kind of noticing you do if it isn't really your house. As maybe it isn't anymore. Now that her son has proved in every way that matters that he's no longer a child—*legally,* she remembers Dean Burris saying; and *legally?,* she remembers herself asking—maybe the house is trying to tell her something. Like *Get out.*

Or maybe she just needs some sleep.

Inside, the pile of mail has climbed past the door sweep. Health care, mostly, and junky catalogs. Living alone, one becomes an expert on the uninvited documents that assault the home, the fusillade of news, tidings, offerings, demands—the grim, the costly, the cheap, the salutary, the redundant, the offensive, the cold-blooded, the hysterical, the superficial. The superficial are best, in her opinion, because you can read them in the checkout line at the supermarket or on the toilet and feel just fine about yourself.

Sam has stepped over the mail and started up the stairs, a bag in each hand. A man in her house again, she recognizes; or an almost-man. She thinks of Norris and internally shakes her head. Bending down over the unlit bonfire at her feet, she begins gathering up the envelopes, magazines, flyers. Thinking, *So many trees.* Seeing, in a flash of autumnal self-consciousness, this unvarnished, refracted image of herself: middle-aged, twice-divorced, sick and alone, picking crap off the floor. Exposed before her son. A truth that causes her to rise too quickly, surfacing like a flailing diver sure to get the bends, one knee audibly cracking, until the fraught contents of her head feel sucked down into a woozy vacuum and she has to reach a hand out to the nearest wall to steady herself.

"Mom?"

She wills herself back into focus: Sam, halfway up the stairs, staring at her.

"You okay?"

"Just a little tired."

About as many words as they've exchanged in the past six hours. Still, for a moment that beautiful worried face of his, unwittingly expressing love, appears childlike again.

He turns and continues up the stairs. She stands listening to the creaking of his footsteps along the hall and into her room, the light thump as he sets down her bag. Then his gangplank passage to his own room, and the closing of the door.

And that's the last she sees of him through the afternoon and well into the next day. He doesn't emerge in the morning to eat breakfast. Doesn't, as far as she can tell, make a trip to the bathroom. She supposes he's still on West Coast time, but then she's forced to remind herself that these are the same hours he's always kept at home.

She has no idea what he does in his room hour after hour. An active young man, a gifted athlete, firmly enclosed now in a twelve-by-fourteen box, with a student's desk and chair, a twin bed, an outdated stereo, a shelf full of baseball trophies, and Red Sox posters and memorabilia from the dark eternal days before the miracle championship. A sweet little cell, if not quite innocent. What alarms her above anything else is the quickness of this move toward self-imprisonment. As if he knows something she does not, sees a future for himself that she is too cowardly or deluded to face.

These thoughts come to her mostly in the car as she rides to the supermarket, while roaming the wide air-conditioned aisles with the other country moms, in her kitchen as she goes from cupboard to refrigerator to pantry disgorging and shelving the contents of her brown paper bags. Everything for two now. Too bad, isn't it, how the things that one has so long prayed for never do happen the way one wants them to, and never without a price.

EMMA

JUST THREE DAYS INTO IT, and a routine has already been established. The woodpecker rapping of her mother's knuckles on her door wake her at seven sharp. She experiences again the cloudy out-of-bodyness of being reborn in her old room, a cautionary figure pulled together not out of cells but of memory fragments beyond her ken.

She gets up slowly. Her mother has gone downstairs to the kitchen. The jeans she pulls on show dirt stains from yesterday's work.

They fix their own bowls of cereal and mugs of coffee. As if—some new reality show—they have no recollection of each other's habits, no proof, are simply in residence like tourists at a hostel.

The first morning her mother made French toast. But when the food went untouched the treaty was tacitly rewritten on the spot: *Okay, so it will be like this. Easier for everybody.* A commonwealth of two—independent but related.

Now while Emma reads *The Huffington Post* on her laptop, standing at the counter, her mother skims one of the local papers at the table. Now like rival figure skaters they perform an elaborate pas de deux in front of the refrigerator and make diplomatic way for each other at the compost bin. Now they both listen in their own free space to the sound of birdsong infiltrating the kitchen from the yard outside, and this, at least, is not a point of contention.

Through the window Emma can see chickadees and a cardinal arranged on the truncated perches of the clear plastic feeder, happily pecking away. The seed compartment full. And she remembers a couple of years when her mother let the feeders go empty and all the birds left. And she remembers those same years when her mother stopped weeding the garden or pruning the hedges or having the lawn mowed, and the neighbors shook their heads and said *How sad* and looked the other way. People habitually remark that they understand how such things happen, but the fact is that no one does. And then Emma went off to college—not so far away, according to Google, just sixty-one miles and still in the state of Connecticut—and stopped coming home, and sometime in there her father left, too, and her mother woke up from a ten-year coma with her eviscerated heart rebuilt out of stone.

The neighbors have come back; that's what her mother claims, anyway.

The house is in decent order now. Of course, it's slowly falling apart like everything else, but in an orderly way.

Her mother is strong now—stronger than all those people who were never destroyed.

That emotionally paralyzed woman who used to add, with humiliating frequency, *Be careful!* and *Drive safely!* to every second utterance, what of her? Sorry, friend, no more. A superhero has moved into the house and replaced her. Wears an exoskeleton, where before all was vulnerable flesh. Lives aboveground instead of under. Moves only and ever forward.

Witness, for example, the following email, received in March:

Emma,
After much thought, I am writing to tell you that I will need you to come home this summer and help me with my business. As you know, it's the most important season of the year, and I'm already shorthanded and can't afford to give up any jobs or hire

more labor, even on a part-time basis. I need someone I can trust to help me.

Making this demand on you is a last resort. I'm aware that you had other plans, and that you would prefer not to spend a weekend with me, let alone a summer. But I have no choice. Over the last few years your father has made a series of catastrophic decisions that have cost him a significant and respected academic career and any kind of responsible stability in life. There are reasons, and we've been over this and I know that your sympathy for both of us is mostly used up. But you must understand how his actions have impoverished us all. The fact is that for us to continue sending you to Yale, even with your scholarship and work study, it falls to me to make the hard decisions that are more than just emotional reactions to what life has done to us as a family.

You will fight me on this, I can already hear you. But it's time to stop pointing fingers, Emma. The situation is what it is and I need your help, and, whatever you say, I believe it will do you good to give it. We can't sit around waiting for your father to recover, because that may not happen.

As soon as you can, please email me the date of your last exam in May, so I'll know when to expect you. I'll get your room ready and promise to give you as much space as possible. Try to see that I love you as much now as ever.

Mom

So this is the battleground, now that she has indeed come home to help. Emma feels like a fool for not having seen it taking shape. That her mother's unsentimental exit from griefhood should leave behind such tender bitterness in herself. That a stone heart can seem so hatefully selfish, just by being stone. That the old, crippling family wound has been so long in existence that it's warped her, too, become a kind of addiction, a scavenged oil drum at which, whenever she needs an enemy, she might warm her frozen hands over the flame of her mother's anguish.

By a quarter to eight they're in the car—her mother's Volvo, a newer version of the wagon she drove home from college—heading to the first job. Emma cracks the window, letting the morning's spring coolness into the car, testing its firmness and clarity, despite the unsparing light that's like looking through a pane of frosted glass. A hard breath taken into the lungs: washing out the unsaid things that seem to clot any room, even this moving one, in which they find themselves together.

"Polly Jamison can be difficult," her mother remarks.

Emma studies her, there behind the wheel. An attractive woman—this she can appreciate on the surface. Hair still blond, bones still elegant. A gardener's roughened hands, with a narrow circumference of paler, faintly indented flesh on the left ring finger, where for twenty-one years her wedding band used to be. Wearing today a slate-colored fleece top, fitted dark twill pants, and green rubber gardener's clogs. She could be forty or even less, except for those hands and the burls of pain lines at the corners of her eyes.

"Unfortunately, I'm going to have to leave you there and get over to the Foleys'," her mother says. "Their son's getting married behind their house in two weeks and they're beside themselves."

Emma looks out her window: they are entering Bow Mills.

"I'm not qualified to work on my own. Nobody hired me."

"You'll do fine. The work isn't complicated. Hector and his crew will be laying the bluestone. Just keep an eye on them, mulch around the trees, do the regular upkeep on the flower beds. Nothing fancy. The snowdrops and the Glenn

Dale azaleas need special attention. If Mrs. Jamison starts complaining about the Carpinus, just tell her to give me a call on my cell."

"Carpinus?"

"The hornbeams. She wants to have them severely cut back so they look what she calls French. But it's not French, it's just ugly, and I won't do it."

Emma watches the small green road signs go by. The names entering her without meaning, though they are not unfamiliar: Larch Road. The Wheldons live there, she remembers, or used to, she doesn't know anymore. . . . And now the memory comes back, sitting in the backseat of the old car with her dog Sallie as her father drives her to Mrs. Wheldon's house for a piano lesson. A fall morning, because of the colors. In the months after Josh. She is small again, and young, and the notes she misplays that day at Mrs. Wheldon's come back, too. And Mrs. Wheldon herself, touching her shoulder with perhaps extra care. And Sam . . . Now Emma is older, they all are; it happens so quickly and so slowly. Sallie, too, is dead. It's that night in Falls Village with Sam again, and she is with him again, he's inside her and they never have to say a word, not to each other. . . . And now she sees plainly how easy it is to despise oneself, how the mind moves without regret or conscience, its own animal, from death and loss to the color of leaves to the sound of broken music to the feel of a boy's skin, as if all of it were equal.

She opens her window more, and the air rushes across her face.

Her father was brave that day. Brave for taking her to a piano lesson when there was no reason anymore to do anything.

His bravery, and the waste of it, makes her feel like crying.

"Here we are," says her mother.

They turn into a driveway leading to a newly built Colonial. The tar dark and fresh. Parked in front of the house are a Lexus and a pickup truck loaded with roughly cut pavers of bluestone.

The house is white like their house in Wyndham Falls, with the same split-rail fencing. But this house has nothing wrong with it. It just sits there, immaculate and scarless. The compact front yard populated with knee-high figurines of deer, raccoons, and woodchucks made out of wrought iron.

"Mom, I don't feel well. I need to go back."

"It's a job, Em," says her mother quietly. "Just a job."

Silence. And she gets out of the car. She closes the door and her mother drives away.

SAM

HIS THIRD DAY BACK.

By agreement, they leave after breakfast. He doesn't own a car so they take hers, which will leave him sitting in the passenger seat for an hour and a quarter tugging at his shirt collar, nothing to do but listen to NPR (her choice), first the news and then the classical music.

She's the chief today, in case there was any doubt. He shaved because she asked him to. Wore the shirt she wanted. Would've eaten the eggs she cooked if he could have done so without throwing up. His sincerity lies most of all in wishing not to make things worse than they already are.

They drive out of Bow Mills to Route 44. The morning overcast, the sky the color of fresh-dried cement. Light so sharp there's no comfortable place to look but at solid things, all of which are moving.

Routes 44, 8, and 7 are the roads over which his life has flowed. Pastoral views occasionally, but just as often not. Most of the farms rough and mechanical when looked at up close, mud-caked, gone to rust, built on the wrong side of the economy. Houses with vinyl siding instead of real wood.

Pointing down a lane running toward a marsh where long ago he caught frogs with a boy named

Eddie Tibbet, his mother says, "Your stepfather is seeing a woman named Wanda Shoemaker. I think he's going to marry her. Her house is about half a mile up that way."

They've passed the lane, continued east. Ahead, a mail truck is pulled to the side of the road, no one anywhere near it, as if the postman just decided to hell with it and left.

"Norris would like to see you," his mother says. "He wanted me specifically to tell you that."

Sam opens the glove box, closes it.

"He has his foibles like anybody else. But he really cares about you, you know."

Foibles. Could be funny, attached to somebody else's life. He looks out his window. The side of 44 shunting past, a pulled string of already paid visits ticking by. He is still young, he knows this empirically, but it feels as if there isn't enough room inside him to hold all these lost things.

It comes rising in him then, nothing he can do to silence it: "I'm sorry you're alone, Mom."

He means this more than he can express, would stake his life on it. But she just turns her head and stares at him as if he's being sarcastic or cruel. Which, in turn, feels cruel to him.

The car begins to drift onto the shoulder. Her gaze snaps back toward the road. On track again but still agitated, she reaches an arm into the backseat, fumbles in her purse, slips a pair of big designer sunglasses over her eyes that have begun

185

to turn watery. "Let's worry about you," she says briskly.

She thumbs the volume on the radio higher, ending the exchange. He might as well have stabbed her.

And 44 is not 44 anymore; it has opened up, turned semi-industrial. The farms gone, the big estates and little shotgun houses. All that looking and he wasn't paying attention. He misses what he didn't know he loved. There are signs for Hartford now, where they will cross the river and merge onto 84. There are signs for UConn.

"Mom, I'm sorry."

He means for all of it this time. Himself. The whole fucking package. She won't look at him again, but her hand comes out and pats his knee.

They ride like that, his love and worry pushing against the back of his throat, a swallowed shout, across the wide blue-metal river and closer, listening to the music.

The notes are familiar: piano, violin, viola, cello. Like the polished green stone egg he used to keep in a lockbox under his bed: he can't see an egg now, or for that matter a bird, without thinking about it, though it was never anything but stone.

The name of the piece—"The Trout"—comes to him in a flash, a memory more of muscle than mind. Until he grew old enough to campaign successfully for something more fun, she used to play it on the stereo in his room every single night as he was fading off to sleep.

Her fingers begin to tap out the rhythm on his knee.

"Remember this?"

He remembers. Schubert was his age when he composed it, though it would not be published until after his death.

RUTH

COLLEGE IS OVER for the year. All month long, commencement ceremonies for the various schools, self-congratulatory speeches given and prizes bestowed, caps tossed into the air. She performed the rite herself once, here in Storrs, back somewhere in the sixteenth century. She can still vaguely recall the days after the big hurrah, end upon beginning, the stupor of it, a public hangover.

Youth's calendar: the arrogant assumption that there will always be time to recover.

It was around that time, she can't forget, that she first moved in with Dwight.

The admissions-building parking lot is two-thirds empty. She and Sam walk across the lined hardtop to the building's entrance, the clouded sun casting a white haze so harsh that nothing seems to hold any defined shape for more than a second or two. The UConn campus—seemingly twice the size and ten times as modern as when she was a student—strikes her as eerily hushed, postmortem.

Dean Burris said that he could see them in his office at eleven-thirty. It is twenty past now, and they walk squinting in the light and through the glass doors that read GORDON W. TASKER ADMISSIONS BUILDING, up the stairs to the second floor. She gives their names to a middle-aged woman with a matronly perm and a dignified air, whose desk has been transformed into an altar of family photographs. The woman has many children and grandchildren, Ruth observes, and they form a family like any other, except that, framed and arranged in this manner, this grandmotherly presence watching over them day after day, they appear safer and more benevolent than most.

"He'll be with you in a couple of minutes," the woman says.

"Thank you."

They sit on a sofa to wait. The grandmother behind the desk returns to her keyboard. Every so often Ruth hears a resonant *ping* as a new email arrives, or a *whoosh* as another message is fired out into the academic ether.

Sam lifts a copy of *Campus* magazine off the glass-topped table. She watches him peripherally, sensing his nerves raised like goose bumps on the surface of his skin; or maybe they're hers. He

188

spends a minute noisily turning pages, then drops the magazine on the table as if he's just realized that he does not, in fact, know how to read.

His folded athlete's legs reach almost to the edge of the glass coffee table. An animal designed to run, here held captive. Even walking across the parking lot, he seemed on the verge of sprinting, each long, fluid stride finished high on the ball of the foot, as if about to take off at full speed in any direction but the one in which she was leading him. As if the possibility of running away is never far from his thoughts.

Is this some recent behavioral change, forged in unhappiness, anger, guilt? she wonders. Or maybe it's always been there and she's just missed it, along with so much else.

Once again the inadequacy of her knowledge of him looms before her, a crash-test dummy of maternal defeat. Of course, there have been victories, too, along the way, but in the parenting game victories and defeats never do feel or mean the same thing. They are not equal in terms of consequence. This is something that Dwight has never owned up to: he's a man who has mistaken defeat for victory too many times to count. Which only makes Sam's decision to seek him out in California that much harder for her to accept. Why? Looking for what? Safety? Absolution? A big brother in disgrace? Did he find any or all of it? She will be the last to know. The only certain thing is that, sure as she's his mother, his not coming to her first is a judgment on her as a mother. She can feel the weight of his verdict without yet knowing the sentence imposed, the cost. Though that knowledge is inevitable, she has no doubt.

"Dean Burris will see you now."

Ruth looks up. The woman, dignified grandmother that she is, standing there, smiling down at them, a much older version of those pretty little girls in the photographs on her desk. And anyone can see that the sentiment behind her smile is not false. That it is sincere. It must be genetic, then, a smile like this, a sense of family like this, some lovely tree whose curled roots reach deep down into time past, all the generations pulling for one another, and whose strong, healthy branches grow out into the time to come, the time not yet known, ready to bear fruit.

Or else it's just a smile.

In any event, Ruth can see in the woman's face—interesting, isn't it, how this once and future smile manages to hold so many questions—that Sam is both a prize and a consternation to her: what can this nice-looking young man have done wrong?

Ruth gets to her feet. She makes sure that her purse strap is on her shoulder, and then she gives her son the look that says *It's time to stand up.* And he stands up. No, she hasn't completely lost

SAM

LEAVES HIS MOTHER in the main lobby
...stairs. He insists; she has followed him
...gh. There is a brief argument and then,
...lly midsentence, she surrenders. Simply
...talking and stares down at the floor, her
...s fluttering open of their own volition, as if
...just released her final hold on the hope she
...had for him.

...the steerage elevator, pressed aside by a
...-clad resident with an unoccupied gurney,
...egins to lose solidity. His body, all he's ever
...going for him really, feels hollowed out from
...inside; his legs are tubes. The urge to turn
...is suddenly acute, but he can only keep
...g. His floor dings, and for a long moment he
...ds disoriented before the multiple directional
...s, the wide fluorescent corridors. A
...sroads. Then to his right the double doors
...the small viewing windows open
...matically outward, and two residents in blue
...r gowns and hair and shoe covers walk out
...ly, one of them saying to the other, "What
...hell's keeping those labs?" in a tone of
...usted complaint, the other replying, "Are
...scrubbing for the three o'clock?" They turn
...n the central corridor, their footsteps
...gely inaudible. In their wake the doors to the

194

control. He unfolds his legs and becomes taller
than her again, more powerful, despite his
frightened, flicking eyes.

We're all scared, she wants to tell him. *Every
single one of us, all the time. That's what makes
us family.*

SAM

LATER, HIS IMPRESSIONS of the dean and their
seventeen-minute meeting will be obscured,
made hazy, by what follows. The dean in his well-
appointed office with the leather chairs, the
Native American art, and the high-end relaxer toy
with the row of five silver balls hanging by
fishing line from an ebony wood frame.

Later, after the visit to the hospital, what he will
retain most concretely from his meeting with
Chas Burris, Dean of Students, is a piece of fine
stationery, cream-colored with a visible weave
and the navy-blue UConn letterhead above the
dean's name in fourteen-point lettering, on which
the dean himself has written in blue-black
fountain-pen ink the names *Nic Bellic, Mirko &
Sonja Bellic,* the family's address and phone
number in Colchester, Connecticut, as well as the
words *Hartford Hospital ICU;* and beneath that,
demarcated by a significantly drawn line, the
names *Jack Cutter* and *Cutter & Associates* of
Canaan, Connecticut, and another phone number.

191

And only later, after the hospital, sequestered once again in the privacy of his childhood room, in his mother's house in Bow Mills, will Sam come to fully appreciate, if that's the word, the artful summing up of his late adolescence and early adulthood that the dean's information sheet has so efficiently achieved.

Leaving the dean's office with his mother, he is careful to hold the paper at the edges. It is his diploma, after all, the only one he's ever likely to receive, and it feels crucially important to him not to stain it with his sweaty fingerprints.

DWIGHT

THE REST OF THE WEEK PASSES. I can give no decent accounting of the experience except to say that my son isn't in it. He is gone from my house and from my place of work, from the passenger seat of my car, from the manicured softball diamond on which we as mutants frolic and fail, from the little spit of backyard sod where I grill my steaks. As if he was a dream—nothing Hallmark, no Iron John epiphanies of male bonding, no movie fireworks, tears, or hugs, just a rogue sort of dream that overtook me for a couple of weeks and then evaporated on waking. The status quo resumed. He is gone, and it's as if each day holds less of him, Wednesday a thimble, Thursday a drop, till by Friday there is no trace left.

And, as I walk my aisles and chart my n and stack my Italian-made bocce sets and my name tag and consider my prostate love life that I no longer seem to ha questions keep returning, the great un above all others, a multipronged koan d I'm coming to suspect, less to enlighten torture: How could I have let him leave telling him anything that mattered? looking out for him more and caring better? Without paying more scrupulous to what now threatens him? Without ins going with him and holding on?

Have I learned nothing?

Of course, there was a time in my l merely not perpetrating direct harm another individual—let alone my another's—might have seemed a kind of for me. But if I ever truly believed such do not believe it anymore. You cannot r years of age and still think that nothing than something, unless you are a fool a an asshole. Despite what the mathe assure us, zero is not a meaningful numl life.

ICU linger open, a mouth waiting to devour him. Slipping in, Sam sees a bustling nurses' station at the center of a large open unit, an orderly chaos of half-curtained beds and portable machines. And he can hear, above the sourceless pings and whispers and a violently discordant note of laughter, the bellows-like breathing of a ventilator.

Of the four paper-gowned medical professionals behind the nurses' station—who are supposed to interrogate him, he knows, and if he is not related to the patient demand that he leave the premises—two are perusing medical records on computer terminals, another is organizing a rolling cart of urine jugs, and the last is on the phone asking for one order of red-dal curry and two of tikka masala.

Ignored by them, he floats past. A phantom. He finds Nic Bellic's chart posted two-thirds of the way down the right-side corridor. There is no one in the vicinity. The curtain making an island of the sickbed is partially pulled back, as if someone has recently passed through.

A body lies on the bed. He barely recognizes the face that he only ever saw once. The intimacy is too stark: a thick clear tube runs out of the young man's gaping mouth. The lips are essentially blue. A thin, wormlike feeding tube runs through one of the dilated nostrils. An IV is threaded into an engorged vein on the back of his right hand, half an inch of blood backing up the dripping saline. Nic Bellic is unconscious or asleep, so heavily sedated that the silent waves of heartbeat on the monitor appear to be breaking in slow motion over an invisible beach in a country that does not exist. Some kind of primitive, sick video game is what it looks like. Maybe he is good-looking, or maybe he is more than that, actually good; with his eyes closed it is impossible to tell.

"You family?"

The large black woman in the white nurse's uniform, voice from the Islands, brushes past him and twists a plastic ring on the IV. Only when he hesitates in answering does she turn and look him full in the face.

Like being picked out of a lineup. *Him. That one there. It was him.*

"No."

"Can't stay, then. Not with no gown on you, neither."

"Can you tell me, is he going to be okay?"

She reaches bluntly past him and pulls the curtain wider: an invitation for him to leave now while things are still peaceful.

"Okay? Hmm. Sepsis not okay—no, mister. But the doctors, they be doing what they can."

EMMA

SHE IS STILL BAGGING the leavings of the day's work—the beggar's harvest of snapped twigs, hacked branches, soil-clumped weeds that she's pruned, raked, plucked since morning—when she sees the car pull into the driveway and her mother get out. Mrs. Jamison appears at once, grabbing Grace Learner's elbow and leading her to the bluestone path that Hector and his crew laid earlier in the day.

"The edges are too high," the woman complains. "There, you see what I'm talking about? Someone could trip and break an ankle."

Someone like her, she means.

"Don't worry. We'll build up around them tomorrow."

"I *am* worried, Grace. I'm not happy."

"It will be dealt with, Polly. All right? Hector will be back first thing in the morning, and we will deal with it."

A voice that Emma can't remember hearing from her mother in years, if at all: a bulwark voice, not unfriendly but hard as bluestone, that declares, politely, *Don't fuck with me if you know what's good for you.*

In any event, effective. With an indignant sniff, Mrs. Jamison retreats to her unblemished house and is not seen again that afternoon.

Lawn sack filled, Emma hauls it and a second one across the grass and heaves them into the leaf-strewn back of the Volvo. They'll take it all back to Pine Creek Road and add it to her mother's compost pile, which by summer's end will be a mountain of rot. (Mrs. Jamison has made it perfectly clear that she does not believe in compost.)

They start for home.

A few minutes into the journey, her mother says, "I'd fire her tomorrow if we didn't need the money. Did she harass you?"

"Not actively."

It's sort of funny, and her mother sort of smiles.

They return to staring out their respective windows. The white, depthless sky has darkened and softened since morning; now it looks like rain.

They pass a deer crossing sign. Then a hump of bloody flattened roadkill—a raccoon. They pass a woman and two girls with a Border collie on a leash walking by the side of the road.

She is suddenly, terribly thirsty. She pulls a metal water bottle from her backpack and drinks close to half a liter. Her jeans are filthy, bits of mulch litter her hair. Her fingers ache. New calluses swell her palms.

"Did you get any lunch?" her mother asks.

"Hector had an extra sandwich. Some kind of weird vegetable paste with sprouts."

"I forgot to tell you he's a vegan. Kind of surprising for a man who can lift a hundred and fifty pounds of stone with his bare hands, don't you think?"

Hector Martinez is short but weighs two hundred plus, a sweet bulldog of a man. His boots are made of rubber and something like hemp. Where he gets his protein is a mystery. His crew consists of his two nephews, Luis and Adrian, seventeen and nineteen, stringbean carnivores who struggled throughout the day to lift the smallest slabs of rock. When not bent over their labors, the two boys stared at her ass as if it was a French rose blooming in a desert cave. This went on for hours, lending the day a certain amusing shape.

"I want you to know that I appreciate how hard you're working," her mother adds after a while.

"You're welcome."

She means it, but her mother just sighs. Formality is a cold distance for them both, Emma sees, as well as a necessary protection.

She opens her eyes: a gas station, the Volvo parked alongside two pumps.

She must have drifted off. Her mother is pulling her wallet from her purse, getting out of the car.

Emma is so tired she feels drugged. Time seems viscous, the world ticking aloud—a clock knocked off its rhythm.

In the large window of the low-slung building to her right, she can see a poster with brightly dancing dollar signs advertising the state lottery; another for Klondike ice-cream bars; a third for Boost energy drink. And so is she able to recognize the Christie's Food Mart that years ago replaced Krause's General Store at the outskirts of Wyndham Falls.

She watches her mother slide her debit card into the pump, pull it out again. Close to three dollars a gallon for regular. She watches her mother begin to pump the gas and turn to stare off at the trees and bramble across the road, thinking God knows what.

Emma remembers the old-style pumps from when she was little, the ones you can never find anymore, like mechanical men with unfortunate shoulders, and that delicate echoing bell ringing off the golden, eye-watering gallons as they flowed into her parents' car.

At the very moment that Josh was being run over and killed by the side of Reservation Road, she was propped on the stinking toilet inside Tod's Gas & Auto Body, panties round her knees, her mother helping her to pee.

For years afterward, her mother would plead with her father every time they had to fill up the car: *You do it. I can't. I'm sorry, I just can't.*

She watches this same woman, her mother, pumping gas and staring across the road. Till there comes, vibrating along the length of the car, the violent upward snap of the nozzle trigger shutting off the fuel supply. Full, finally. A faint electronic prompt inquires whether a receipt is desired. It is. And her mother gets back into the car.

What can you say? And to what possible end? When something so long wounded in a human being becomes, through time and the gradual unremembering of love, healed.

Except that it isn't.

The getting out of bed, the getting dressed, the brushing of hair, the washing of dishes, the feeding of birds, the pumping of gas.

"What is it?"

"Nothing."

Her mother starts the car. "Long day."

As they're pulling out of the station, another car is just pulling in: a dark-green Subaru wagon. The two vehicles move slowly past each other in opposite directions.

Unawares, Emma catches a glimpse inside: dreamlike, the unfolding pictorial vision as clear as a series of magnified stills.

It's Mrs. Wheldon driving, she would swear.

And Sam Arno riding beside her.

DWIGHT

IN MY LIVING ROOM this balmy Friday evening, with beer and organic blue-corn tortilla chips, I watch ESPN as if it carries nothing less than the word of the Lord. I try Sam's cellphone again. I pop an Ambien. And still the wakeful night hangs on like an unwanted guest who, though abused by his belligerent host, stubbornly refuses to leave the premises. I already have Saturday's TV sports schedule memorized, golf and baseball, late-round basketball playoffs, track and field (I've been known to watch darts and curling when pressed); and right in my head, as I finally pass out in darkness and wake again in daylight, programmed to the hour, floats my immediate future.

But Saturday morning, before all the screened entertainment kicks in, is undeniably desolate. I roll my hand-push mower (bought on eBay for a song) a few turns over my backyard goatee. I spray Roundup over the weeds growing around my cement patio. My kitchen I scrub as if I'm a reincarnated fifties housewife from Des Moines. I make my bed the way the government taught me.

There's nothing like new wrinkles in the game plan to make the crushing monotony of one's existence too obvious to bear. Sam's absence this morning feels hellish; like all negative ghosts, it casts a savage light over my solitary routine and, more generally, over the blind mole-rat behavior of my life.

You go to sleep and wake with a start time in your head—a sporting event on television, say, no more and no less. When that hour comes there will be, oh yes, paid announcers to tell you what's going on and what to think, how fast the pitch or how rough the lie. The statistical odds of success or failure. The weekend morning, meanwhile, stands between you and then. A pass-through zone, spray-coated and nonstick, designed to see you across the suburban tundra to the next nursing station, where if you're lucky some noble, slobbering Saint Bernard might give you a neck barrel of brandy and revive the life that you never really wanted in the first place.

Years can go by like this, and have.

By late afternoon, the final pairing of the PGA tournament in Walla Walla stands on the seventeenth tee. The number of Buick ads I've visually consumed—with Tiger Woods driving a car he'd otherwise never be caught dead in—has reached double figures, outpacing, even, the number of beers I've drunk. I am deep in the heart of America's living room, a place far more seductive than my own home. With their polite hushed voices, the announcers in their crisp network blazers are like priests murmuring words of absolution through the obscuring scrim of my very own confessional. Forgiveness is on the way, coo these pigeon voices, just for sitting through and buying it all, for being the good rehabilitated boy who refrains from pointing out the dead elephant in the room.

Well, it's nice to think so, isn't it? Even if you know that thinking it will be the end of you. And so the human circle comes round, or seems to. And you turn your terror's attention for a minute—because, being for some reason still alive, you can't not—out your open window to the high, unchecked voices of the neighborhood kids playing Transformers on Hacienda Street.

It takes me a fair while to realize that the grown man I hear blubbering into his hands is myself.

RUTH

SHE MAKES HER MOTHER'S MEAT LOAF, mashed potatoes, and thin coaster-size disks of grilled eggplant with extra-virgin olive oil, and they sit down to Sunday supper as if it's old family times. The only missing ingredients are: (a) conversation, (b) appetites, (c) a bottle of good red wine, and (d) old family times. Add to that any sort of legitimate male authority figure—

a species she last set eyes on in the Museum of Natural History in New York City, sometime around the first Gulf War.

"More meat loaf?" she asks her son.

"No, thanks."

"It's not very good. I forgot the salt."

"I'm just not that hungry."

A few seconds, then the scrape of his chair against the floor.

"Don't get up." Her unseemly plea at once too loud and too late.

Already standing, he looks down at her from his full height, which makes her feel like a dog begging for scraps. Her face grows warm. With no other options, she decides to double down.

"Please?"

He sighs, scratching the back of his head with a rough hand, and finally lowers himself back onto the chair.

"May I ask you a question, Sam?"

When in a position of doubt or anxiety, Ruth Margaret, she suddenly remembers her ninth-grade English teacher admonishing her after an especially awkward class presentation, *it behooves you to speak politely and firmly, as though from a podium of formidable rectitude and calm wisdom.*

Sam offers up the least generous of ironic smiles. "Do I have a choice?"

"Why did you go to your father, of all people?

Why didn't you come to me? That's one of the things I'm trying to understand."

She sees the question, the basic concept, take him by surprise. She does not understand how this can be, after all the time he's had to reflect. Yet he's clearly caught off guard, his eyes glued to his hands—his default safety mode as long as he's been sentient.

She waits. But his surprised, hiding silence is like a magic trick he's performed right in front of her: she saw him enter the curtained box, but she won't see him leave.

"All right," she murmurs in defeat.

Her heart aches. This is not just a phrase. She picks up his plate, still filled with the bland food she cooked, and stacks it on top of her own and gets to her feet. Her bones are sixty, eighty years old. She is almost to the kitchen when his voice stops her:

"I felt like him."

She turns around slowly. His eyes are on hers now, and they look too old and scared to be who she still believes he is.

PENNY

SHE STANDS AT THE KITCHEN COUNTER, early on a Sunday morning, her daughter still catacombed in sleep in the back of the house. Not in the poetic mood, no, or anything like that. Last night, somewhere around the witching hour, she understood that she wasn't going to get much rest, and so it came to pass.

She pours herself another cup of coffee—then, thinking twice, dumps it back into the pot and pours herself a glass of fresh carrot juice instead. The juice, which she didn't really want, remains undrunk.

Through the window above the sink she observes her street. Small, artificial houses like punctuation marks without words, framing nothing. There was that time, back in the sixties, when one of her poet heroes—the beautiful, angry one with the shepherd's clothing and the godlike gaze, according to the old dust-jacket photos—simply stopped using punctuation at all. The words, he said, should be clear by themselves; commas and periods and capitalizations were distortions, cotton wool over the senses.

And, whether he was right or wrong, she would like to learn to live like that, without punctuation, hearing just the words themselves. But that is not how she seems to be living.

She puts her glass of juice on the counter.

Dwight's car has come to a stop in front of her house. The top is down. Sitting in the passenger seat beside him is a black carry-on suitcase. There is a pause, almost a hiatus, while Penny studies him through the window, during which he remains with his hands on the steering wheel, his gaze level, as if he's still driving, though the car is stopped.

He is still there when she opens the front door. Only then, and heavily, does he climb out and walk around to meet her on the grass.

He is, she thinks, perhaps not like other boyfriends or husbands, ex- or otherwise. He does not, for instance, say "Good morning," or "How are you?" or "I'm so sorry for taking you for granted."

He says, "I've got some hard things to tell you."

And what surprises her is not the dramatic, if prosaic, opening, but how expected it is, finally, after so many untold secrets. An intuition, she suddenly realizes, that has been darkening her vision and her heart for weeks, keeping her from any hope of rest.

"I'm listening."

"I served two and a half years in prison." He takes in air through his nose and folds his arms tight across his chest, forcing his body still. "I ran over a little boy. Ten years old, knew my son at school. It was an accident, but then I drove away. The boy's father witnessed it. He saw his son killed. He spent months trying to find me. And then, finally, he did."

Dwight falls silent. He takes in more air. The sentences have come in quick, inward stabs of pain. He's bleeding right in front of her.

"There's another thing. Sam was asleep in the car. He woke up, but then I floored it. I told him we'd hit a dog. I lied to him every step of the way. The morning I turned myself in was the last time I saw him till two weeks ago."

She stands staring at him. He has finally blown her away, her regular guy. Stunned nearly senseless by his confession, her dazed mind retreats; for a few strange moments, she becomes a satellite parked overhead, littering the clear blue sky, a Cyclops of sad, incredulous wonder at what human beings will do to each other.

Then she is grounded again. She finds Dwight back behind the wheel of his car. He has mistaken her silence for her final verdict, and he is already driving away.

DWIGHT

THE SUN IS GONE by the time my plane lands at Kennedy. I grab a *grande* Starbucks, pick up my rental, and head north. In an hour I'm on Route 8 in Connecticut, following the disappearing tunnel of roadside lights.

Restless as a teenager, I keep pushing the radio's seek button, landing finally on the Red Sox, that frequency hardwired into my gray matter at birth.

They're into the seventh-inning stretch at Fenway by the time I hit Torrington. And in the gap where the game's been going I find myself in an uncomfortable place, picking at some of the loose threads of my son's narrative, his and mine: Sam busing himself to Torrington and back five days a week during his high-school years, so desperate is he to claw his way out of the small-town swamp of shame and disgrace and gossip that I left him mired in, to write himself a new identity at fourteen, so that there might be something to live for that doesn't have the stain of his old man's name attached to it.

The irony being that during this same period the old man is just a hop, skip, and a jump away in Hartford, scraping by on janitorial jobs and weekly manos a manos with his probation officer.

Until, one unhistoric day, with nothing else to hold or lose, the old man lights out for California on a Greyhound bus to (as they say) seek his fortune.

It's past evening when I finally drive into Wyndham Falls. I've been traveling all day, and I'm hungry and thirsty for a hard drink and more than a little anxious about my intended plan of action.

I half circle the lightless oval green—not round, you understand, but oval, which is more historic (or so the residents explain it) and thus somehow more perfect—and then branch off toward Bow Mills. A lesser town, a hamlet. No one around tonight. Along the unlit roadsides the mailboxes are strange cranelike figures, totems, or maybe just boys waiting to be punished. They stand like sentries in the shadows, and I pass them one by one.

Twelve years since I've been back.

It all comes haunting, especially in the dark. The place called home is the one place you can drive into at night after a lifetime away, with no light to see by, and still know exactly where you are.

Down at the bottom of Larch Road, I slow the car almost to a stop. I've begun to sweat badly, and I power down my window to get some air. Somewhere nearby a dog is barking that old biblical warning—*intruder, intruder*—as Ruth's mailbox appears in the spread of my headlights. On its sidepiece three ducks are flying. They are mallards, and it was Norris's conceit to have them painted beneath his name.

I turn into the driveway, and the ducks disappear behind me. I switch off the engine, sit listening and watching. The dog has stopped barking.

Outwardly, the house hasn't changed. The front porch, like a stage between shows, has the same neighborly presence and intent as when I built it almost twenty years ago. Behind and above it the double-paned windows are dark now, all but two: the kitchen, and Sam's old room upstairs.

I get out of the car, closing the door softly.

I stand looking. Not trying to hide, but not trying to be seen yet, either. A coward's way of coming back to a place that's spit you out whole: you can make it through years of exile only to find in the end, with your feet again on the old bloody battlefield, that you'll always need a few minutes more to gather yourself. As if these last banal sights and sounds can somehow protect you against what you otherwise know.

Through the kitchen window I can see Ruth sitting at the table, a magazine open before her. Not reading but watching a small TV on the counter across the room. I can't make out the show, just the flickering of colored light. Every so often she raises a mug to her lips and takes a sip of something. Herbal tea, probably.

And upstairs, in Sam's old room, the shade is drawn. A white schoolhouse shade, pretty standard-issue, behind which, backlit like this, the smallest of human gestures might appear as the magnified Kabuki acts of a crazed giant. The kind of screen against which, when he was little and still in my care, on the rare occasion when I got home from work in time to put him to bed, I used to perform finger-puppet shows for his amusement, making him laugh out loud with every dumb rabbit shadow I could muster.

The extent of my limited parental know-how; the very best I could do at the time, I still try to believe.

No shadows tonight. He isn't asleep, clearly, but what else he is or isn't, I can't see.

There are invited guests, and there are the other kind. Most every place I've ever been in my life I've had to force or connive my way. This is true about people as well as places. It's true about Ruth, whom I had to court like some straight-up Jimmy Stewart before she would agree to move in with me. It's true about Penny, whose phone number came my way only in return for the considered use of my employee discount, and whose sense of full-disclosure honesty I have undermined from the beginning, I now understand, with the persistent withholding of my own. It's true about Somers, that rathole shitbox with its grated windows and acres of razor wire. It's true about my son, whose early blind trust in me—the kind of belief so without the taint of preconceived deliberation that it must be evolutionary, biological, if not something even higher and deeper—I repaid with breakage and betrayal, with abandonment, slamming the door of hope that his birth so miraculously opened.

It is human nature to want to get inside where it's warm. To want not to be left outside the shelter, in the cold. It can be a rock cave or a tree house or a person so much better than you that your view of him or her can only ever be from your knees. Which is still preferable to someplace locked away or underground. All you know for sure is that you will keep trying to reach the warmth as long as you have strength, whatever the cold darkness you know about yourself, your own lack of deserving. Because if you are not taken in, if exile is as guaranteed as death, then you are kicked out and alone.

Who will have you then? Who? The fire is no more. The fire that was love.

PART THREE

SAM

HE HEARS VOICES DOWNSTAIRS, a man's and a woman's, and comes stealthily out of his room, where for the past half hour he's been tossing a Jason Varitek–signed baseball again and again into his Mizuno glove, the repeated sound of the soft webbing enveloping him, soothing him, rounding unwanted edges, virtually making him disappear.

He stands in the hallway at the head of the stairs, not quite believing his ears.

"You couldn't at least have called?"

In response, an audible male sigh—ponderous, weary, possibly embarrassed.

Then his mother again: "I can't believe this. Where were you planning to sleep?"

A mumble.

"What? Oh, in that case be my guest. *Jesus!*"

But her sarcasm is subtly animated, Sam would swear—as if this unanticipated man-invasion, however much a pain in the ass and an insult to her intelligence, is already producing a galvanizing reaction, bringing strange purpose to this little outpost of waiting and despair.

"How long are you planning to stay? At least tell me that."

"Any chance a guy could get a beer?" The first clear words the man's spoken.

An odd snort from his mother. Which sound it takes Sam a moment to realize was actually laughter.

And so something has begun.

He light-steps it back to his room, quietly closes the door, and sits at the schoolboy desk where, on his laptop, ESPN.com's home page continues to offer the first ten lines of a story about Barry Bonds and steroids; a piece about a female decathlete with one leg; a sidebar on some lunatic Cape Cod fisherman who caught a hundred-and-forty-pound bluefin tuna from a plastic kayak: *"I thought the effing thing was gonna pull me all the way to effing Portugal!"*

With his finger on the trackpad, he navigates backward to the Wikipedia page he was looking at before he started obsessively throwing the ball into his glove:

SEPSIS is a serious <u>medical</u> condition that is characterized by a whole-body <u>inflammatory</u> state (called a <u>systemic inflammatory response syndrome</u>, or SIRS) and the presence of a known or suspected <u>infection</u>.[1][2] The body may develop this inflammatory response to microbes in the blood, urine, lungs, skin, or other tissues. . . . Approximately

20–35% of patients with severe sepsis and 40–60% of patients with septic shock die within 30 days.

He clicks the bloody dot in the upper left-hand corner and the webpage vanishes—just as he hears his father put his full weight on the bottom stair. The screen goes gray. His father is climbing, and with each step the whole house seems to shift under its foundation. And Sam's gray nothing screen, which holds a kind of existential terror for him, is abruptly filled with his chosen saver: a downloaded thirty-year-old photo of Freddie Lynn in midswing, arms fully extended, the baseball a white stuttering trace of itself, a stop-motion ghost, flying so fast off his bat on its way over the Green Monster that no camera will ever be quick enough to catch its true, singular shape.

DWIGHT

I STOP IN THE DOORWAY of his room as at some invisible electrified fence. He's sitting at his desk, half turned to the door, waiting and not waiting. The color photo on his laptop screen makes me look twice: Freddie Lynn hitting what appears to be a sure home run.

Freddie Lynn: Boston hero, superboy, grace of the gods—till he wasn't. An historical figure to my son, who of course never got to see him play in person.

"Hey."

Snapping his computer shut as if it's porn he's been looking at, he sits staring at the brushed-metal cover.

"Ever answer your cellphone?" I pause, studying him, not really expecting a response but willing him to look at me. "So . . . How're you holding up?"

Finally he turns. "How long are you staying?"

The question stings a little, and I attempt to deflect it with a painted-on grin. "You must be related to your mother."

"It's her house."

"And don't I know it." My tone is still jaunty, but my right hand has begun strangling the doorjamb; I make the fingers release. I think about going farther into his room, maybe sitting on the bed. Instead, I stay where I am and keep talking, the words coming out rambly and nervous.

"Tony sends his best. I told him, you know, that you had a situation come up all of a sudden back home. I didn't get into specifics or anything, but I think he understood. He got it. I'm taking my week of summer break a little early."

Understandably, Sam doesn't respond to any of this. So I just stand there, my monologue delivered and the air sucked out of me, everything quiet except for my own battering heart. His room is essentially unchanged from when he was ten; this is what I'm seeing. Which could be laziness in him, or fear, or maybe a curious form of bravery. His own little Cooperstown. The Sox forever and ever. On a shelf above his head his sports trophies are arrayed, at least half a dozen, their fool's-gold skins dulled with dust.

What does one do with it all after the fact? What's any of it still good for? His vibrant boy's spirit reduced to artifacts, to trinkets.

The problem is that once I start thinking this way it's hard to stop. To keep myself from perceiving every last thing through a darkening tunnel. To not see my son the way my faults and failures have taught me to see the world and myself, to tar him with that stinking brush. When all the kid's done is leave his room the same, which is no crime.

RUTH

SHE STANDS IN A STATE of suspended belief, watching him climb the stairs. Each lumbering step a small explosion that, being somehow personal, threatens to bring down the entire structure. Which collapse she would deserve, absolutely, for letting him stroll in here unannounced like this—into her house—to stage his big mock-heroic riding-into-town moment, as if he truly has anything to add to the pot. She knows this man: he's no General MacArthur, or even General Schwarzkopf. More like having that silly cartoon clown fish Nemo arrive to mooch off the wreck of the *Titanic.*

Before her on the front-hall rug, his black carry-on sits upright on its rubber wheels like an overtrained poodle. Enough clothes for three days, she estimates by size—unless, of course, she offers to do his laundry for him during his uninvited stay.

Over her dead body.

She observes herself give the suitcase a good, solid kick, and it falls over onto its side.

Next, she walks into the kitchen and bitterly hunts down a single bottle of beer in the fridge—the last survivor of the twelve-pack she bought for Sam's visit over Easter weekend—eventually finding it nestled with the broccoli in the humid vegetable drawer. She twists the top off with such animus that she tears her pinkie nail. And the lightly hissed *Fuck!* she hears then can only have come from her own mouth. No, it isn't her night. She puts the bottle to her lips and forces down a few ounces of sour brew, just to prove she can. That little belch was hers, too.

Then, calmer for some reason, she carries what remains of the beer upstairs.

The door to Sam's room is open, Dwight

loitering in the entrance. Apparently he's made limited headway in his caped-crusader parenting mission, and now hopes to beat a hasty retreat to the nearest sports bar.

She taps him on the back. "Here's your beer."

He turns eagerly, his face alight with canine gratitude—more for the interruption, she suspects, than for the drink—though she notices him squinting quizzically at the amount of liquid missing in the bottle.

"Thanks."

"It's the last one in the house. So I'd take it slow." She tilts her head around the roadblock of his body and peers at her son, slumped at his desk in front of his closed laptop. "Everything peaceful in here?"

"Why wouldn't it be?" Dwight grumbles.

"I can't imagine. Listen, I'll make up the sofa in the den for you. But after tonight you make your own bed."

"Wouldn't have it any other way."

At this she raises an eyebrow but keeps the tart fruit of her reply to herself. A matter of personal privacy. She walks down the hall to the linen closet.

EMMA

SHE HAS NO INTENTION of telling her mother about Sam Arno. An old habit; also simple common sense.

Sunday she works all day, returning home at six with her back so stiff from eight hours of weeding and brush-clearing in Lakeville that she doesn't think she'll be able to rise in the morning. Her mother's suggestion of two Motrin and a hot shower sounds reasonable enough, but crawling up to her room she decides she needs something stronger.

An inspired summer-vacation gift from her college roommate Sarah, the single Vicodin pill has been kept these past couple of weeks, wrapped in a pink Kleenex, in the zippered pocket of her makeup bag.

She washes it down with Diet Coke and waits.

By six-thirty, she can just about stand upright and pain-free. By seven, sitting down with her mother to a dinner of store-bought *pasta e fagioli* and sourdough bread, she's smiling intermittently and can't get herself to shut up. Words pour from her lips—*Carpinus*, for instance, rolls off her newly versed tongue as though she's Olmsted himself; as does a strange disquisition on poisonous tree frogs and a long monologue on the various ways that pioneer women dealt with their periods while out on the wagon trail, and half a dozen other informational obscurities that don't bear mentioning, the live product of one of the best (as the brochure trumpets) liberal-arts educations in the world. As much to say to her mother, *See what your money's buying?* Or, alternatively, *How cool is it that a conversation doesn't actually require the participation of both of us!* Which under the circumstances would have to pass as a full-fledged epiphany—and amazingly, in her own mind at least, does.

But in truth she's not in command of her thought flow to the extent of making any kind of grand point. She doesn't care. All she can really do, the only real control she possesses, is to continue hoarding her semiprecious secret that she saw Sam Arno with his mother pulling in for gas at the Christie's Food Mart outside town. That he's come back to the deathly nest, for whatever reason, just as she has, and now must be close by.

Her mother, meanwhile, unaware of any sighting—unaware of so much—nursing a single glass of white wine to Emma's half bottle, stares in amazement at this unprecedented display of conviviality by her daughter, such a rare show of, well, humanness.

The drug wears off around ten. The magic talking babe she's become is unceremoniously deposed by a pain-racked mute, whose head is a hollowed-out gourd. It's more than sad. Her mother—in her bedroom by now with the door closed, probably reading *The Year of Magical Thinking* for the third time—observes none of this. Which strikes Emma as the essence of mutual loneliness; unless somehow, like that famous unheard tree falling in the forest, it's a perverse kind of enlightenment.

She limps through the creaking house, turning out lights.

RUTH

FROM BEHIND THE CLOSED BATHROOM DOOR at the end of the hall, she can hear a gurgling faucet and some haphazard splashing. And the fact that her son's awake at six-thirty in the morning is so atypical it affects her like a tremor, some physical disruption of the house's natural geology.

Nonetheless, knotting the belt of her ratty bathrobe, she proceeds downstairs as though secure in the illusion that it's just another day.

Which pantomime is soon dispensed with. Because, approaching her kitchen, she begins to smell her own coffee being brewed (Green Mountain Breakfast Blend); and then, entering, catches sight of the burly visitor at her table, hunched over a plate of burned toast heaped with the French strawberry preserves that her pupil

Adam Markowitz's mother gave her after winter recital at school—that she's been saving, unopened, for some more auspicious occasion not yet arrived.

"Morning," says Dwight, chewing a mouthful.

She says it back, absorbing the scene. His hair is damp and he needs a shave. He looks—she doesn't want to be ungenerous here—vaguely as if he's spent the night in his car; but then so, probably, does she. And although she's trying her best to acclimate, his presence is too distorting, to the point where she can't even muster any real annoyance over the violated jar of preserves.

Wild strawberries, no less. Whatever.

She pours herself a mug of coffee, no sugar, and, blank as a mental patient on double meds, sits down across from him.

"Can I get you some toast? Eggs?" he asks politely.

She stares at him in a kind of wonderment. Is this Tommy's Diner and she's simply misread the signs?

"No, thank you."

"You should eat something."

She turns and looks out the window. Sees the Newmans' black Lab nosing along the bushes between the two houses. After mild urinary suspense, old Toby lifts his leg and does his business.

"How'd you sleep?" Dwight persists.

She observes that his eyes are clear, focused: he is a man she was once married to, and he seems to really want to know.

"Mixed."

Ten minutes later, he's at the counter pouring himself a third cup of coffee—a veritable caffeine sponge, she's had time to note, despite his supposed healthful California existence. Holding the full mug, he slouches back against the counter and fixes her with a gaze whose meaning only he can fathom, the slightly left-of-center vertical crease between his eyes deepening to a brain patient's crevasse; as though he's struggling to remember a single cogent thing about her, comparing her with some other her in his uncertain playbook.

She pats her pinned-on hair reflexively, while her other hand falls to checking and rechecking the knot on her robe in case she's been flashing him by accident. All in all, she's starting to feel like Norman Bates's mom in *Psycho*:

My mother's not herself today.

"Why are you staring at me like that?"

"No reason. Just looking at you."

"Please don't."

He looks away, but not by much. She takes air into her lungs and slowly releases it. The wish to knock him out of his comfort zone sits high in her chest, a kind of reduced life goal. At the same time, there is logistical business to attend to, things that need to get conveyed now that he's here, or risk further complications later. The lawyer she's going to see this afternoon is his old partner, the best man at their wedding, and decidedly a former friend. Which will not go down well. There's a history there. Though it's Dwight's history, not hers, she's going to remind him, and if he has a problem with that he'll just have to deal with it like a grown-up.

"Sam and I have a meeting with Jack Cutter over in Canaan this afternoon," she announces, apropos of nothing, in her willfully brisk voice.

As expected, she watches the warmth drain from his brown eyes, till they're like those hard glossy chestnuts you find in Central Park in December, if your parents were loving enough to take you to New York City for a *Nutcracker* weekend, as hers were.

"Why him?" Dwight practically barks.

"Because the dean recommended him."

"And why the hell would the dean recommend Jack Cutter of all people, out of all the lawyers in the state?"

"I don't know, Dwight. Probably because he knows I know Jack and he happens to think he's good at what he does. His reputation."

"His reputation," Dwight repeats, adding a guttural sound at the back of his throat. "Cutter's never been anything but a small-town huckster, and you know it."

"A huckster who hired you when you were untouchable around here, in case you've forgotten," she shoots back before she can think better of it. "Which makes you what, exactly?"

Too far: she sees his eyes go from cold, which she can defend against, to something faintly wild, which she cannot; his expression a laser beam of raw, uncalculated anger. And she knows without the slightest doubt that if she wasn't already sitting across the room from him safe and sound she would retreat a step or two backward to protect herself—from her memory, if from nothing else. And that, humiliatingly, is all it takes for her to relive the occasional—maybe three times in all—moments of being physically afraid of him during their marriage. The recall a jagged piece of amber suddenly jammed into her chest, the old skin-prickling fear inside it, perfectly preserved.

Which makes her want to bloody him somehow in return, yes it does.

"You asked if you should come, remember? 'To help.' And I said no. But you came anyway—to suit yourself."

"I came for Sam," he protests.

"Of course you did."

"He's my son, Ruth. He's got my name."

The idiot patriarchal smugness of this last

remark alone—what has Sam's name ever brought him but grief?—is enough to make her crazy.

"Not even you could be that much of a narcissist."

"He came to stay with me."

"Because he'd just done a stupid, terrible thing and was scared out of his wits! And you were the farthest possible place he could think to get to. But intermission's over now. Time to face the music."

She is trembling, the air in the kitchen rippling with unstable energy. And the worst part is that her tone of certainty is such an obvious sham.

He turns away from her and, with an air of rigid disgust, splashes what's left of his coffee into the sink.

A moment later, she hears his mug clatter recklessly against the blue-veined porcelain, hard enough to chip her dead mother's stoneware beyond repair. It's too much—in a flash she's on her feet, lashing out at him as she somehow knows he wants her to:

"This is *my* house, dammit! Either show some respect or get out!"

He says nothing. The room gone still and quiet, his anger seemingly replaced in the space of a few seconds by hers. Roughly he runs the flat of his hand over his face as if to scrape off the invisible muck, then turns and goes to the windows and stands brooding over the yard.

And she? Does she enjoy even a momentary spark of victory at this reversal? Sorry, none. Too tired to move, more like it. As if an entire day, not just thirty minutes, has passed in freakish mortal combat, and she's here bleeding from the spleen even as she stands staring over his shoulder at the yard they first planted together when they had no money to speak of and a child on the way. Oh spring, that hypocritical bitch, is being good to them today: the flowers bright from sun and rain, the hedges lush. The Newmans' dog has wandered back inside for his breakfast, and a gray squirrel is scampering up one of the tall oaks. All this is in front of them, she sees, incontrovertible, subject to no one's mistakes or lies or rage.

She takes a deep breath to anchor herself to the floor, and speaks to him with as much truth as she can imagine.

"Please, just listen to me. I don't have the energy to fight with you. My heart's not big or tough enough. Probably it never was. Sam's known Jack Cutter since he was born. And if things get worse, my God, Dwight, if that boy dies, he's going to need a lawyer who believes in him. Do you hear me? People who believe in him. That's it, and it's my decision."

Behind her the coffeemaker exhales like a dying old woman.

Dwight makes some reply, but it's so soft and

mumbled, with his body turned away from her, that she doesn't catch it.

"What?" She stands staring at his broad back. "What did you say?"

He repeats himself sorrowfully without turning or revealing his face to her, the words coming out like a pitiful confession.

"I believe in my son."

She doesn't understand her need to console him then, to lay her hand on his back and maybe even be consoled by him in return; or how, in the end, she's somehow strong enough to fight off this urgency and stand there and not touch him at all.

SAM

ENTERING THE KITCHEN, he finds them standing close to each other by the window. Their faces twitch round on him in unison, before his mother retreats a few steps to the table.

"You're up early." The smile she tries on for his sake so clearly needs an oilcan that it shames them both. Still, because he loves her more than he knows, he walks up to her and kisses her cheek.

"What's that for?"

He doesn't answer *I was upstairs and heard you yelling your ass off at him and I'm proud of you, Mom,* but that's the essence of it.

"Morning, Sam," mumbles his father from his outpost by the window, so close yet so far.

"Morning."

In the general silence that follows he goes to the counter, takes two slices of bread out of the package, and drops them in the toaster. He has no appetite, but he understands viscerally that this is what one does: you start the day, or you never get up.

Within seconds, the insides of the appliance begin to glow and tick.

And so the family—what's left of them, anyway—stand captivated in their separate places: waiting for the expert who might disarm the bomb that holds them there.

DWIGHT

ESTATE AND TAX LAW was my legal specialty, if not precisely my area of expertise. A subfield I'd chosen during my final year of law school, much as an anxious med-school student from the wrong side of the tracks might decide to go into proctology—not because he finds the study of the anus riveting per se but because he figures there will always be plenty of anuses to go around and so, on the demand side at least, his particular line of practice should be well covered in times of general depression.

It was Jack Cutter, two years ahead of me, who

urged me toward estates (the anus analogy is his, I readily admit). Following some early hotshot years at a big firm in Hartford, during a subsequent low period in my life—which turned out, in retrospect, to be merely a stage of descent—I went to work at Jack's tiny but successful firm, Cutter & Trope, housed in a handsome Greek Revival building on the outskirts of Canaan. According to the circumstances of the time this was a huge break for me, what I suppose you'd call a saving grace. Logically, I know this. But, looking back, I can't seem to take it that way.

Clients came to me early in life, just married, on the verge of having kids. They came to me late in life, too—especially late, and especially when they believed they were dying. They came with their eyes wide open and their skins thinned by fear of oblivion; they came exposed and vulnerable and, in their clumsy agedness and terrified wonder, a lot like children. They came to me with cataracts and arthritic joints, some with cancer. They came in pain and rage, and they came in something like hope. They came with grievances petty and epic. They came with enemies in mind, and long-lost loves. They came jingling stuffed coin purses from bygone eras or hefting folders thick with stock certificates of the great companies of American capitalism. They came with debts to hide, tales of bankruptcy and shame, and nothing much to talk about but my exorbitant fee. They came with private vaults stuffed with bullion and hidden bloody knives and shelves of dusty tomes on how to turn horseshit into gold. They came with twins and triplets and grandkids in the double digits. They came with but one living relative who ever gave a damn, the hard-core gay nephew who, all dressed in leather, represented the definitive end of the line.

Some jobs you can't shower off at the end of the day. Over burgers and fries at Tommy's Diner, Jack and I would joke about having blood on our hands after some irascible widow had blown through the office, waving her hatchet of vitriol and wanting to leave the world to her cat. We facilitated her wishes, of course, and the blood that we laughed over belonged to all those relatives who were going to try to kill one another (after drowning the cat) the minute the old crank was in the ground, to get her pile of loot (a pile not insubstantially diminished by the money owed for our services). Which seemed funny for a while, until it wasn't.

Things just change. You can booze it up for years, pour the turpentine down your gullet every morning, afternoon, and night for decades—and then one day out of the blue a single sip of beer will send you screaming to the ER, and the beginning of the end has begun. You will never know why. You can think you're best pals with someone, sit across from him at lunch week in and week out yucking it up over the same tired jokes, then the next thing you know one afternoon the mere sight of him chewing with his mouth open makes you sick. Or maybe it's him who grows sick of you first, and you're just too far gone to realize it.

Out in the real world nothing but a vetted legal contract is writ in stone, and even then someone—your wife, say—is surely waiting in the wings to sue your lights out. Like the med student who comes down with every disease he studies, the lawyer without a rock-bed conscience (in terms of numbers, take the American Bar Association and multiply by two) is inevitably susceptible to the view of morality that he has helped bring into practice—i.e., whereby the best man at your wedding ends up being the same fuck who never once visits you in prison.

SAM

FROM SOMEWHERE HIS MOTHER IS CALLING him. He comes out of his room and down the stairs, and there by the front door stands his father.

"Where's Mom—my mother?"

"Out in the car."

237

"You're coming, too?"

"You okay with that?"

Sam walks past him. In the driveway, the car's already running: his mom hates to be late. A morning talk show, disembodied above engine noise, floats out the window and across the yard. Faintly self-impressed, politely interrogative, the radio anchor's voice reminds him of the shrink he was sent to after his dad, all of a sudden and four months too late, turned himself in to the state troopers for accidentally running over Josh Learner and leaving him dead by the side of Reservation Road.

The shrink with the pale freckled skin and thinning Creamsicle-colored hair, always the same brown corduroy jacket and uncool Wallabees. The room where they met two times a week a former school bathroom—windowless, pipes sticking out of the walls where the urinals used to be, it was easy to imagine the piss smell if you let yourself.

Worse, as he walks to the waiting car, actual words come back, not an exchange of views or feelings but a psychiatric one-way street—something he hasn't thought about in a long time and doesn't want now, drowning out the radio chatter in his head like some advertising jingle that you swear you'll never be loser enough to remember, yet end up singing to yourself anyway:

And how did it feel when you learned what your father had done?

Sam?

Was it that he didn't tell you himself? Prepare you somehow? That he lied to you about something so huge? Was that what hurt most, that you had to hear about it from other people? How did that make you feel?

Sam, if you won't talk to me, I can't help you.

He never did talk, not to the shrink or anyone else. Him in a nutshell: plenty to think about and nothing to say. Which maybe was the thing about sports, the on-the-spot sense of acceptance it gave him at fourteen, fifteen, after—here, finally, was pure doing, not saying. Learn to do something, do it right or wash out; train your body till it knows nothing else; do that thing again and again till the mind separates itself, grasps its own pathetic worthlessness and quits the body. Out on the field, any field, if you stop to think, you lose.

Though every theory has its limits. Of which he is his own solid proof: he never even took a swing when it counted most.

"Why's *he* coming?" he asks his mother in a low voice.

Exhaust fumes the air between them. Her bare

arm rests on the sill of the open car window. Staring at her wrist, with its drugstore Timex on a cheap leather strap, he's haunted by the wish to buy her a fine watch one day, something with real diamonds. Sentimental tears instantly threaten—in his heart he knows he'll never buy her that watch—but he fights them off.

Behind him, his father shuts the door of the house and clumps down the porch steps.

Quietly, in a tone that gives nothing away, his mother answers, "He says he wants to be there for you."

Sam gets in the front passenger seat, leaving the back for his father.

Nothing to say, but things get said anyway.

"Now, Sam, I'm going to ask you a couple of questions, and I want you to answer me with total honesty."

Jack Cutter, Attorney at Law, sits behind a wide antique desk, the family threesome, such as they are, spread before his Majesty—mom and son on a two-cushion sofa, dad on a hardbacked chair he hardly fits into.

Dad butts his nose in: "Just hold on, Jack—what are you implying?"

The lawyer's gaze sharpens to a practiced courtroom icicle, sizing up the antagonistic voice and its owner, evidently ruling thumbs-down on both. With the flat of a meaty hand, he smooths his green rep tie over his stomach.

He turns to Sam with a tight smile. "My professional advice is just ignore him, son. That's right. Now, first question."

DWIGHT

THREE YEARS I SPENT in those offices, just down the hall from Jack Cutter. That they weren't happy years wasn't his fault. Yet, coming back now and finding new carpeting on the floor, the latest computer hardware on the desks (I was a whiz with an abacus in my day), my old secretary and occasional bedmate long gone, and a plaque with the name of some recent law grad on my old door, I'm guilty of holding it against him anyway. Maybe because he's still an upstanding figure in the community, this self-inflated small-town buckaroo, himself to the nth degree and roguishly proud of it, and stacked up beside him in his own digs I can only feel like some shrunken head brought back from the Dark Continent in a burlap sack. Maybe because it's not the friends who leave you early in the game whom you never forgive; it's the friends who leave you late. Even his coming into work on Memorial Day especially for Sam's sake—a fact that he manages to mention at least three times—seems a blowhard's ploy to me.

But then, discredited and way out of touch, let's

just say I'm not an ideal judge in the matter. There isn't a single word spoken by Cutter during his interview with my son, starting with Sam's name, that doesn't make me want to put my hands around his fat throat and squeeze the breath out of him.

"You're positive he hit you first?"

"Yes," answers Sam.

"Did you get a look at him before he hit you?"

"No."

"You were talking to his girl."

"No. She was talking to me."

"Was she drunk?"

Sam nods.

"Were *you* drunk?"

"Maybe a little."

"Wound up? Pissed off?"

Sam is silent.

"Was *he* drunk—the other guy? Loaded?"

"I don't know. I didn't see him."

"Till you turned and clocked him with the baseball bat?"

"He hit me from behind—twice."

"Hold on a sec. I'm a little confused here. Tell me again what you were doing with a baseball bat in a bar?"

"Objection."

"Dwight," Ruth warns under her breath.

"Ignore him, Ruth." Cutter exhales. Then he turns back to Sam and repeats his question.

"Why'd you have the bat?"

"I still had my gear from the game with me." Sam shakes his head as if unhappy with his own explanation.

Cutter waits for more, but there isn't any. "So what was the bat in? Some sort of team bag?"

"Duffel."

"Was the duffel open or closed?"

Sam hesitates. "Closed."

"And you had to unzip the duffel to get the bat out?"

Sam is silent, staring at his hands.

"Son, look at me, all right? We need to focus here. This is pertinent. Did you *unzip* the duffel to take the bat out?"

Sam nods.

There's another pause, longer. Jack's lips are pursed. Ruth is glaring at me as if she knows by now how badly I want to unpurse those lips with my fist, and I look away from her.

"One more question," Jack says. "Anybody else in the bar see you unzip that bag?"

"I don't know."

"Where was the bag, exactly?"

"On the floor, under the bar."

"So not easily visible?"

Sam shakes his head.

"Were there people close by?"

"I guess."

Jack sighs. "Okay, let's move on for the

moment. You unzipped the bag. What happened then?"

"I guess I swung at him."

"You guess? That's a helluva guess. And hit him where?"

"Stomach."

"Below the ribs, you'd say?"

Sam was silent.

"Say we call it his 'midsection' and leave it at that. Clear, but not too clear."

"Quit screwing him up, Jack."

Cutter swings his big head around. "When I want your assistance, Counselor, you'll be the first to know."

"Put your ego aside and let him tell it like it happened. Or he'll never sound like himself on the witness stand."

"For God's sake, Dwight, butt out," Ruth snaps.

"Tell you what, Ruth." Angry pinkish blotches have appeared on Cutter's walrus cheeks and, quivering like a soufflé, he takes a moment to Buddha himself. "My ex-partner's behavior is understandable, if not exactly remedial to the situation at hand. I have sympathy for the guy, I do. Lasting feelings of impotence are a common side effect of incarceration."

I stand up.

In the old days Cutter would've been on his feet, too, never caught flat; but he's heavier by fifty now, deeper into heart-attack land and, like

244

all good lawyers, too smart to get into any dogfight he doesn't already have the answer to. So he stays put. Scanning the legal pad on the desk, he clears his throat a couple of times.

I sit back down, the chair cracking under me as if it might collapse.

"Nic Bellic," Cutter begins again with Sam. "He was your year at school?"

"Yeah, but I didn't know him."

"You sure about that?"

Sam hesitates, then shakes his head. "He tried out for the team, but got cut first week."

"What about his family?"

"His parents are Serbian immigrants. That's what the dean told me. They don't speak much English."

"Do they have any money?"

"The dean said they're pretty hard up. His dad does part-time construction work. His mom makes dresses, something like that."

Cutter nods sagely, a transitional gesture signaling a move into the next stage of his performance.

"Fortunately, Sam, I happen to be a UConn benefactor and am on reasonably good terms with Dean Burris. The head of surgery at Hartford Hospital's a friend as well." He leans forward, the edge of the desk shelving his gut, and fixes Sam with his Atticus Finch gaze. "Okay, I've done a little sniffing around these Serbs during my holiday hours. Your pal Saint Nic's already had a couple of run-ins with Colchester's finest. That's right, you can chalk up another two bar fights, as well as a charge settled out of court for pilfering from the plumbing-supply store where he worked last summer. So you gotta figure the last place he and his parents want to see him is in a heart-to-heart with the UConn cops—or in court. Definitely to be avoided at all costs. And the university's got little choice but to follow the family's wishes on the matter—unless and until, that is, the kid's injuries, or conditions stemming from the alleged original injury, should prove fatal."

Here Cutter takes a few moments to check his notes and allow for applause. Looking up again, he does everything but bow to the wings.

"So let's review the medical situation, shall we? Approximately two hours after receiving a traumatic blow to the midsection, the patient self-admits to hospital, complaining of severe abdominal pain. Kid can barely stand up. Says he was in a fight and got gut-whacked with a bat, but he claims total ignorance about the identity of his attacker. Pretty much standard ER behavior for bad boys who don't want anything to do with the cops, even if they're dying. Two days later, after unsuccessful observation and worsening pain, the docs open him up and look around. Duodenal hematoma promptly discovered. They sew him back together and in a few days he starts looking better. A little color in his cheeks, that petty-thug personality coming back to delight society once again. But then—bingo—sepsis hits, his blood's poison, his BP's nosediving, and his ass goes straight back to the prime-time ICU. That's hospitals for you—if you're not already dead, they'll find some way to kill you once you get there.

"And then what does the idiot resident go and do? Prescribe the wrong antibiotics! The kid doesn't improve, keeps sinking, now he's just barely hanging on—till finally somebody has a George Clooney moment and figures out they're headed for a doozy of a malpractice case. Which is the only time, I can assure you, that anybody will ever be motivated to do anything constructive in this great nation of ours."

By now, Cutter is enjoying himself so much he's actually grinning. I want to knock his teeth out.

"This fun for you, Jack? You like being the star of your own fucking reality show at my son's expense?"

"Shut up," Sam says to me, and to me alone.

He doesn't repeat it. He doesn't have to. He stands up and walks out of the office and leaves us there.

247

SAM

THE AIR OVER ROUTE 44 fuses his perceptions, muggy and bright. The shoulder is narrow; traffic passes close. He turns east, breaking into a desperate jog. It can't be more than five miles to his mother's house.

But he runs lumpishly today, unable to locate his stride, eyes hugging the gravel-strewn ground in front of him: an athlete in civilian clothes, his shoes heavy and flat.

It would seem a simple thing on the surface—that a child is not an event, alleged or otherwise, a mistake or accident or crime, his or someone else's. That he is by definition more than this, sum rather than division, a living promissory note. That he might love his parents helplessly, in spite of who they are; just as, if he's ever to find his place in the world, someday he must accept himself helplessly, in spite of who he has become.

He slows, then stops, a painful stitch digging into his side. He bends over. Not in shape, after all. No kind of "prospect." Just another washout without a life plan.

He remembers stabbing a freshly sharpened pencil into the hand of a boy at school. It was Eddie Tibbet, his friend. They were ten. There was no logical reason for the attack, no apparent motive.

It is still fresh to him: the look of disbelief on Eddie's face, his high, startled cry of pain. The teacher grabbing him by the wrist, dragging him off to the principal's office.

To separate him from the others, she said: so he could not hurt anyone else.

A fuel truck lumbers by at close range, trailing gasoline vapor. Painted on the back of the stubby silver tank, for some reason, is a palm tree, brown coconuts nesting in green fronds.

He thinks of California.

And then, heading west in the opposite lane, he sees a second vehicle, a converted pickup, its flatbed vertically sectioned by large panes of clear glass—a roving window in search of a house. And for the instant it's even with his position he is granted, as if by some higher power, insight through its crystalline lenses to the other side.

He snaps this mental picture, not knowing what it means.

Then the truck is past, and all views everywhere revert to the obscure.

The tips of his father's brown lace-ups are badly scuffed from his mad dash along the roadside: the man's been out running, too, chasing his son. Pale dust coats his pantlegs to the shins, and dark islands of sweat stain the armpits of his white button-down.

"I still know some people around here—" His father bends over—hands on his knees—to catch a wheezing breath, then slowly straightens again. "Come on . . . I can find you half a dozen lawyers better than that pompous asshole."

"Forget it."

"Sam, listen to me—"

"No."

"Dammit, we need to do everything we can here."

" 'We'? "

His father looks away. Sam repeats the question, his anger growing, as a yard away a minivan passes them in a rush of dust and fumes.

His father breathes out. A public service, in essence: trying to expel something potentially harmful to them both.

"You don't want to go where I went. Never. You don't want any part of that."

"Doesn't look like it killed you." Out of bounds now, Sam lets it fly. It almost feels good. His father stares at him, takes a step closer.

"You don't know what the hell you're talking about. It'll ruin your life. Rot you from the inside out."

"Too late," he says softly.

(He is five again, and across the room his parents are killing each other.)

"Listen to me—"

He turns to get away. But a hand shoots out, grabs him high up on his left biceps. Strong blunt fingers that know what damage is dig into the soft tissue between muscle, sending a knifelike pain shooting up his shoulder and down his arm.

Before he can stop himself, his fist flies out: he punches his father in the face.

They both see it at the same moment: his father's fist cocked in the stunned air, about to deliver the return blow.

And then his father, running.

RUTH

DRIVING EAST ON 44 from Cutter's office, on the lookout for her son, she is thrown back to an afternoon a good decade in the past: raised voices out on her front lawn, a man's and a boy's, where Norris is tutoring his indifferent stepson in the mysteries of the short game in golf. Then a sudden loud clatter—her husband's prized pitching wedge tomahawked into a tree—and by the time she peers out the bedroom window to see what the fuss is about there's only her son's sweatshirted back, tearing up Larch Road at a jackrabbit clip.

Sam disappears from sight even as Norris, arms akimbo, flails in the driveway like a discombobulated traffic cop. And, observing her husband from this judicial distance, Ruth is finally able to conclude what she's probably known all along: that here is a man who doesn't know anything—*anything*—about kids.

Meanwhile, her son has run away. For more than two hours she drives around the area alone, trying to guess where he might have gone. (Norris remains at the house, ostensibly in case of Sam's early return, but really so he won't miss any of the third round of the Masters on TV.) And when, still searching, she senses darkness beginning to fall, hot waves of grief roll across her brow and down her neck as though she is suffering the early onset of menopause. Yes, it is before and after, youth then age. She returns home an old woman, prepared to call the police, only to find her son sitting on the porch steps as if she is the child who went missing and he the haunted parent.

And for a rageful moment, rushing at him from the barely parked car, slapping his face actually seems possible. For terrorizing her as no one should ever be allowed to terrorize another. But by the time—maybe five seconds—she's actually got her hands on him, the threat of her anger has been sapped; the threat of her, period. She can no more imagine hurting him than letting him grow free.

"Don't you ever do that again," she whispers

harshly, pulling him to her and squeezing the breath out of him.

He promises he won't. He says he's sorry.

Out her windshield, half a mile east of the law office, she spots him, a man now, dressed in the respectable clothes she demanded, sitting hunched on a bench that the proprietor of Maya's Arts & Crafts established beside her odd little kiosk of a store. Oblivious of passing traffic, he's staring at his hands gripping each other in an awkward joined fist between his knees.

He doesn't look up till she beeps the horn.

She shoves open the passenger door, and he ducks inside.

"You okay?"

He won't even glance at her.

"Seat belt, please," she says.

She pulls back onto the road. He brings the belt around, fastens it. The knuckles on his right hand are raw, as if he's burned himself. She stops herself from inquiring about it, instead redirecting her focus, seeking an acceptable angle.

"Did your father catch up with you?"

His grunt is more or less affirmative.

She waits, but he won't elaborate. Her eyes go again to his inflamed knuckles, then back to the road. The truth is that a good part of her doesn't really want to know.

She makes herself ask anyway, assuming she won't get an answer.

"What happened?"

He's silent.

"Where is he?"

"I don't care."

She sighs. "All right, Sam."

She drives on. The sun hazy, the afternoon growing late. They pass the Elks Club. They pass the two-lane bowling alley, probably to be closed soon, now that all the kids prefer hanging out in front of their keyboards to actually getting together. They pass Fanelli's, a locals' bar she's never liked. They pass Gray's Ice Cream stand, outside which on steamy summer afternoons when Sam was small he and his friends used to hold contests to see who could eat an entire double blackberry cone before any of it dripped on the ground. Their faces violet as clowns by the end. He never won that she can remember, though maybe that was the point.

A mental scene that morphs into another, older and still more unaccountable: Sam with his father on the beach in Cotuit, engaged in an elaborate "wipe-out" contest. Dwight the self-proclaimed champion, allowing himself to be comically pummeled by one wave after another, big rag doll of a man, flopping and hamming it up in the shallows for his son's delight, Sam laughing so hard he has seawater coming out his nose.

While, in a sunroom in a house long sold, her mother is speaking to her from the grave: *For God's sake, Ruth Margaret, quit arguing with your life all the time! You'll never win.*

She's relieved when the commercial buildings are soon behind them, the road running straight for a mile between gray stone walls before crossing the creek and doglegging north into Wyndham Falls. A town deeply familiar to her, if not exactly her own. A town plucked out of some high-end catalog of towns. A town innately organized to martial into a livable pattern all those stray memories that otherwise will peck you bloody like Hitchcock's birds as you try in vain to imitate the healthy people who can take it or leave it.

She, unfortunately, has long proved herself to be not this sort of healthy person. She can take, all right, but leaving is something she has never mastered. She's of the stubborn bag-lady genus: bringing it all with her wherever she goes, hoarding the past not because it's better but because it's the only thing she seems to own.

"Mom?"

Beside her Sam's voice is soft, almost pleading, unlike the superhero's body he possesses. But she's driving over a tricky stretch of road and doesn't feel she can risk peeking at him. Her hands choking the steering wheel. The tires clattering across the little iron bridge stretched across the creek. She turns the wheel and the car follows the sharp curve, at the end of it more stone walls, and the clean white houses of one of the prettiest towns in Connecticut.

DWIGHT

I RUN TILL I CAN'T RUN ANYMORE. Run from my own hands, which keep following me—no getting rid of them. Run till the sweat's leaking out of my hair and I'm bent over the littered side of 44.

Cars shoulder past going east and west, a furniture truck. Eventually I raise myself and stand looking up the road, hands on my hips. Two football fields distant is a bar I used to haunt. An after-work sort of place, Fanelli's, with a pool table and a TV. Off-duty state troopers from the Canaan barracks used to drink there, house builders and roadworkers, the odd white-collar. I head for it now, my lungs gradually settling, the sweat drying on my face. A neon Pabst sign flickers in the unwashed front window. The place is open, and I go in.

My eyes are slow to adjust to the gloomy, secondhand light. Two solitary men hunched over drinks at the bar in the long narrow room, and a single couple nursing beers at one of the back tables. Nobody speaking. The less-than-regulation-size pool table where grown men used to play pickup games with stacks of quarters for cheerleaders. Barren now. The old jukebox gone; speakers built into the nicotined ceiling ooze easy-listening country.

I take a seat at the end of the bar, as far from the wall-mounted TV as I can get. Oprah's on. A young man about Sam's age with a soul patch under his bottom lip shuffles over to take my order. He's sporting a heavy-metal T-shirt under an open flannel shirt, and has a wad of dip stuffed between his cheek and gum. On his way to me he stops and with pinpoint accuracy spits a stream of brown juice into an empty Snapple bottle on the backbar.

"What'll it be?"

I order a double Jim Beam with a draft on the side.

He stands there a few moments, staring at my face a little too long, in a way I don't care for. I'm about to ask if he has some kind of problem, when he moves a pile of bar napkins in front of me.

"Your lip's bleeding," he offers in a confiding tone.

I thank him for the information.

He goes off to get my drinks while I dab a napkin at the corner of my mouth. It comes away streaked red. I keep dabbing till the blood stops, by which time the napkin is almost entirely ruined, the blood's starting to dry and darken, and the bartender has returned with my drinks. He glances at the bloody napkin before he goes away, but not at me.

I drink my order. And when those drinks are finished I raise a finger, and before I know it, without intervention, fresh drinks arrive. I drink those, too.

What I see is my own hand cocked in the air as I stand by the roadside. My hand that is a fist. The violence in it already born. As if the rest of me that's always wanted to be good is just dead skin over the old, true self, which is the fist. The skin sloughed off in an instant, revealing the fist, and all the fists before it. The fist raised by me against my own son in the falling light of day.

PENNY

AS IT HAPPENS, the day following Dwight's confession and departure, the nagging hollowness that she feels in the pit of her stomach while delivering her annual lecture to the undergrads on the last days of Sylvia Plath has little to do with the tragic happenings in anybody else's oven. It is purely her own drama, and all the more confusing for it. An unacceptable, even shameful, gap seems to have opened between her understanding and her heart. She never knew the boy Dwight killed, of course, and, no matter how hard she tries, can't seem to create an image of him in her mind. This is the gap in herself that follows her from the lecture hall to her office; from her office to her car. That sits with her in traffic on the drive home. That overcooks her daughter's dinner. That takes a shower with her, and watches *The Wire* with her. That stays up much of the night with her, because it, too, can't sleep. It resides, somehow, where she believed her judgment of him would rise up in moral outrage. But instead of judgment there has been this strange, urgent welling of compassion for him, a compassion not unlike love.

SAM

HOME AGAIN IN THE LATE AFTERNOON, he makes straight for his room, taking the stairs two at a time.

His father hasn't returned yet.

He stands in the middle of the room. Daylight, shadowed but not yet disappearing, seeps through the two front-facing windows, exposing his nostalgic arsenal of trophies and sports equipment for what it is: the littered remains of a failed belief system that he wasn't even aware, until now, of having bought into.

He sits down at his desk because it's there. After a while he opens the single drawer, revealing two ballpoint pens and a blunt yellow pencil that belonged to a boy he once knew. These he aligns in a row, as if solving a puzzle of his own design. And there are loose paper clips, too, which he herds into small piles; and the ticket stubs to an old Sox game; and a black-and-white speckled composition book that for a few weeks when the boy was thirteen and on the verge of some ascending darkness he used as a journal.

The book, never close to being completed, appalls him now; as does the handwriting on the cover, like the ragged scrawl of an unschooled child.

In the last moments before the sun dips behind the visible line of trees, he opens his laptop and discovers her email:

Sam,
I'm here for the summer.
Get in touch if you feel like it.
Hope you will.
Emma

For a long while he sits with her message, as his room—everywhere but the glowing screen with its five lines of print—gradually withdraws into shadow.

Finally, he types back:

What are you doing tonight?

And with a long outbreath like a sigh, clicks *Send*.

RUTH

THE KETTLE BEGINS TO MOAN, those last few seconds before true boil. She reaches the stove in time to disarm the apparatus before its shriek can crack her glass house of repose. She pours the water and the steam wafts up—

"Mom?"

The calming scent of lemon verbena still in her nose, she turns and sees him standing in the doorway. One of his feet extending into the kitchen, the other planted sideways like a tug-of-war contestant, geared for resistance, already pointing out the front of the house toward some misinformed notion of freedom. He's replaced the decent clothes he wore for their meeting with Jack Cutter with torn jeans and a gray hooded sweatshirt, along with thick-soled work boots.

"Can I take the car?"

She checks the wall clock—almost nine. "Where were you thinking of going?"

"See a friend."

"Anybody I know?"

The slight movement of his head means yes— or no, impossible to tell.

An old hand, a professional, she waits him out.

"Just a girl," he says to the floor.

She studies him, the points of his cheekbones inflamed as if by fever. "You okay?"

261

"Fine."

She lets the response stand, holding it up to the light so they can both see the holes in it. "Where are you meeting her?"

"Fanelli's."

"Sam, do you really think you should be going to a *bar* under the circumstances? You think that's the smart choice?"

He shrugs as if he honestly doesn't have a clue.

She is starting to hate the sound of her own voice; hate her idea of what a question is, or its purpose. She takes a spoon from the dish rack, scoops the tea bag from the cup, and drops it into the sink. She's given up using sweeteners, but she would like something sweet now.

"The keys are on the dash. Be home by midnight."

He comes into the kitchen. He seems to want to hug her to show his gratitude or maybe his pity, but she does not want to be touched at the moment, not even by him. And this is the saddest thing.

"Go," she murmurs, waving him away as she might have when he was little, a fluttery shooing motion of the kind that says *Now get along, honeybun, I've got muffins to bake;* except there's honest-to-God pleading in her voice, unmistakable to them both.

Well, she's still his mother, isn't she? Will be as long they both are breathing. And he goes.

She drinks her cup of tea, fires up the kettle for

another. Keeps the television on, the little cook's set with the rabbit ears and the fuzzy-wuzzy reception—showing *Law & Order*, the sound on low. So many different kinds of *Law & Order*, and—on TV, at least—the guarantee of a neat resolution to every problem.

Earlier, she went up and stood outside his room and asked through the closed door whether he'd like some supper, and when he said no in such a small and tired voice she ached for him, believing he must be like her, gutted by the afternoon, his insides turned upside down. But now she understands that she was mistaken—he is not like her. She's been in the kitchen since late afternoon, numbly watching talk shows and news and reruns, drinking cup after cup of herbal tea, each time trying like some matronly Buster Keaton to reach the kettle before it can shriek her lights out, eventually eating a single-portion can of lentil soup, while all along he was up in his room getting himself prepped for a night at a bar. She's been down here replaying in her mind Jack Cutter's carelessly cruel, yet undoubtedly accurate—she can't question the man's intelligence, only his heart—rendering of the probable legal realities facing her son, while the son himself was already moving away from those realities, surfing the Internet or texting with some girl, dreaming his way right out of her house.

Maybe the main thing, the only real goal, is to

not get trapped alone with one's feelings; to continually start and restart reality in the hope that the next episode might offer greater resolution, clearer meaning; that although the show will still appear on the same old channel they might somehow all come back different, better, wiser, younger, able to start again, rewind to the beginning. . . .

She gets down on her knees then, yes she does, right there on the kitchen floor.

EMMA

SHE PAUSES IN THE DOORWAY of her mother's studio, trying once again to account for the changes. From her childhood she's preserved a mental picture of several antique lamps, an interwoven jungle of spidery hanging plants and lithe potted palms, and a large, overstuffed reading chair with a slipcover of green velvet worn in spots like a favorite pair of old jeans. Here, however, is spare, industrial efficiency, enforced geometry, and highly focused halogen lighting. The lack of soul is general. Only the original drafting table remains, as if to say *This one last thing will I still honor.* Everywhere else, hard new metal has replaced old soft wood. This room that for years was the last haven for her mother's dreaming and private moments, for curling up with the contents of her head or the hand-drawn plates of some nineteenth-century monograph on shrubs, today more accurately resembles a diamond cutter's workroom, a temple of purposeful precision.

A second table, metal, is set up for an iMac with a twenty-four-inch monitor and a color laser printer. The only chair is a modernist Swiss thing that looks about as comfortable as a park bench. And what plants remain are sharp-edged and sculptural, cactus eye candy, lovely enough as long as you don't try to touch them.

Bent over a drawing, hard at work, Grace Learner is oblivious of her daughter's cataloguing presence. A welder's beam of halogen light spills off her blond head and into the shadowy corner of the room.

Emma takes another step. A floorboard creaks, and her mother raises her head sharply.

"Oh, it's you!"

"Sorry. Just coming in to say good night."

"You're going out?"

The gaze focuses rapidly, taking in the glove-tight jeans and sexy stretch top, then jumps to the digital clock on the computer table.

"It's getting pretty late."

"Now was the only time Paula could get free." The lie pops out of Emma's mouth so easily it leaves no trace on her tongue.

"Oh. How is Paula? Still with that awful boyfriend?"

"That was a couple of years ago."

"Where are you meeting her?"

"Is that a new project you're working on?"

An obvious diversionary tactic; yet depressingly, as foreseen, her mother can't help warming to this rare interest in her work.

"It's for Sue Foley. She says she'll have me redesign their entire four acres if I can come up with something that will persuade her husband." Her mother pauses to realign the tracing paper she's been working on. "The job would mean a lot." A tentative half smile squeezes out. "Well, it would be great."

"I hope you get it." Emma means this—but at the same time, physically, she has begun drifting backward.

"Em?"

Halfway out of the room, she gets reeled back. And here is her mother at the canted table, face outwardly composed but blinking now in familial Morse code a haggard SOS: *Don't. Leave. Yet.*

"You'll be careful? End-of-the-holiday weekend. You know how wild people get."

"Of course."

"Thank you."

"You're welcome."

The empty, formal phrases trotted back and forth; no end, seemingly, to how many times they can be recycled, or how much erosion they can cause over time.

Then, out of nowhere, her mother takes a deep, complicated breath. "I ran into Wanda Shoemaker at the supermarket this afternoon."

Emma doesn't want to be rude exactly, but her foot has begun to tap against the floor. She's already late. Sam might leave before she gets there. She might never see him at all.

"Who's Wanda Shoemaker?"

"The woman living with Norris Wheldon. Probably going to marry him, I've heard."

"Sam Arno's stepfather?" Suddenly, Emma is listening with both ears instead of just one.

"Wanda told me news that just knocked the breath right out of me."

"What news?"

"It seems that a few weeks ago, just before he was supposed to graduate, Sam Arno got into a fight with another UConn student at an off-campus bar."

"So?" Emma's tone—by design or accident, she doesn't know which—emerges almost cavalier. Like: *Guys in bars get in fights all the time.* But look closer and you'll see that her foot has stopped tapping. She takes a step farther into the room and remains there, taut and waiting.

"So—" repeats her mother with sudden irritation, as though it's now incumbent on her to make an obvious and unforgivable point. "So the boy he beat up is still in the ICU in Hartford. And from what Wanda told me he may not pull through. He may *die,* Em. And Sam Arno may well end up going to prison like his fucking father."

The room goes quiet; the word *fucking* seems to linger like a crude aftertaste. Behind its invisible, altering presence it's possible to hear the tree limbs shifting in the breeze in the front yard. Emma's face feels cold, stamped on like a sheet of tin.

Her mother is staring at her fiercely. "Did you hear a single thing I just told you?"

Nodding, Emma turns and walks out of the room. She flees the house. She drives to Canaan as fast and recklessly as she can, in her safety-first Swedish car that doesn't know the meaning of recklessness.

RUTH

INTO THE RUNNING BATH she pours a generous dose of dark-green sea kelp foam and watches it catch like a flame under the tumbling water. Greenish white bubbles flare to the surface as if breathed into by an invisible glassblower. They grow rapidly, with a barely audible, sibilant fizz, till the water's surface is covered. The air in the tiled room already turning humid, the scent pleasantly marine.

On the closed lid of the toilet beside the tub, she's gathered her necessities: the latest issue of

Vogue, a fresh mug of tea, a cuticle stick, and an oval pumice stone of the kind, thirty-five years ago, her mother taught her to use.

She slips the robe from her shoulders and, naked, eases herself into the bath.

Down below, distant and outside, there are footsteps on the front porch. A moment later, the door to the house opens and closes. Then Ruth hears more footsteps—*too heavy for Sam's*—in the entry hall.

Shutting the magazine she's been reading with a transporting avidity, she sets it on the toilet lid, her wet fingers leaving snail's tracks down the front of the glowing, mineral-hard model on the cover, ruining her ten-thousand-dollar dress.

The bathwater has cooled. She isn't ready to get out yet. She needs more time. She turns on the tap again. Warm fresh water trickles out, turning hot. She increases the volume, adding more bath foam. New bubbles form and spread, and soon she can no longer see any part of herself.

"Sam . . . ? Ruth . . . ?"

Downstairs, she hears him calling out tentatively to the house at large, somehow making their names sound like trick questions, when they're just names. She lies back, the weight of her head eased by the smooth rounded rim of the tub, and listens to him gamely tackle the stairs.

With each step the house tremors faintly; the liquor he's drunk is in his overreaching feet. He gains the landing and there's an abrupt, guilty stillness that she recognizes, too, and then he's knocking on Sam's closed door.

"Sam . . . ? You in there . . . ?"

Sam's not in there, and in the still emptiness, his dejected need for company by now architecturally palpable throughout the house, she audibly follows him on the next stage of his long march against loneliness, down the hallway in her general direction. "Ruth?" he calls. "You asleep?" Well, not anymore. He's like the mummy in those old Peter Lorre movies—heavy-footed, inadvertently comical (if you've never been married to him, that is), murderously unstoppable.

"Ruth?" he calls again—this time from her bedroom, not fifteen feet and a half-closed door from where she lies in a state of unseemly aquatic exhibition.

With both hands, in case he's lost his mind, she quickly attempts to froth up the patchwork bubbles into a decent coverlet. Shouting, "Don't come in, I'm taking a bath!" The warning unnecessary: she hears the aging springs shudder and twang as he lowers himself onto the bed in the next room—all two hundred pounds of him, spread out horizontally by the sound of it, on the side that used to be Norris's.

Poor old Norris. Were he around to witness this little *réunion de la nostalgie*, he'd probably require an emergency angioplasty on the spot. More likely, though, ten o'clock on a holiday night, he's out duckpin bowling, shopping for golf shoes online, comparing actuarial tables, or microwaving lite popcorn with his new family. Or all of the above. Well, people are different, aren't they? A girl never can predict who might wander into her boudoir during a bubble bath.

She turns on the tap again. The hot water trickles down and the heat warms her toes.

"Where's Sam?"

A surprise: Dwight's breathing once he hit the bed was loud enough that she assumed he'd passed out.

She turns off the water and tells him matter-of-factly where their son has gone, as far as she knows. There is no immediate reaction. She can't see him, but they are close enough that soft voices will do; there's no need to shout. While she waits for him to challenge her, start something, he merely shifts around on the mattress, sending the springs crying as if he is no more than the weight he carries, no more than that. His lack of fight is so opposite his typical bully brand of strength that in spite of herself she begins to feel sorry for him.

She lies in the tub and listens to his silence, her fingers making tiny ripples in the bathwater. In

271

the next room, as far as she can tell, he has stopped moving entirely. She begins to think he must have drifted off again.

"I hated my old man," he says suddenly—as if, shivering awake, he's just spit out whatever bad dream was on the tip of his tongue. "Christ, I hated him. But I never took a swing at him."

She lies there, picturing again the angry raw knuckles on Sam's right hand that she observed in the car—and realizes what must have happened between them on the roadside. A depleted feeling of imminent sadness drains her, like an hourglass about to run out of sand.

She says, "You would have, if he'd lived long enough."

Dwight grunts. "Maybe."

"Sam doesn't hate you. He tried, but he couldn't do it."

"He'd have his reasons."

"Yes. He would."

His silence then is his confirmation. She still knows him. Maybe if she lives longer, maybe in thirty years, she'll start to forget who he is. There are people everywhere who marry again and move on, growing older and older, farther and farther from where they started, and begin, at first gradually and then with annihilating finality, to forget, forget all of it. But in her case that seems unlikely. It is not about love. It is about physics. She and Dwight are like two speeding cars that collided head-on before ever knowing the world. What's left of each, the wrecks of their hearts, all that's not scattered by the roadside and in the fields, has been fused by the force of impact, made into one thing, which no longer at its core resembles the old things. What's between them isn't useful or beautiful or good. It simply is. It exists. She has never separated herself from him as she imagined.

"I'm sorry," he says.

Still thinking, she makes no reply.

"How I handled today, all of it. I deserve what I got. Worse. Sometimes . . ."

He doesn't finish. Maybe there's no end to it.

"It's all right," she says, not unkindly.

"I'm trying."

"I know you are." She takes the pumice stone off the toilet seat and balances it on her raised knee. Just as she used to do when she was twelve and her mother was still there to teach her how to live.

"I'm just no good, Ruth. No fucking good."

She could tell him it isn't so. But they've always known each other better than that.

They are quiet then, the two of them, in separate but connected rooms, hardly moving, listening intimately to each other for the first time in many years.

SAM

OUTSIDE FANELLI'S, the night is moonless but clear; a warm breeze has swept the clouds from the sky. The parking lot is clotted with weeds, and shards of broken bottles glitter underfoot. Above the sound of his boots scraping the dirt, Sam hears the chirping of crickets rising out of the marshy derelict field, and the vaporous bass thump of music escaping the bar.

He comes to his mom's Subaru, keys dangling from his fingers.

He sees her then—a few yards away, leaning against an old Volvo wagon with her arms folded across her chest, her blond hair smudged yellow by the safety light from a phone box at the rear corner of the lot.

"I waited an hour," he says, his voice caught awkwardly between anger and relief. "How long have you been out here?"

She doesn't answer. Hugging herself, though the night is anything but cold.

EMMA

SHE FOLLOWS HIS TAILLIGHTS toward the center of Canaan. It's after ten and the town is dead. A small-town law office, shuttered for the night, could stand for a funeral home; Tommy's

Diner, with not a light on, looks as good as bankrupt. At the junction with 7, traffic signals swing in the breeze from their stretched wires like arms waving to the dark. The audience gone. It's just the two of them now, in their separate cars, and the birdcall of rusted hinges coming out of the black sky.

Then his left blinker speaks to her. She replies with hers, and soon they're heading south on 44 toward Salisbury.

A car passes going the other way. For a second, the back of his head is a silhouette in her vision— something to aim for—then a blinding slash of yellow, then just more darkness paled by the wash of her own headlights, and the two ruby eyes by which he's leading her.

SAM

"WHERE ARE WE?" SHE ASKS.

"Someplace I used to come when I was a kid."

He speaks softly, the words weightless; but still his voice seems to ring in the night as if he's calling her out of some shelter to meet him in the dark. The dark a kind of wilderness, the two of them inside it. He reaches for her hand, feels her lace her fingers through his. No thought to this— thought comes the moment after, his mind running in his heart's rutted wake.

In his other hand he holds a small flashlight he

275

found in the glove box of his mother's car. The weak trembling beam lighting in body-length patches the unmarked dirt tracks they've driven down to get here, ending now in meadow. Incipient dew gives the thick grass an optimistic shine. Mole tracks cross the field at random. He spots a burrow of some sort, maybe a woodchuck's. Ahead loom the tall shadows of trees, interspersed with low humps of shrub. He's lost track of where they are, but guesses it must be somewhere near Dutcher's Bridge. The Housatonic must be on the other side of the trees. The river of his childhood.

They are the same in this, he wants to believe: born into a place not of their choosing, they carry its fixed but living pattern inked on their skins as they grow and break away, wild for some other home to make. The river remains where it's always been, moving constantly but never changing, waiting for the inevitable day when they will come crawling back to its banks in supplication. Because it knows more than they do, and always has.

He can't remember the last time he was close enough to hear the rippling whisper of its steady flowing—as he can now, holding his breath in the dark, walking beside her.

EMMA

THEY REACH THE RIVERBANK. He lets go of her hand and switches off the flashlight, and for ten seconds that stretch like a hundred the night blacks her vision. She feels on the cusp of panic until the edges of a knowable picture begin to emerge, half-familiar sensations, beauty of detail and scent. Thick ankle-high grass and damp loamy soil underfoot. The tarry water flowing by with its mica flecks and earth whisperings. The long shadows of elderberry shrubs on which clusters of tiny blue-black berries impose islands of bewitching lacquered darkness.

An owl hoots warily in the distance. And she recalls her mother telling her how some indigenous cultures believe that the elder tree offers protection against evil and witches.

Sure.

Sam's been staring at the river, but now he turns to look at her. A facet of light appears on one cheek; she has no idea where it's coming from, but for some reason it moves her deeply.

It's then that she hears herself asking him the first of the questions she's brought.

He tells her. Tells the whole thing, and when he's done she speaks about extenuating circumstances, questions of self-defense. But he is reluctant to talk about excuses or ways out. What he needs to do is draw from his acid pool of self-recrimination a portrait of his own flawed conscience, a drawing intended to posit that, according to some moral proof of his own reckoning, inside the heart of his violent mistake must live the real person.

Which, if true—the X-ray correct and the guilt earned—then inside the heart of the real person can live only the violent mistake.

She leans closer and kisses the mark of light on his cheek, the unconscious brand of his goodness.

SAM

HIS HANDS UNDER HER TIGHT-FITTING TOP, flush against her skin, his fingers piano-scaling her rib cage to the under-stone coolness of her breasts. Kissing her, his tongue deep in her mouth, her taste some herb he can't name, her tongue silken and firm. Her hair freshly washed, soft as hair can be. Her beauty more resonant than his memory imagined—a mysterious collage of slender but forceful definitions that, under his fingers now, in his mouth, are, at long last, open to him again.

Until she pulls her head back, stands looking at him from inches away: "What's wrong?"

He shakes his head, tries to kiss her again.

But his heart isn't in it.

• • •

So he is discovered. Betrayed by himself, after two years of dreaming. His physical desire a shameful no-show, the bat again left on his shoulder. He stands before her buried alive by these thoughts—trapped not in reverie but in a lost city whose forced excavation, performed alone under her honest questioning gaze, is hard and painful work that leaves him on the verge of grief.

He's about to turn away when she reaches out and presses a hand to his cheek.

"Breathe."

For a moment, he has no idea what she's talking about.

"Smell that? It's elderberry."

And suddenly he smells it in the humid air, emanating from the shrubs behind: as if her naming the scent is the key that unlocks his knowing it. And with this simple recognition comes an equally simple, and rather vague, memory of his mother baking an elderberry pie. He can't remember the year, or the pie getting finished, or eating it, or the taste, or whether life was good then or more like it is now; just his mother in the kitchen with her sleeves rolled up, flour dusting her forearms to her elbows, while he sits doing his homework at the kitchen table, a radio playing low.

And over the river a sudden breeze pinches the

water's black skin into intricate flashing scales, like tiny silver minnows leaping in the holographic night—until, as quickly as it's risen, the breeze dies and the scales are swallowed back into the smooth oil-black liquid, where all is moving as well as still.

He places his hand over Emma's hand, against his face.

There is still the possibility that she knows him better than he knows himself, can read him without words. Who else, if not her? They who were there by chance when the world went wrong. He doesn't need to own or claim her, only to hold on to the fact of her. To stand with her on the scented bank of the river, naming the things that can still be named, touching her hand, till the night finally runs out of darkness.

RUTH

FOR MORE THAN TEN MINUTES as she finishes her bath, Dwight's deep regular breathing is the only sound coming from the next room. Not even the drain's centrifugal rant manages to interrupt his descent into the depths of a calmer place where, for minutes or hours, he might hope to inhabit someone who is not himself. Almost like old times.

She stands in the bathroom rubbing moisturizer on her body—everywhere but on her breasts, which, just these past few days, she's turned superstitious about touching. She puts on her robe and turbans her hair with a towel. On the robe are forget-me-nots, seasonless and charming, giving the impression, in a certain light, if one rules out a host of other factors, that she is every age she's ever been.

Escaping the mirror, she walks into the next room.

He's rolled onto his side, toward the middle of the bed. On the pillow by his chin there's a liver-colored patch of dried blood and a larger absorbed blot of darkened cotton where he's drooled in his sleep. His bottom lip looks swollen and painful.

She stands watching him. To see him sleeping on this bed again is to see a part of herself that's never quite woken up. A wave of feeling for that young woman moves her. A part of her is animal, too; neither of them is static. Under his eyelids and rough stubbled cheeks now, the pale, surprisingly hairless skin at his wrists, the powerful twitching shoulders, Pyrrhic battles are still being fought: even in repose, his muscles quiver and rage at invisible enemies, who will never be beaten.

The difference, she is starting to believe despite her instincts, is that he's finally learning to live with his hands gripping only his own throat. The only person he dreams of hurting now is himself.

With delicate, almost loving concentration, she unlaces his shoes and pulls them off. She covers him from the waist down with the quilt sewn in the Crown of Thorns pattern that's come down from her mother's mother. Like a baby blanket obsessively clutched for too many years, it has turned ragged at the edges and is slowly disintegrating. She covers him with it anyway. And then she turns off the lights and leaves him to sleep in the once familiar darkness.

DWIGHT

I WAKE IN MY MARRIAGE BED. It's deep night or early morning and I find a lamp on the bedside table and switch it on. A quilt is draped across my legs. My shoes have been removed. My mouth aches, and the lower half of my jaw. I turn my head and see an ugly rust-colored smudge where my cut lip's been pressing against the white pillow while I've been sleeping.

Ruth, though not physically present, is all over this room: her needlepoint throw draped over a chair; her TV on a mahogany chest of drawers come down to her from her Aunt Marlene; her ivory bra hanging on the closet doorknob; her shoes with the heels worn down along the inside edge; her silver tray holding two small bottles of lavender water.

Eau-de-vie, I remember calling it once, till Ruth

shook her head and with a sly grin said, "I think that's the liqueur you're talking about."

We conceived Sam here. His bassinet stood in the corner by the window so he could watch the stars twinkling up in the blue-black sky if he felt the urge to see other worlds, which he often did. He slept and dreamed under an airplane mobile I put together from a kit.

After a while, I shuffle into the bathroom. Where, hours after the fact, the air still smells of Ruth's bubble bath—like her, bracing rather than flowery. The scent of a morning walk along a Cape beach in summer, the tide out and the seaweed left to dry on the yellow sand, the sand yellow like my wife's and son's hair, on a Fourth of July weekend of the last perfect year, the three of us shot from behind in an endless, vanishing wide shot.

I sit on the edge of the bathtub, breathing it all in. Then, like the animal I am, I get up and stand for a minute pissing into the toilet. And go to the sink and stare into the bright clear mirror at my fifty-year-old face. The lower lip fat now with blood, a small blue star blooming in its corner.

EMMA

BACK HOME, alone in bed, the warmth of Sam's hand remains on hers. This is actual, she believes. And awake as she's ever been, with an hour or two left of the night, she begins to study the warmth under the microscope of her feeling. Gradually she twists the dial, increases the magnification. Looking at the kind of warmth it might be, its source, its conceivable longevity. What it might signify, what it might not. If there might be answers in it as well as questions. Whether it's even sexual, after all, despite her longings and his. Or whether the sexual part might in fact be more remembered than real, a kind of shared aura trailing them from the past, a reflection less of where they're headed than of where they've been.

It's morning and time for work before the truth comes down on her in all its sadness and possibility: that she loves Sam Arno not, as she has long assumed, with the full heat of her passion but instead like a brother. And it's for this that she knows she will forgive him anything.

SAM

IT'S THE WALL OF HIS ROOM he sees when he opens his eyes in the morning, but it's not the wall he feels.

He doesn't move. He lies there, staring at the wall, an odd, probing warmth on his back.

In the dream, what there was of it, his mother's house was a different color, dark green. No reason. There was a rocking chair on the porch. He cannot in fact recall such a chair. But he can recall the thin dark-haired boy who sits on it, rocking slowly, just the tips of his black sneakers touching the floorboards (and only on the downward rock), his elegant, precociously musical hands resting secretively, maybe haughtily, atop the black violin case in his lap.

He walks past this boy. They do not acknowledge each other. He enters his house, climbs the stairs, and goes to his room.

The Red Sox memorabilia is gone. No, it's not the Yankees—this isn't a horror movie—it's merely nothing. Bare white walls. Another pointless incongruity. It's still not registered on him yet, the identity of the thin dark-haired boy downstairs, all four feet of him. The boy who sits rocking on the chair that was never there. The boy who—he can hear it now, rising from the porch and entering his open window—is humming to himself, yes humming, in a soft high voice, as if to unburden himself of his life, and at the same time to tell the world a story: the voice burnished as in church, practiced and choral, with something like a soul in it.

It's the music Sam can't get rid of. That keeps coming back to him like a curse, here and here and here and here, whenever it feels like it. As if he was the one who'd gone and killed everything.

DWIGHT

IT WAS A CLEAR NIGHT, but it's a gray morning. What I can see of it, anyway, pressing dully around the drawn shades in Sam's bedroom.

I've turned his desk chair around so I can sit observing the twin bed, cornered against two walls, where he lies facing away from me on his side, one knee raised almost to his chest as if he's hurdling some obstacle in his sleep. On the floor, his clothes are dropped in no special order. I notice some caked dirt on his boots and the knees of his jeans—he was out in a field somewhere, I guess, or down by the river.

I sit watching him, the throaty, priestlike calls of mourning doves coming in through the partially open window.

At some point, he rolls over and blinks at me. He doesn't seem surprised by my presence, and I have the vague feeling that he's been awake for a while already, just lying there, hiding in plain sight. We stare at each other, until I turn my visible attention to the computer sitting on his desk, as if it has something important to tell me. Next to it is a speckled school-composition notebook, and near that, on the floor, Sam's baseball glove, an expensive Mizuno, with a fresh white ball still caught in the webbing, an illegible autograph scrawled on the ball's exposed face, between the sewn red seams.

Across the room, the door to his closet stands open. Up on the top shelf, jutting out starkly amid a riot of old clothes and sports equipment, is a trumpet case of hard black plastic.

"Ever play the horn anymore?"

He shakes his head. Slowly he raises himself to a sitting position and leans back against the tongue-in-groove wall: I can see the tic-tac-toe ridges in his abdominals smooth out as the angle of his torso widens. There is a tear at the left hip of his blue boxer shorts. His muscled chest is practically hairless, and the bruises he had when he arrived at my house in California have faded away to nothing.

"I wasn't any good," he says, after a while.

"You always sounded pretty good to me."

"You probably weren't the best judge."

"No," I agree.

We fall silent. Sam begins picking at the bedspread with his long fingers. And merely to do something and maybe, against tall odds, to lighten the general atmosphere, I get up and move to the window and raise the white shade. And, unexpectedly, the subway-car noise of the roller going up, its pins and ball bearings, brings back to me with a painful stuttering strangeness my mother in her last days. Sad decent woman, who every morning during the housebound months she was dying of stomach cancer used to raise her bedroom shade so that she could watch me leaving for school. She never failed to wave to me as I climbed on the yellow bus, even when my old man screamed at her to get back in her sickbed.

The day is brightening. The lawn needs mowing and the doves have gone away. I turn and look back at my son, who's looking down at his hands.

"There's nothing you can't ask me, Sam."

He sits staring at his hands, a small swab of muscle pulsing in his jaw.

"Do you dream about him?"

"Yes."

"His family?"

"All of them," I say.

"Then what? What do you do then?"

"What I can. I get up and go to work."

He looks up at me. "Do you hate yourself?"

My mouth is dry. Carefully, I sit on the edge of his bed.

"Some days. Other days are better."

He nods as if he understands, which makes me sadder than anything he could have said.

He is my son. He's within reach now. Soon, I think, I will try to touch him, but not just yet.

RUTH

SHE STANDS AT THE KITCHEN SINK finishing
last night's dishes, her back to the windows that
look out over the front yard. It was a point of
contention with the house when they bought it all
those years ago: how it seemed ungenerous, and
maybe even cruel, to deprive the one person who
was to spend a good portion of her life cooking
meals and washing up for the family of a
reasonably pretty view while she worked. After
months of grudging, Dwight gave in and said that
as soon as they had the money they'd redesign the
kitchen, turn the sink around, make it however
she wanted. The money eventually came, but,
despite numerous promises, the new kitchen
never materialized. She watched Dwight build
himself a fancy workroom in the basement and
buy loads of junior sports equipment for Sam,
who wasn't yet even three feet tall. She saw the
Newmans next door do a gut renovation,
complete with portable wine cellar and the latest
German appliances. Which was okay; envy
wasn't her particular sin. It was just that some
days, living in the "country," as they called it, she
missed nature the way she missed her mother.
One eventually grew tired of brown backsplash
tiles palimpsested with 1990s marinara sauce.
She wanted to be able to look up one day—

simply raise her head—and see that the world was larger and more inviting than her house kept telling her it was.

The last pot done, she sets it on the dish rack and turns off the water.

She hears it then, behind her and outside: what she has not heard here, at home, in a very long time. It takes her a few moments to understand.

Norris had no gift for it. He didn't like having objects thrown at him. The only ball he ever related to was tiny and never moved unless he himself decided to strike it.

She turns and looks out the window at the lawn.

She sees the white baseball, hard-looking in the morning light, speeding through the clear air toward her son.

She sees her son, as calmly as if he's considering an itch under his chin, tip his glove like a casual salute and envelop the ball, make it disappear. He doesn't even glance at it; he knows it's there. He reaches down—a magician now—and plucks his trusted rabbit back into the light; he grips it and unlimbers himself and hurls the object back whence it came.

She sees the ball speeding backward in time.

She sees his father, standing on the other side of the lawn, catch it without struggle or regret.

PENNY

STIRRING A POT of miso soup Wednesday evening, she notices, to the right of the stove, the corner of a yellow scrap of paper poking out from underneath the blender. She pulls at it with her fingernail, and a Post-it emerges. Written there, in Ali's cramped print, are the words "Dwight called."

The message is stained with some sort of cooking oil and decorated with juvenile doodles in purple ink; it is not even close to fresh.

There is nothing left on the answering machine but this morning's automated message from GEICO, informing Penny that her quarterly car-insurance premium is coming due, and suggesting online payment as the most convenient and secure method. Whatever Dwight had to say to her has been erased by her daughter.

She slams her hand into the machine, so hard that the thing flips over twice, and the small plastic hatch to the battery compartment pops off. She stares at this minor wreckage as at another's handiwork. She thinks of marching to her daughter's room and forcibly extracting her face from the screen of her desires and demanding to know exactly, *exactly,* the message that was left by a man who may, or may not, be asking for some kind of comfort.

Reaching for her purse on the counter, she shouts to Ali that she's going out.

There is no response.

A light shines from above Dwight's front door, reaching to the small patch of grass; a precautionary measure in his absence, it would seem, meant to deter criminals. An example of grim psychological conditioning, Penny speculates to herself, or maybe just good practical sense.

And sitting in her car parked on Hacienda Street, reading his house as though it's a poem in disguise, Penny attempts now, in desperate earnest, to take a hard look at her own psychological conditioning, such as it has been. The glittering false premise of her many years of adult training: the insistent sifting for patterns and symbols that can be broken down into constituent theories, to be coolly sorted and weighed for meaning in the clinical laboratories of the mind.

To somehow find a way, *his* way, to throw away all that. To call it what it is. To be able to say, tonight, simply because she needs it to be so, that maybe this light shining in the darkness is just that—a light in the darkness—and enough to live by.

SAM

HE EXCUSES HIMSELF precipitously from dinner. His parents are sitting on either side of him, one at each end of the table, and when he stands and picks up his plate of half-eaten food both sets of eyes, for their own reasons, grow unnerved and meaningful: *You're going to leave us here, together? You must be kidding. . . .*

Outside, in fast-lowering dusk, he walks the front yard. It is two days since he's been off the property.

You reach a stage where you don't want to be seen anymore, by anyone. . . .

Above the trees, in its rightful place, the evening star is an all-seeing eye hammered into the world's bruise.

And under his feet now, in the corner of the yard, a good-sized rectangle of lawn—about ten feet by five feet—shows a persistent degradation of growth: a worn green carpet striated with streaks of brown dirt.

On this area over countless years his stepfather spread thousands of dollars' worth of fertilizer and specialized lawn products. For it turned out to be beyond Norris's imagination to accept that there are some places whose troubled history cannot be cured by tonics and potions and other people's seed. His grass-growing failure he took personally—it was almost funny—never understanding how the problem was never his to begin with.

A jungle gym had been here once, put together by Sam's true father. Sam retains blurred, fragmented memories of playing on its tilted swing and rickety slide, under sunshine that may or may not have existed.

And then, at some still unformed age, he has no idea why, he simply refused to go near it anymore. And that part of his childhood was over.

The contraption remained, a monument to inept mechanical love and other, more complicated secrets, until the day his father angrily took it apart. Piece by unhappy piece, the jungle gym was transported to the junkyard.

Which was when his father, showing an optimism singular in his history, began an interminable wait for the lawn to repair itself, to grow full and thick again, in this place as in others.

A wait that has outlasted them all.

On this very spot, half night-shaded dirt and half meager grass underfoot, Sam is standing when his phone rings in his pocket. Out of an otherwise quiet evening, the repeated, vibrating cacophony seems to originate deep in his own chest: his heart rattles in its scaffolding, and his knees tremble.

"Are you sitting down, son?"

"No, Mr. Cutter."

"Well, I am, son. I'm sitting down, and I'm an old pro in the game of life. So my advice to you right now is to go find yourself a good, sturdy chair to sit down on, and to listen damn carefully to what it is I have to tell you."

EMMA

THURSDAY MORNING, she says goodbye to her mother—who believes her to be going to meet an illustrious professor about a possible research position for the fall—gets into her car, and drives up Pine Creek Road. But instead of taking the shortcut for New Haven she continues to the outskirts of Wyndham Falls, where she parks in an unreserved spot behind the post office. From there she walks east a hundred yards along the edge of Route 44, stopping by the 35-mph speed-limit sign on which someone has scrawled the trenchant words WHY NOT ME? with an indelible marker.

A not unreasonable question, it seems to her as she waits beneath it for her ride—if, say, like the hooker standing outside heaven's gate in the tired old joke, you're only granted one question to get what you always thought you wanted. It dresses up nice, existentially, and is suitable for just about any occasion.

. . .

Several minutes later, a white rental car pulls over in front of her. Sam is behind the wheel, and she climbs in beside him.

"They moved Nic Bellic out of intensive care last night."

She turns and studies him. Handsome from the side, as he is from the front. The flickering car-window light on him today like the inside of a grotto. So here it is: she's been waiting for the explanation, why he called her near midnight, waking her up, to inquire in an offhand voice, which she immediately X-rayed, whether she might be able to change whatever plans she had and go to Hartford with him in the morning. And, seeing through that voice, she said she would. For which agreement, first thing this morning, she made the requisite arrangements; nothing being simple in this land. Preparations required, fractional white lies.

"Does that mean he's going to be okay?"

"It will take him a while to recover. But 'no lasting effects anticipated.' According to my lawyer."

"Sam, that's amazing."

He doesn't look amazed, however, or even relieved, his jaw set and his gaze unswerving, as they motor grimly on toward Hartford and around them, all along this two-lane country highway, the pastoral landscape gradually sheds every last atom of its pastoral nature.

They drive by a wholesale furniture outlet with a GOING OUT OF BUSINESS sign; and a Dairy Queen; and an Italian sub shop. Two gas stations. The pet store where her father took her one day to buy fish. She remembers how the pimpled young man ran his tiny feminine net through the tank, coming up with her first guppies. He blew air into the clear plastic bag before knotting it. And all the way home she worried about the fish, trapped inside with that strange unwanted breath, which was not like or of them.

Sam slows down; there's traffic bunching ahead.

"My lawyer told me not to go to the hospital again."

"Why?"

"Because—his words—at this point it's incumbent on me as someone who's still a potential defendant in a potential criminal proceeding to maintain total separation from the potential plaintiff. That even so much as a semblance of a record or pattern of personal involvement with said potential plaintiff must be avoided at all costs, because it could leave some kind of motivational trace that a jury could later interpret with a negative bias."

"That's one of the most hateful things I've ever heard."

He shakes his head to himself.

"Well," she says, "we're here anyway."

They drive on. Her left hand on the armrest, inches from him. He drives as though on an extraordinarily long trip, with continents still ahead of him. He drives as if he has no company in the world, including himself. If she were to touch him now, she thinks, it would simply be to bestow faith, or what she knows of it, to show him something good about himself, something like the news he's just gotten.

"It means a lot to me you came," he says, after a long silence.

"So what did you tell him? Your asshole lawyer."

"I thanked him for calling. And then I told him he can go fuck himself."

She laughs out loud—a sudden joyousness, like dancing.

He smiles at her then. Like a gold coin buried under the sand that you gave up looking for so long ago you can no longer remember where or when.

The smile she hasn't seen since they were children.

SAM

HE KNOCKS SOFTLY on the open door and tips his body inside: a shared room, divided halfway across its length by a hanging curtain pulled almost to the far wall. Up front, a small man with a cap of sparse white hair lies on a forty-five-degree bed watching TV. The volume is off and the screen shows a news anchor mouthing above a stock ticker.

The old man turns his head in stages: olive-pit irises planted in drought-ridden soil, hoary stubble bristling over sunken cheeks, a grizzled tuft of chest hair bursting the hospital gown's declining neckline. An odor of forgotten surrender permeates the room: potatoes going to rot in a dank basement.

A crooked finger directs him toward the curtain.

A murmur of thanks, and he crosses the foot of the bed, slips around the edge of the curtain. Then one more step, before he stops.

On a chair beside the bed a fiftyish woman with a sharp nose and blunted Slav cheekbones sits vigil over her sleeping son, on whose still gaunt face lifelike signs have sprung up like petals out of ash: full, pinkish lips, eyelids no longer the color of gray Plasticine. An IV remains, but the breathing and feeding tubes are gone.

And Sam stares confounded: the soul-sapping paradox by which a patient—no, victim—miraculously beginning to live again, may appear more like a ghost than when he was dying.

Meanwhile, the woman glares back. Which he cannot contend with, so physically complete is her authority over her dominion. Her plain brown dress—too heavy for the season—and thick-soled brown shoes remind him of the Portuguese woman in Winsted who used to sell his mother bluefish at cost. A dark-red head scarf lumpily contains her graying dark hair. On her lap she holds a canary-yellow blouse and a spool of yellow thread.

Licking his dry lips, he quietly announces himself:

"Mrs. Bellic, I'm Sam Arno."

Simply from this he's drained. In return she remains mute, as immovable as a frieze in a ruined church.

"Mrs. Bellic, I'm very sorry."

Suddenly, she is standing, blouse and thread dumped on the floor. . . .

"Ma."

They both turn as if called: her son, awake in the hospital bed.

The mother's face transformed; you could imagine her smiling, almost.

"Ma, go down the hall and get me something to drink, okay? Coke—not diet, regular. You need money?"

She shakes her head.

"Go ahead now, Ma."

A canvas sewing bag goes with her. She walks past him without a glance and around the curtain, trailing the smell of another country, cedar and dust.

Sam bends, picks up the spool of thread, the yellow blouse. He stands awkwardly, not knowing what to do with these things. All he knows is that he can't bear to leave them on the floor.

"Chair," Bellic snaps.

Sam places the things where he's told, folding the blouse as best he can, though one of the sleeves immediately falls loose.

He faces the bed with his empty hands. "I'm sorry, Nic."

"Don't call me Nic. You don't fucking know me."

"You're right."

"Some mystery guy, the nurse tells me a couple days ago, sneaking around the ICU? Think I wouldn't guess who?"

He doesn't know what to say.

"So how did I look? Since you were there."

"Like you were dead."

It is just the truth he's telling. But the truth seems to cave Bellic in: his head sinks into the pillows. He looks as if he wants his mother to come back.

"Get the fuck out," he begs softly, and turns his face away until Sam leaves.

DWIGHT

IN THE UPSTAIRS HALL SHOWER, the soap mostly rinsed off, I hear my phone ringing. I step out, dripping, and answer.

"Where the hell you at?" the voice starts in.

"Tony . . . Hey."

"Called your house yesterday to see if you wanted to play some golf. Jorge was up. Could've had us a game."

"I'm in Connecticut."

"Still? When you coming back?"

"Don't know yet."

"How's your kid doing, anyway?"

I'm standing by the bathroom window. Initially the heat from my shower left the panes steamed white, but while I've been talking to Tony the thin, obscuring film has evaporated off the glass, providing a clear view down to the driveway, where a pale-blue Honda minivan has just pulled in. The driver's door opens and a balding, gangly man in a seersucker sport coat and chinos gets out, pausing to tug his yellow socks taut over his asparagus calves.

"Christ. It's fucking Norris."

"Who?"

"My ex's ex."

"That's you," Tony points out.

"Not me, the other guy. He sells insurance."

"Yeah? His rates any good?"

"Tony, look, I gotta go."

"Monday back at the store, right?"

"If I can."

"Monday!"

I click off. The water has dried on my body, leaving behind an invisible chill. Norris is in the house: I can sense his insinuating, low-wattage ambience like a cheap scented candle. I open the bathroom door and hear Ruth's voice drifting up the stairs, telling him that Sam's gone out for the day but she'll be sure to let him know about the visit.

I tiptoe out to the top of the staircase to hear their conversation better.

"I bet you didn't even give him my message."

"I told him you wanted to see him," Ruth replies calmly. "I gave him your new number."

"Did he say he'd call me?"

"No."

"I've got something important to tell him."

"What is it?"

"I'd rather tell him myself, if you don't mind."

Creeping on the balls of my feet, I descend a few steps, bending low enough to be able to safely observe the situation through the scrim of the upper balusters.

Down in the front hall, I'm satisfied to see that Norris has managed to get only one leg inside the house. Ruth, looking pretty and firm in a plain navy shift dress, stands before him with her arms crossed over her chest—a Pop Warner blocking position that I remember well from the days of our bliss.

Norris gives a loud, emotional sniff. "Wanda and I are getting married."

"So I've heard." Ruth's tone is matter-of-fact. "Congratulations, Norris. I'm happy for you."

"Thank you." He can't hide the disappointment on his face. "I'd like Sam to be in the wedding."

Ruth studies him.

"Having him there would feel right," Norris adds.

My lower back's aching from crouching so low. Aiming for a more comfortable vantage point, I take another step down. My foot lands on a loose board, the wood lets out a loud crack under my weight—and I watch Norris's head quick-pivot in my direction and his mouth pop open like a human PEZ dispenser.

Ruth is gawking at me, too, and not in an admiring way. "Jesus, Dwight. Get some clothes on, will you?"

I rise to my full height and come down a few more steps.

"Norris," I greet him.

Mortally dumbfounded, he looks at Ruth, whose response is to rub a hand over her face and contemplate the floor, disowning both of us. This goes on for a while, till Norris clears his throat and rallies.

"Dwight . . . Well, this is a surprise."

"I'm here to see my son," I say, a little defensively.

"You mean Sam?"

"That's right, Norris. My son."

"That's interesting, Dwight. I mean I have to say, it's been a while, hasn't it?"

"You know it has. And you know why, too."

"I do know, Dwight, I do," Norris says amiably. "Or at least part of it. I guess what I'm a little confused about—forgive me for prying—is why a visit now. All of a sudden, I mean, after a whole decade without so much as a stopover."

"He needs me."

"Needs you. Hmm." Norris's mouth draws a line harder than I thought possible in him, and he takes another step into the house. "Okay, I guess we can have a gentleman's agreement on that one. But just tell me this, Dwight, while we're at it: Where've you been when Sam really needed a father? Where've you been all these years, Dwight? That's kind of the million-dollar question, wouldn't you say?"

I stand looking at him. The chill that briefly came over me upstairs, then abated while I was watching and lazily mocking him in my thoughts, now returns in force: I almost shiver.

But it's nothing, just myself.

Norris, meanwhile, seems to loom more manly and resolute in the doorway of the house he was

305

so unceremoniously kicked out of not so long ago; he appears, for maybe the first time in his personal history, like a man in sober possession of himself. All his life his goofy bonhomie and ineffectual waffling have been his hallmark and chrysalis, but that's visibly gone now. It's as if, somehow, the cumulative personal failings of our broken little circle—the countless ways, independently and together, that we're doomed to continue to get it wrong—have finally killed off the innocent in him.

I listen to him drive away. Then I sit down on the stairs where I am. Hard thoughts have sprung upon me, and questions I can't answer.

RUTH

SHE FEELS ALMOST PROUD of Norris for his little speech—and, of course, is relieved that he's gone.

Turning, she finds Dwight sitting on the stairs. With his little towel skirt, his big shamed head and primitive naked chest, he might be the deposed king of some Pacific atoll. But the picture doesn't incite or amuse her as it might once have. Actually, he has his face in his hands and looks rather sad.

Not her problem, she tells herself firmly, deciding to go to her room. She'll pass the time as calmly as possible until Sam's return from the hospital. Confirmation is what she needs, as soon as possible, and about twenty fingers and toes to cross while she's waiting. She doesn't have time to worry about Dwight. She walks toward the stairs.

"Excuse me."

She attempts to step around him. He makes no effort to move, however, his wide body blocking her path. Inadvertently, her right leg bumps his right shoulder. Which she should ignore, obviously, just continue on as if nothing's happened. . . .

But for some reason—number one on the List of Inexplicables—she stops and meets his gaze.

Meanwhile, his bare shoulder, still damp from the shower, as though guided by its own circuitry, has coerced the hem of her dress from her knee up to the middle of her thigh. She can't fathom whether the sudden heat she feels at the point of contact is coming from his skin or hers; only that, after so many years, it shocks her down to her feet, robbing her of the power to keep climbing. The one thing she can think to do is remain where she is, leaning into their combined heat with everything she has, trying, in fact, to deepen the seal between them and create more heat, this red flame sparked out of nothing, out of two inanimate nodes, cool and harmless on their own but incendiary when pressed together.

"What do you think you're doing?" she breathes, as though insulted.

His eyes, for the first time in all the years she's known him, appear boyishly stunned.

Not me, they say. *You.*

She knows this is so, but has no wish to stop herself. Her hand reaches out and grips the back of his neck. Then she leans down and kisses him hard on the mouth.

DWIGHT

SHE UNSTRADDLES ME. I can smell the sex we've just had, and under it the softer, less complicated lavender water she's wearing, now transferred to me. Her rumpled dress is hiked up to her waist and she's tugging at the hem to try to cover herself. Already not looking at me, her eyes darting around the room.

"Try the stairs," I suggest, meaning her underwear, which I can tell she's hunting for. I make an effort to keep my voice unassuming, just the helpful facts. But this does not seem to be what comes out. She frowns, her gaze suddenly stunned with regret, and slips out of the bedroom.

When she returns a few minutes later, her dress smoothed back down to her knees, she's apparently made the decision to meet my eye in the manner of kindergarten teachers and white-collar prisoners. The hitch in the plan is that I'm still lying naked in her bed, half covered by the sheet.

"I have no idea how that just happened," she begins in a voice of assertive calm. "And neither do you."

"I think you mean why," I reply with a lightness I don't feel. "The how part would seem pretty cut-and-dried."

"Is that supposed to be funny? That wasn't us, Dwight. It was two other people. And if you try to tell me it was us I'll have to deny it to your face."

"It was me," I say simply.

Ruth stares at me. "It was a mistake, obviously. One of those kamikaze things people do during wars just to prove they're alive."

"We're alive, all right. I can verify that. But there's also no law that says we've got to talk about any of it. We could just go on with the day and see how it feels later. That's my recommendation."

"Your life philosophy in a nutshell."

"If you think it'll make you feel better to paint a target on my chest, go ahead. Fire away."

She falls silent. Shaking her head to herself like an explorer who, after years of hacking through malaria-infested jungle and scaling craggy peaks, has suddenly discovered that the New World is really just the Old World in new clothes (or no clothes at all).

Then she comes closer. I watch her approach. She lies down next to me on the bed, dressed in her clothes, on top of the sheet, and after a while she takes my hand where it rests between us and holds it in both of hers.

"I won't say I've missed you, because technically it's not true. But I guess this feels okay. For today."

She lays her head on my chest, and I feel the weight of her drifting down into me, becoming my weight; until, finally, I begin to float.

She is gone when I wake. The bed empty even with me in it, the room. I call her name, but there's no answer. Naked, I go down to the den and put on some clothes. Then, needing to occupy myself, I take the stairs to the basement.

Down there, a lifetime earlier, I built a home workshop fitted out with a bench-top table saw with a ten-inch carbide-tipped blade, a professional power sander, and a double-tined wall rack full of Craftsman tools to make your mouth water. I put together the setup on weekend days over the course of months. It was expensive and time-consuming, my hobby and my goal. And then it was finished, and I used it at most a dozen times, all except once for meaningless things, tiny handyman jobs, none of the big artisanal projects I thought I'd attempt—no hand-turned tables or toboggans or birch-bark canoes made the old Indian way, nothing that would ever last in the world or in memory. And then my habitation in this house came to a premature, though deserved, end.

And, with the entire life system needing emergency repair, there seemed no point in taking my tools with me to continue my pursuit of small-time fixes elsewhere. What's a little tear in a sleeve when the coat itself needs replacing? Why stop the faucet drip when you're up to your knees in floodwater? Who gives a shit about a workroom when the house has burned to the ground? And then eventually, deep in a lockdown hole, say, you start to think—always a mistake—that all those beautiful American tools maybe never really existed in the first place, nor the famed blueprints toward which they were going to be put so nobly to service; that there never was going to be any table or toboggan or birch-bark canoe, that it was all just an excuse masquerading as a dream, an empty reason not to spend your weekend hours with your wife and son while you had the chance, a dead-end escape hatch down the stairs, a basement in your head.

At the sound of footsteps, I turn. Ruth is standing halfway down the basement stairs. Up behind her the door to the rest of the house is open, daylight from unseen windows reaching down over her shoulders and head, singling her out in the otherwise fluorescent glare. I have a block of sandpaper in my hand, and I set it on the bench.

"Sorry about the saw noise."

"I didn't hear it. I went for a long walk."

"Where'd you go?"

"Nowhere special." She's clasping her hands, looking at me from a slight angle. "What're you doing?"

Instead of answering, I step aside so that she can see the birdhouse I've almost finished making. The kind of basic home project taught in every shop class in every grade school in America. Seventeen-odd years ago, Sam and I made one—or, rather, I made one and Sam passed the hours handing me tools, watching and talking and growing bored and drifting off and coming back and standing by my leg, right here, while I cut and nailed and sanded and stained. And when we were done we wrapped the birdhouse in brown butcher paper tied with rough twine, and gave it to Ruth for Mother's Day.

"Oh," Ruth says. "Look at that."

I found the spare wood in the boiler room, where I left it long ago. The sanding is almost complete.

If I'm still in this house by evening, I think, I will stain the birdhouse and nail it to a tree in the backyard, beside the older one ruined by weather.

SAM

IT IS LATE AFTERNOON by the time he pulls into the driveway beside his mother's car. To his consternation his parents are sitting out front on the porch steps with drinks in their hands. They are not next to each other—a couple of feet of space separates them—but their drinks appear the same, made by the same hand—rum and tonics, he guesses from the golden-brown liquid in the glasses and the visible wedges of lime—and their postures are ominously at ease, languorous almost, which gives the contradictory impression of a certain jerry-rigged unity, some new amorphous history shifting beneath his feet, and for a long minute he remains in the car, as if protected, watching them through the windshield, unsure after all that's happened that he can face the end of the day.

His father sets his drink on the porch. They are watching him, too, waiting for him to come out.

He closes the car door, and out on the lawn a cardinal flares like a struck match. There's a rabbit frozen in green quicksand by the sight of him—can't go forward, can't go back. And he understands. Feels it all too much, can no longer defend the position; whatever armor he had in that department is gone. He is skinless. He takes a few more steps. The sun is going down.

His mother smiles anxiously. His father shakes his head as if to ward off disbelief.

Because he suddenly understands that it is meant for him, Sam sits down in the space between his parents.

A long moment passes: the three of them, sitting in a row, looking out at the yard.

Then he feels his father's arm around his shoulders. No more than that. And he is undone.

DWIGHT

HE IS SOBBING. He falls forward as if trying to wrench himself free of his own body. His head comes onto my lap and I hold him there on the porch. I hold him a long time. He is my child, his pain pouring into me.

PART FOUR

RUTH

THE APPOINTMENT HAS BEEN ON HER calendar for weeks: *Friday, June 2nd, 11:30 A.M., Dr. Orenstein.*

After this they'll come regularly, every three months, for the next five years, for the rest of her life. But first you have to get there. This kind old doctor who lost his wife to the very thing he's trying to help her beat back, he will have to lay his hands on her, feeling for dark stars in her body. She will have to peel back her robe and submit herself to the machine. X-rays will see inside her as no human eyes can. *Lie still, my heart, lie still.* The rest is fate. Or just dumb luck. You bare yourself and say, *Do your best, please; see what you can find.* And if they find nothing you will live to come again. And if the constellations return, dark as dark matter, soon enough they will stop looking. And that will be the end.

To live, then, means continually opening her most hidden self up to clinical scrutiny. No other way to do it:

Put your hands on me. Turn me inside out. Make your accounting. And then, either way, let me go free.

She remembers the day she made the appointment, studying her date book at the reception desk of the Breast Center on the first floor of Smilow Cancer Hospital. She picked a Friday because she thought it more likely that Sam, whose post-graduation plans were still unclear, might be around to accompany her. She chose late morning because she imagined, hopefully, that if he was home he'd want to sleep late as usual.

Calling up from the front hall now, she asks if he's ready.

He appears at once at the top of the stairs. If she wasn't already anxious about what lies ahead, his alacrity—and the fact that he's shaved for her sake—would be enough to tip her over the edge. It's as though a skull and crossbones floats above her.

Instead, she smiles at him, which immediately improves her spirits.

At that moment, Dwight emerges from the den. He's shaved, too. He hovers there nervously, not quite looking at her.

Finally, just to calm everybody down, she says flatly, "For God's sake, it's only a checkup."

DWIGHT

IF YOU LIVE ALONE, you probably spend less time in waiting rooms than most people. This could be, of course, because you have fewer people, maybe no one, to wait for. You are your own stoic messenger, delivering only to your home address: whatever the news, you will bear it yourself.

And then, one day, you will enter an exam room where a highly trained medical specialist will tell you a story based on a chart or a picture. One story, with a couple of possible endings, none of them necessarily what you'd choose to write on your own. But that's how it is. You will thank the man and get dressed. You will reenter the waiting room, this time from the opposite side. And the room will be populated by strangers, every one of them waiting for someone who isn't you.

Compare this, for a moment, with today: this spider's web of transitive love that holds you fast.

Someone much dearer to you than yourself has taken her place inside the exam room and been strapped into a machine. The results are pending; they always will be. And it's you stuck outside, waiting among last month's magazines, neurologically soothing artworks, and the odd plastic plant, for her to come out and tell you the story.

"Clean," Ruth says. "He said I was clean."

She is smiling, facing us in the waiting room. Slowly, she puffs out her cheeks and expels the air.

• • •

Approaching her car in the cancer hospital's parking facility, she holds the keys out to me.

I get in behind the wheel, Ruth takes the passenger seat, and Sam gets in back.

I start the car and ease us to the gate.

My foot is gentle on the gas at first. We make our way out of New Haven, a city I've always hated till today, northward to Route 8.

It is just the three of us, riding home: as if it's a real place, after all.

Our beleaguered state of Connecticut running past—uncommon today, and beautiful.

EMMA

FRIDAY AFTERNOON, she drops her mother at Sue Foley's and continues on to the tree nursery. A good hour spent picking out shrubs on her mom's shopping list—India hawthorn, Chinese witch hazel, black chokeberry, summer sweet, Burkwood viburnum—then buying and loading six thirty-pound bags of mulch into the car, then stopping at the garden-supply store to replace a lost trowel. By the time she starts back to the Foleys' it's a little past four. She drives with the windows open, the wind in her hair, the radio on loud.

The song ends just as she arrives. She gets out of the car and stands leaning against the warm ticking hood, looking over the property.

The L-shaped, cedar-shingled house sheltered from the road by old-growth privet. The driveway framed by evergreens, some sick and some healthy, the air smelling of pine sap and turned soil and the roses climbing the front of the house, a riot of all the wrong colors. On one side a small overgrown pond, its surface simmering with dragonflies. On the other, a sloping irregular field where piles of metal pillars and a haystack of white tarp lie ready to be assembled into a wedding tent.

"Hope you haven't been waiting long."

Her mother, standing on the front steps, a pair of gardening gloves folded in one hand, her face shaded by a straw hat.

"Just a couple of minutes."

"How'd the errands go?"

"Okay, but they didn't have the same kind of trowel; I had to get a different one."

"I'm sure it's fine." Her mother slides onto the passenger seat. Around her mouth some buoyant twitchiness, Emma notices, like a baby bird about to leap from a branch for a first risky flight.

She starts the car and pulls out onto the road. The radio off, but the Fray's "How to Save a Life" still haunting her head:

> *And I would have stayed up with you*
> *   all night*
> *Had I known how to save a life*

"I got the job," her mother says.

She glances over. The smile out in the open now, cut loose, the little bird bravely, improbably aloft.

"They're willing to go all in. We'll start as soon as the wedding's over."

"Mom, that's great. How's the money?"

"Decent. Good enough, anyway." She pauses. "I might just be ready to do some serious work again."

Emma drives on. End of the week: long hours of labor behind them, dirt under their nails. Her mother no longer actively smiling but looking ahead with level chin and a gaze softer by the minute.

And this to see: atop a perfect red barn a sailboat weather vane pointing true north; a chestnut mare and her foal staring over a split-rail fence; a man with a wheelbarrow planting forsythia.

She breathes in deep, the country in her lungs. She drives by Pine Creek Road and keeps going.

"Em, you just missed the road."

"We're not going home yet."

"What do you mean?"

"Supermarket," she explains.

"But we've got plenty of food."

"Not this kind of food, Mom. This is special. Tonight we're going to celebrate."

DWIGHT

WE WALK THE AISLES of the Stop & Shop together. Friday late afternoon, in the Northwest Corner. All the neighbors out, known and unknown, heading home from work, stocking up for the weekend.

Sam wheels our cart loaded with three New York strip steaks, a sack of mashing potatoes, bunches of herbs to rub over the meat, a bag of prewashed lettuce, a ready-to-heat apple pie, and a tub of vanilla ice cream. A dinner to celebrate Ruth's good health. Ruth to Sam's left, intently scanning the shelves for other treats to add to the evening's haul. I watch her drop back and pick out a bottle of aged balsamic vinegar, then walk ahead and toss it into the cart.

Her step appears light and dancing to me. She looks hungry again, you'd say, as if the meal to come might just turn out to be the pleasure she doesn't know she's waiting for. And the sight of her like this makes you want to eat that meal with her, whatever it's going to be. To sit down at the table with her and pay serious attention, not to miss it.

Muzak's playing cloyingly over invisible speakers, some little appetizer medley of Americana. The tune at present is "Take Me Out to the Ball Game"—neither of whose creators, I recall reading once in an in-flight magazine, ever went to an actual ballgame before writing the song. Theirs was the mythic, not the particular, game; certainly not the game at which, in the bottom of the third inning one Sunday afternoon at Fenway in the spring of his fifth year, my son magically caught his first foul ball.

Still, hearing the tune wherever you happen to be, even in a supermarket, you know that summer has to be close. That it isn't far away. That spring is just the bridge you walk over in your sleep to reach this place where the song's playing. Soon, any day now, the barbecues will all be going, and you'll be able to talk baseball with anyone you meet.

I am trying to be in the moment, not to make plans. There's no backward and no forward, no day other than this. You fill your cart as you go, and that's that.

I have never been any good at this.

Clean. He said I was clean.

The heart can hardly hold it all.

Sam and the cart reach the end of the aisle. Ruth's right beside him. I see them start the hairpin turn to the right, to pass along to the next aisle—frozen foods, I guess it is—and then, as if they've run smack into a wall, they simply stop where they are.

SAM

HE WATCHES HER FACE CRUMPLE. Josh Learner's mother. Then she turns and runs. Back of the supermarket and the aisle long as a bowling lane and down its bright catwalk spine other women, moms lost in ruminations on fish-stick brands and ice-cream prices, their shopping carts thoughtlessly parked on the diagonal, horizontal, some of the rides with small kids dangling off the rear fenders, a carnage of traffic and road obstacles blocking passage, making escape that much more difficult or impossible. She runs it anyway. He's never seen the like, elegant woman in a kind of jerking sprint, her shoulders shaking as she goes, her left arm raised to her face as if she's just been shot in the forehead. And people, every last one of them, stop and stare. Fucking town. Not the house on fire but the mother inside, burning alive.

She reaches the exit and disappears through the automatic doors, gone into daylight.

Left behind, her daughter lowers her head.

Long seconds tick by.

All the life gone from his father's face.

Years from now, it is these breath-held moments he will remember most sharply: the interstice between what he knows of the world and what he will do; the getting ready.

He is tired to death of having no comfort to give to those who truly need it.

"Emma."

She looks at him.

He walks up to her. He puts his hands on her shoulders and his cheek next to hers.

"Go after her," he says.

And she does.

EMMA

THROUGH THE KITCHEN WINDOW, in the gathering dusk, Emma can see her mother on her knees in the garden: the closed nautilus of her back, the furiously working arms, beside her a mound of pulled weeds.

She flips a switch by the sink, and outside a pool of light laps her mother's bent, praying back and brings her closer.

Her mother does not pause in her work. She keeps pulling.

Knotweed is pernicious, everyone knows, it will keep coming: you have to remain vigilant, mustn't let your guard down for even a day.

And so the garden is just a big metaphor, is that it? And yet not.

The dirt is real. The weeds. This woman with her hands in the dirt and her heart still in pain.

She is going to make her mother a cup of tea. She is going to pour her a glass of wine. She is going . . .

She goes outside: around the light thrown up by the house, the dusk is coming. It's coming. The air is sweet with flowers. The birds are thinking of rest.

All this weeding might just finally do the trick. You never know.

"Mom."

Her mother does not stop. The pulling of each weed has a sound: in this small death, one more life.

Emma gets down on her knees to help.

PENNY

AT THE END OF THE DAY, outstretched in the Eames chair, a glass of white wine beside her, her leather journal open on her lap, her fountain pen uncapped, Penny writes:

A hand searches for another hand, not knowing it is already full.

She looks up. Ali is standing in the doorway, dressed in her flowered pajamas. Her eyes are soft and needy. Her face is vulnerable once more.

Penny puts aside her pen and notebook.

Ali enters the room. She sits on a chair a few feet

from her mother, turned away from the built-in desk. She draws her knees up to her chest.

"What is it, sweetie?"

Penny leans forward, trying to get as close to her daughter as possible. Thinking that love has a memory, too. It knows how to come home.

DWIGHT

WE COOK THE FOOD, try to do it right. We sit down at the dining table. I pour wine for the three of us.

But the celebration is over before it ever really begins, and no one eats or says very much.

Ruth is gazing into the corner of the room as if she's lost something there.

Finally, she looks at our son.

"I'm just curious. How long have you been in contact with her?"

"It's not like that," he says.

"Are you seeing her?"

"No."

He falls silent.

Then: "We understand each other."

Then: "I can't explain it."

Ruth drinks the last of her wine; she folds her napkin and lays it on the table. And I do the same. As if we're normal people finishing a meal in a family restaurant. But we are not in a restaurant.

We are just ourselves in this house that has held so much and so little, everything possible and never enough.

I see Grace Learner standing under the cold light of the supermarket: staring at me in shock and hatred, terrified and enraged that I've come back to haunt her, that I will always be here, that I will never leave her in peace.

I see her boy, frozen in time. The family she lost because of me.

We think we are solid and durable, only to find that, placed under a cruel and unexpected light, we are the opposite: only our thin, permeable skin holds us intact.

Hemophiliacs walking through a forest of thorns.

I look at Ruth. It's a long look, as if we are tied to each other by a cord, which we are. What I want her to know is more than I can ever say.

"I can't stay here, Ruth. I can't do that to them. I'm going to leave in the morning."

She is silent, her face impassive. She pushes back her chair and gets slowly to her feet.

"I'm truly sorry."

Sam has been staring at his hands. Now he looks at me.

"I'm going with you."

RUTH

SHE REMEMBERS HER MOTHER saying to her once, years back: *Ruth Margaret, you must earn everything that comes to you, or it is not worth having.*

And it is sound advice—you cannot refute it. Though it's not until now, inside her echoing head, that she finally needs to demand in return:

Yes, but haven't I earned it yet?

And if so, tough girl, then what? When they're going to leave you anyway. Leave you for the other parent who's earned not half of what you have over the long haul, nor sacrificed half as much. Leave you with a glance and a single throwaway line. Leave you by yourself, when you're just getting addicted to the company. Leave you as you've always predicted you'd be left. Leave you when you can no longer really blame them for leaving you. Leave you with your bill of good health, still uncelebrated and a matter of some optimistic conjecture. Leave you so abruptly and so completely that you can't imagine what to do with their leaving but hold it up and study it in its natural light and shadow, in daytime as well as dusk, observe it like a philosophy, take it to heart, alone now they're telling you, honestly struck by how the light passes through it to the side on which you remain, here, in bittersweet and solitary wonder.

"Mom."

She cannot speak, or look at him.

"I'll come back. I promise."

She wipes a hand across her unseeing eyes.

Dwight says, "I'll send you a ticket to come out, Ruth."

A ticket. She will need a ticket to see her son. She begins stacking plates.

"There's his diploma," he goes on, warming to his cause. "I have a friend who might be able to work out a way for Sam to finish up his credits at UCSB. You'll come out for graduation."

Will she? Go out to California for Sam's graduation? Probably, though it's hard to believe.

She has been to California, and it is not the promised land.

But then neither is this place—Bow Mills, or any other town in Connecticut, any place anywhere. They are simply places you live. You're born there, or one day, pushed or drawn or dreaming, you move there. You live there, and get married there, and raise children there. And there, if you stay long enough, things happen to you and the people you love that no one can imagine. And either you survive them or you don't.

She carries the plates with their uneaten food into the kitchen and lets the door swing shut behind her, leaving the men to themselves, to sort it through or not. She stands there alone, suddenly wishing she had a dog, a puppy, who might eat these leftovers with a pure and jubilant hunger, so none of it would go to waste. . . .

Waste is something she has grown to hate as she's gotten older, waste and indifference. . . .

She will wake up tomorrow and her son and his father will be gone. The house and her life will be hers again, not a waste. And she cannot be indifferent to any of it, this she knows. . . .

She and the pup she's going to have will go outside and the yard will be green as a Swiss field in summer, and she will watch the puppy run and frolic. . . .

A cardinal will flutter onto a branch of the old oak, and for the first time in months the color that pops into her head will not be *blood*. It will be *rose*. . . .

And then she will go back inside and sit down and write her son a letter, to try to tell him how much she has loved her life while she's lived it.

She returns to the dining room. Where her men are still at the table.

Dwight with his chair pushed back, that graveling voice, in tandem with those powerful arms, caught in the middle of a story about a legendary home run smashed over the wall in Fenway Park, some game-winning hit that will never be forgotten. . . .

While, beside him, Sam sits listening, his eyes on his father and his mouth cocked in what might just be a smile . . .

Ruth goes up to her boy, who is a man, and kisses the top of his head.

"I'll help you pack."

ACKNOWLEDGMENTS

One writes alone, but never in a vacuum. My particular gratitude goes to my editor David Ebershoff, who so gracefully combines his impressive gifts as a novelist with those of an ideal reader. As always, the wise and bracing counsel of my longtime agent, Binky Urban, helped see me through, from beginning to end. Jen Smith, at Random House, once again offered a clear-eyed reading of my manuscript at a crucial juncture in its development. And working with the wonderful Jynne Martin in publicity has turned the sometimes confounding experience of promoting a book of serious fiction into a pleasure.

My warm thanks as well to Gerry Krovatin and Dr. Cara Natterson, dear friends and experts in their respective fields of practice, who helped round out my legal and medical knowledge in the writing of this novel.

This book is dedicated to my wife, Aleksandra, and our son, Garrick, for all that they do, and all that they are.

ABOUT THE AUTHOR

JOHN BURNHAM SCHWARTZ is the author of four previous novels: *The Commoner, Claire Marvel, Bicycle Days,* and *Reservation Road,* which was made into a motion picture based on his screenplay. His books have been translated into more than twenty languages and his writing has appeared in many publications, including *The New Yorker* and *The New York Times.* A past winner of the Lyndhurst Foundation Award for mastery in the art of fiction, Schwartz has taught at the Iowa Writers' Workshop, Harvard University, and Sarah Lawrence College, and is currently literary director of the Sun Valley Writers' Conference. He lives in Brooklyn, New York, with his wife, Aleksandra Crapanzano, and their son, Garrick.

Center Point Publishing

600 Brooks Road • PO Box 1
Thorndike ME 04986-0001 USA

(207) 568-3717

US & Canada:
1 800 929-9108
www.centerpointlargeprint.com